"Soon I shall be mistress of an Irish castle," Clementina confided to her friend Leonora, but six months after Clementina's return from Bath, she had still heard no word from her Irish lover. With a heavy heart, Leonora watched her friend pine for the man she had so foolishly loved, the man to whom she had so recklessly surrendered.

As summer turned to autumn, Clementina grew pale, weak and listless. One misty November morn, Leonora's beloved friend died of a broken heart.

Leonora laid a posy of white flowers beside Clementina's headstone and whispered, "Your secret is safe with me, dearest friend. But I give you this solemn promise. If ever I chance to meet Sir Max Fitzarren, I shall not rest until I have taken revenge for the suffering he has caused you!"

Other Novels by Caroline Courtney

Duchess In Disguise
A Wager For Love
Love Unmasked
Guardian of the Heart
Dangerous Engagement
The Fortunes of Love

Published by
WARNER BOOKS

CAROLINE COURTNEY

Love's Masquerade

WARNER BOOKS

A Warner Communications Company

WARNER BOOKS EDITION

ISBN: 0-446-94292-8

Cover design by Gene Light

Cover art by Walter Popp

Warner Books, Inc., 75 Rockefeller Plaza, New York, N.Y. 10019

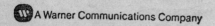 A Warner Communications Company

Printed in the United States of America

First Printing: February, 1980

10 9 8 7 6 5 4 3 2 1

One

"Melissa, look! Oh, is that not the most shocking sight!" cried Leonora, her lovely amber eyes wide with distress.

Lady Melissa Pagett turned her elegant head and gazed from the carriage window, murmuring, "You really must not point in that vulgar fashion, Leonora. Now what is disturbing you? I can see nothing amiss. Covent Garden looks precisely as it always does at eleven o'clock in the morning. As usual, it is noisy, there are far too many carriages for the narrow streets—"

"Over there, by the steps of the theater!" exclaimed Leonora impatiently. "Have you not observed that enormous man setting about that young girl? See, he is boxing her ears! Oh, and now he has seized hold of her long red hair. I am convinced he will pull her poor head from her shoulders. The brute!"

Melissa shrugged disdainfully. "Do not waste your sympathy on her, Leonora. Look at her ragged dress and filthy face. She is probably a common pickpocket, receiving her just deserts from an angry father." She sighed. "Heavens, the congestion of carriages here this morning is taxing my patience. I declare, we have been stuck here in Drury Lane now for nearly half an hour!"

"The girl may be poor, but she is not a pickpocket. I am certain of it," asserted Leonora, pushing a wayward

5

strand of golden hair from her forehead. "When I was here at the theater recently with Sir Max Fitzarren, that selfsame girl came and tugged at my cloak, and returned to me a gold brooch which had fallen from my gown. In all the crush and confusion I had not even realized I had lost the brooch. The girl could quite easily have pocketed it, and I should have been none the wiser. But she was honest, and sought me out in order to hand it back."

"How can you be so sure that it is the same girl?" enquired Melissa, watching with languid disinterest as the big man slapped the girl's face.

"By that bright red hair," declared Leonora with conviction. She winced as the man pinched the girl's cheeks, making her scream out with pain. "Oh Melissa, we must do something to help her!"

"Leonora, do not be absurd!" snapped Melissa, tucking a dark curl back beneath the blue velvet of her bonnet. "You must not interfere in other people's battles. And you know Cameron would be furious with you."

"Fiddlesticks to your pompous brother!" cried Leonora. She drew a sharp breath. "Mercy, he is trying to drag her down the Lane. But she is fighting back!"

Leonora clapped her hands in encouragement as the red-haired girl delivered a well-placed kick on the big man's shin. He howled in fury. Seizing the advantage, the girl shot out her hand, and clawed him down his leathery cheek.

"She's drawn blood! Oh well done, well done!" called Leonora.

Melissa covered her ears.

As her persecutor let out a bellow of rage, the girl wisely took to her heels. She fled down Drury Lane, her red hair flying in the wind as she dodged between the smart carriages, and round the back of the coffee stall. The big man lumbered after her, waving his fist, threatening to skin the girl alive when he caught up with her.

Still running, she emerged from the coffee stall, her eyes huge and terrified with fear.

"I'll roast your hide for you, you see if I don't!" roared the man, hot in pursuit. "You'll rue the day you cross-chopped me, you cat-witted hussy!"

The frightened girl sped on. Nimbly, she sidestepped round a passing Simon, with a steaming trayful of hot pies balanced on his head.

Observing that the pieman was, for a few precious seconds, obscuring the big brute's view of the girl, Leonora hastily flung open the carriage door.

"Quickly! In here!" she called urgently.

The girl hesitated.

"Come on!"

Responding to the authority in Leonora's voice, the red-haired girl lingered not a moment longer. Taking a deep breath, she threw herself in a quivering heap on the floor of the carriage.

Melissa delicately swept her skirts out of the way, so that not so much as an inch of muslin was in contact with the ragged individual on the floor.

"Stay down there for the moment," advised Leonora, slamming the carriage door shut. And not a moment too soon. She threw back her golden head and laughed softly as the big man stood, red faced and perplexed, searching this way and that through the crowd for his elusive quarry. He mopped his perspiring face, cursing anew as he examined his tattered handkerchief and viewed the blood caused by the red-haired girl's nails.

At this point, to Leonora's relief, the congestion in Drury Lane eased. The driver cracked his whip, and the carriage rolled forward once more. Within minutes, the girl's attacker was left far behind.

"You are safe now," Leonora gently informed the shivering girl. "Come and sit by me."

Melissa raised her eyes to heaven as the urchin girl scrambled onto the velvet seat. Leonora, however, took no notice of Melissa's disdainful display. Despite the dark-haired woman's affected airs, Leonora found her a good friend and an amusing companion. And she was well aware that deep beneath that fur trimmed cape, and the fashionably styled muslin, there beat a kindly, loyal heart.

Indeed, Melissa's gray eyes had already darkened in sympathy as she regarded the bruises on the girl's pinched face.

The girl looked up at Leonora and stammered, "Thank you . . . miss . . . my lady?"

"I am Lady Leonora Pagett," smiled the golden-haired girl, "and my companion here is the Lady Melissa Pagett."

"And how are you called?" enquired Melissa kindly.

"Daisy, my lady."

"That man you were running away from. Was he your father?" asked Leonora.

Daisy shook her head. "That's my Uncle Jack. I'm an orphan, you see. I was found in a field up near teeth. That's why they called me Daisy."

"A field up near *where?*" murmured Melissa.

"Teeth. Hounslow Heath is what you'd call it, my lady. Where I come from we often talk in rhymes, to confuse outsiders . . . or the Law."

Melissa shook her head in amazement.

Lenora laughed. "It sounds fun! But now tell me, Daisy, why was your Uncle Jack abusing you in such a dreadful fashion?"

Daisy twisted her fingers, and was silent for a few moments. Then she blurted, "Because I wouldn't go thieving like he does! He says now I'm fifteen I should be earning my keep. I wanted to get work as a scullery maid and earn my living in a decent way. But he wants me to go diving."

Leonora raised a puzzled eyebrow. "You mean under the Thames?"

"No, no my lady. Picking pockets," explained

Daisy. "That's what we were fighting about just now. I told him I didn't want to, and if he made me it would do him no good as I'd only make a queer diver . . . that is, I'd bungle it and be caught by the Law. That's when he started laying in to me. I thought he was going to kill me. I kicked him on the leg, and scratched his face. There was murder in his eyes, then, and I realized I'd better shin off. It was like a miracle when you threw open your carriage door. Otherwise Uncle Jack would have caught me in the end. Oh, how I hate him!"

Daisy's blue eyes filled with tears. She searched in the torn pocket of her dress and pulled out a filthy piece of rag to mop her eyes. Hastily, Leonora handed the girl her own lace handkerchief.

"Here, use this."

The carriage drew to a halt outside Layton and Shears, the fashionable textile merchants of Henrietta Street.

"I shall only be a few minutes," said Melissa, descending from the carriage. "I desire to inspect their new Indian muslins."

Watching Melissa sweep into the shop, Daisy enquired hesitantly, "If I may make so bold . . . may I ask, are you and Lady Melissa sisters?"

"No," smiled Leonora. "Lady Melissa was married to my cousin, Julian. He was killed in a hunting accident a year ago, not long after my own dear father passed away. As we both then found ourselves alone, Melissa asked me to leave my country home in Gloucestershire and come and reside with her in Grosvenor Street."

Daisy nodded. "Is your mother still alive, my lady?"

"She died when I was born," replied Leonora softly. "So you see, I understand something of your plight, Daisy. I know how it is to grow up without a mother's love and care."

Daisy said wistfully, "It was all right until a few months ago. My Aunt Mary—Uncle Jack's wife—she looked after me. Aunt Mary wouldn't let him take me

9

thieving. She taught me how to sew, and generally make myself useful. But just before Christmas she slipped on the ice, fell in the river and drowned. Since then I've had no peace from Uncle Jack."

As she spoke, Daisy darted nervous glances from the carriage windows, clearly terrified that at any moment Uncle Jack would wrench open the door and drag her screaming into the street.

"Whatever happens, I'm not going back to live with him, my lady," declared Daisy fervently. "I'd rather go begging on the steps of Covent Garden than face him again."

"Have you no other relatives who would take you in?" asked Leonora, a worried frown creasing her delicate brow.

Daisy shook her tousled head. "I'll survive, my lady. I may be only a poor girl, but I've a tough hide, and quick wits about me."

Leonora sat in thoughtful silence until Melissa returned.

"It's quite shocking," she said as she seated herself in the carriage. "Ten shillings a yard for Indian muslin! Such a price! I don't know what the world's coming to."

"So you made no purchase?" Leonora asked, smiling.

"Well," admitted Melissa, "it was so pretty, I told them to send round five yards. I confess, I couldn't resist it." She turned to Daisy, and said pleasantly, "I can assure you, there is no sign of your dreadful uncle in the street. It is safe for you to leave now."

Daisy obediently reached for the door handle. But Leonora motioned her to remain seated.

"I think it best that Daisy returns home with us, Melissa."

"Leonora, you are going too far!" protested Melissa.

Leonora said persuasively, "Melissa, be reasonable. You observed what a towering rage her uncle was in. He will tear this area of London apart trying to find Daisy.

Much better, then, that she returns home with us until his anger has had time to cool."

Melissa sighed. "Very well. But I must make it clear that this is against my better judgment."

Leonora smiled. "That's fixed, then, Daisy. You are to accompany us to Grosvenor Street, and have a rest, a good meal—"

"And a *bath*," added Melissa firmly.

By midafternoon a bathed and fed Daisy lay fast asleep between clean sheets in an attic room of the elegant house in Grosvenor Street.

Mrs. Harris, the housekeeper, informed Leonora, "The poor little thing was fair worn out. I must confess, my lady, I was taken aback when the footman brought her in to the kitchen. What a scruffy, grubby little urchin, I thought. But once we'd cleaned her up and washed her hair, she looked quite presentable. In a sharp kind of way."

Leonora smiled. "Thank you for attending to her, Mrs. Harris. When she awakens, could you find her a fresh dress to wear?"

"Of course, my lady." Mrs. Harris's plump hands smoothed her apron. "I, er, I took the liberty of burning her old dress on the kitchen range."

"I think that was quite the most sensible thing to do," said Leonora, satisfied that Daisy was being well looked after.

Melissa, however, was far from content.

As the two girls sat by the drawing-room fire on this raw March afternoon, Melissa exclaimed, "But you cannot be serious! Taking in this wretched creature and giving her food and shelter for a night is one thing. But now you say you propose to engage her as your personal maid! The notion is absurd." Her hand trembled as she poured the tea.

11

"I do not see why," replied Leonora calmly, buttering a muffin. "Not only is she quick-witted and eager to learn, but I believe she will display steadfast loyalty to me. I am convinced that under Mrs. Harris's excellent tutorship, Daisy will suit me admirably."

Melissa let out an exasperated sigh. "Leonora, it is just not the done thing to pluck a girl from the streets and take her into your personal service. You know nothing about her, except that her father is a common thief, which does not strike me as a particularly strong recommendation for employing his daughter. She has no references. You will be bringing trouble down upon your own head."

Observing Leonora's implacable expression, Melissa turned appealing eyes on the tall, dark-haired man sitting on the other side of the fireplace. "Cameron, can't you instil some reason into Leonora's pretty, but obstinate, head?"

Lord Cameron Rothwell regarded Leonora for a moment, an amused expression flickering in his gray eyes. Then, stretching out his long, well-muscled legs, he said, "I have told you before, Melissa. I refuse to become embroiled in your domestic arrangements. It seems to me that Leonora is perfectly free to choose whomsoever she likes as her personal maid."

Leonora lowered her beautiful amber eyes to conceal her surprise. It was a rare event indeed for Melissa's elder brother to take her side in an argument. Leonora had known and sparred with Lord Rothwell since her schooldays. He had been fond, then, of striding into the schoolroom, looking over her shoulder and informing her that she had placed Italy in the wrong place on her map of Europe.

Later, when she put up her hair and made her social debut, Cameron had been present at every ball, assembly, and rout. Not as her escort necessarily, but a watchful figure in the background . . . telling her not to dance once more with Lord Tressler, he was the most fearful rake and would wreck her reputation . . . advising her that it was unseemly for young girls to wander unescorted in the moonlit shrubbery . . .

"Stop telling me what to do and how to behave!" she had stormed at him on more than one occasion.

"I'm not telling you, I'm advising," he had replied, with a smile on his rugged face which had infuriated her even more. "You are a young, headstrong girl. I am merely giving you the benefit of my experience in the ways of the world."

Leonora had blazed back: "I should be obliged, Lord Rothwell, if you would allow me to live my own life. In my own fashion. And make my own mistakes!"

It had been an enormous relief to her when, two years ago, the long French wars were ended and Lord Rothwell had removed to Paris. She had looked forward to coming up to London each year for the Season, and devoting the rest of her time to her beloved father in Gloucestershire. What a joyful prospect it had seemed, to be free of Cameron forever at her elbow, with his "advice" and obstructive remarks.

Yet, perversely, while Cameron was in Paris she missed him dreadfully. Wild horses would never have dragged the admission from her. But she had found London society dull without Cameron's acidly amusing comments on the antics of the *ton,* and his vivid descriptions of the gaming parties he had attended.

Now all their lives had changed. Her dear father was dead. Melissa was widowed. She herself was living permanently in London. And Cameron had returned from Paris and reopened his magnificent house in Park Lane.

Yet from his agreeable tone, Leonora surmised that he had mellowed toward her. No doubt he appreciated that since she was now twenty-one, she was perfectly capable of organizing her own life without any interference from him. However, Leonora was never able to suppress the mischievous streak in her nature, and she could not resist challenging Lord Rothwell with the remark:

"Really, Cameron, I should have been surprised if you had offered any opposition to my employment of Daisy. It is, after all, your fault that I am losing my present personal maid, Evelina, because she is marrying one of *your* footmen!"

The glimmer of a smile touched Lord Rothwell's gray eyes. "Come now, Leonora. That is quite illogical. You cannot hold me responsible for the *amours* of my footmen."

Melissa noisily banged down her teacup on the rosewood side table. "This is getting us nowhere!" she declared impatiently. "Quite apart from Daisy's unsuitability for the position of personal maid, there is the unpleasant fact that her Uncle Jack is sure to come looking for her. Someone is certain to have seen her entering my carriage. If they have the wit to recognize the family crest on the door, Daisy will soon be traced here, to this very house. And then you, Leonora, will most like be charged with abduction!"

Melissa's eyes were moist. "Imagine the disgrace, the scandal! I shall never be able to hold up my head in society again!"

"Calm yourself, Melissa," smiled Leonora, her beautiful face luminous in the soft lamplight. "I shall, of course, send round a footman to Uncle Jack's lodgings, with a letter explaining exactly what has occurred."

"Leonora, I think it most unlikely that this Uncle Jack will be able to read," said Lord Rothwell, taking the brass poker and stirring up the glowing coals on the fire.

"Goodness, do I have to dot every i and cross every t?" exclaimed Leonora. "Naturally, if the wretched man can't read then the footman will explain the matter to him. From the sound of it, he will consider himself well rid of Daisy. He was only interested in the girl if she were willing to steal. When she made it plain that she was not, then he began abusing her."

Melissa closed her eyes, a long suffering expression

etched on her fine-boned face. "What I cannot comprehend, Leonora, is why you should be so concerned with this particular girl. There are hundreds of unfortunate girls to be found on the streets of London. What is so special about Daisy?"

"I feel responsible for her," replied Leonora, her amber eyes grave. "You recall that when I was at the theater with Lord Fitzarren, Daisy found, and returned to me, a gold brooch which had fallen from my gown. When I questioned her about the incident, she admitted that her Uncle Jack was so enraged with her for not keeping the brooch, he gave her a sound thrashing. I saw the weals myself on her poor thin body. So you see, I feel it my duty now to take her under my care and protection."

Lord Cameron Rothwell was leaning forward, listening intently to Leonora's account of the episode. Melissa reached across and touched his arm.

"What are we to do with her, Cameron? She has a positive obsession with the waifs and strays of this world."

He smiled. "There are worse vices, Melissa. Though I do recall once visiting young Leonora in the schoolroom. She had rescued a moth-eaten puppy from one of her father's farms, and hidden it beneath her desk. The little monster leaped out and sank its fangs into my leg."

"There is no cause to speak about me as if I were not here," said Leonora loftily. "Besides, I should have thought a man of your experience, Cameron, would have appreciated that the puppy was teething. He merely viewed your mature calf as something nice and hard to chew on. His action was not meant to be taken personally."

"Thank you for the benefit of your advice," replied Lord Rothwell mockingly. "Next time I chance upon a stray dog I'll do the decent thing and offer it my hand to bite."

Melissa shook her head. "Whatever you say, Cameron, you will never deter Leonora from her defense of the unfortunates of this life. You are probably unaware that whilst you were away in Paris, I came across Leonora at Lady Pinsley's ball, selling copies of Sir Walter Scott's loyal poem *'The Field of Waterloo.'* She was demanding a guinea a copy from all the gentlemen to aid the widows and destitute children of our war heroes."

"It was a good cause!" protested Leonora. "And everyone present at the ball could well afford a guinea."

"How much did you collect?" asked Lord Rothwell with interest.

"Close on fifty guineas. Then Lady Pinsley discovered what I was doing, and set up a fearful ruckus. She alleged I was abusing her hospitality by accosting her guests in such a common fashion!"

Lord Rothwell repressed a smile. "Then what did you do?"

"I informed Lady Pinsley that I could no longer honor the ball with my presence. I swept out, and went home."

"In the carriage?"

"No, I was so livid I wanted to walk to cool myself down. Lady Pinsley lives very near, in Grosvenor Square, so it was only a short step."

Lord Rothwell leaped to his feet, his eyes blazing. "You reckless little fool, Leonora! To walk alone, at night, through the streets of London with fifty guineas in your possession was sheer madness! You could have been robbed, attacked—"

Leonora faced him boldly. "The fifty guineas were in my reticule, safely concealed beneath my cloak. No one could have perceived it was there. And as you see, I am alive and well to tell the tale. You are fussing unnecessarily, Cameron."

Angrily, he turned to Melissa. "And where is your sense of propriety, allowing Leonora to do such a foolhardy thing?"

Melissa replied indignantly, "There is no cause to take on with me, Cameron. You know as well as I that to try to deter Leonora from her chosen path is as fruitless as Neptune attempting to hold back the waves of the sea. She is forever slipping out on her own, and there is nothing I can do to stop her."

"You are both behaving as if I were invisible again!" cried Leonora. "There is no point in attacking Melissa, Cameron. She is not my keeper. If you have any remarks to make, kindly address them to me!"

The tall man's face was white with rage. "What is this I hear about you wandering around London unchaperoned? Do you not take a maid, or footman to accompany you?"

Leonora shrugged. "Sometimes. But often I prefer to be on my own. I never take unfamiliar paths. I may go for a stroll in the park, or shopping in Bond Street. What is the harm in that?"

"You headstrong, infuriating girl!" shouted Lord Rothwell. "Surely you are aware that London is teeming with villains who would regard an unchaperoned young lady as very easy prey. And quite apart from those dangers it is most unseemly for an unmarried woman to be seen abroad alone."

Taken aback by the force of his words, Leonora could only murmur in her defense, "But Melissa sometimes walks abroad by herself. And no one accuses her of impropriety."

"I usually take Sarah, my maid, with me," said Melissa.

"Besides which, Melissa enjoys a different status to you," said Lord Rothwell.

"But she is only five years older than I," protested Leonora. "I do not see what enormous difference five years is supposed to make."

"Melissa," said Lord Rothwell patiently, "is a respected, respectable widow. You, on the other hand, are a young, unmarried girl. You must be observed to behave with decorum and restraint."

"Fiddlesticks!" cried Leonora rebelliously. "What

17

you are saying, Cameron, is that because I happen to be unmarried, I must lead a boring, tedious life, whilst Melissa has all the fun. It appears to me that if I am to enjoy myself at all I had best get myself wed with all possible speed!"

Lord Rothwell sat down. "That is something else I wished to discuss with you, Leonora. As all of London is aware, on the death of your father you inherited a considerable fortune. Which means you are not only one of the most beautiful girls in the capital, but also one of the richest."

Leonora stared at him in disbelief. She knew, of course, that she was now an extremely wealthy woman in her own right. Her father's financial advisers had impressed that fact upon her.

What amazed her, however, was that Cameron should call her beautiful. In all the years of their acquaintanceship, he had referred to her as many things: an ink-stained hayseed during her schooldays in the country . . . a frivolous silkworm during her first London season, when she had been so entranced by the number and variety of drapers' shops, she had drifted from one to the other, viewing the wares, but with no intention of buying . . . and once, when she had spent hours dressing for a ball, and was more than satisfied with her appearance, she had asked him how she looked, fishing for a compliment. "My dear," came the mocking reply, "you look as grand as the Countess of Puddledock!"

But never before had Lord Cameron Rothwell so much as hinted that he found her beautiful. She listened with particular attention as he continued:

"It is not just the common rogues of whom you must be aware, Leonora. There are in London many men with titles and high social position who, having squandered their own inheritances, would be more than interested in acquiring yours."

Melissa nodded. "Cameron speaks truly. When choosing a husband you must be wary of fortune hunters."

Leonora replied nonchalantly, "Have no fear, Melissa. I believe I am capable of separating the chaff from the wheat."

Melissa gave a little cough. "I should like to believe that to be so. But we . . . that is, Cameron . . . has grave doubts about one gentleman of your acquaintance."

"I see!" Leonora glared accusingly from brother to sister. "You have been discussing my personal affairs behind my back!"

"Only for your own good," replied Melissa hastily, looking to Cameron for support.

Leonora enquired icily, "And may I be informed which of my beaux has incurred your disfavor?"

Lord Rothwell said, "To be frank, Leonora, I am not at all happy about the amount of time you are spending with Sir Max Fitzarren. He appears to me to be a raffish, totally unsuitable fellow. He gambles—"

"But so do you!" cried Lenora. "You yourself told me it was a harmless activity enjoyed by all classes of people in England. Peasants, lords, doctors, lawyers, all of them gamble you said. You even told me how when they took up the floor of the Middle Temple the workmen found nearly a hundred dice that had fallen through the cracks in the boards!"

Lord Rothwell held up a hand to stem her indignant flow. "I also said that there was no harm in gambling *in moderation*. Sir Fitzarren is anything but moderate. His losses are enormous. And he doesn't just play the tables. He is a well-known figure at Newmarket. It is also common knowledge that he'll accept a wager on anything, however absurd the odds."

Leonora bit her lip. She had herself been present when Sir Max had accepted Lord Tressler's wager on which drop of rain would reach the bottom of the dining room window first. On that occasion Sir Max had won, and called for another bottle of port to celebrate.

"I admit, Sir Max Fitzarren likes to enjoy himself," said Leonora, choosing her words carefully. "But I do not see that you can accuse him of fortune hunting. Why, he owns vast estates in Ireland. I should not be surprised if he is far wealthier than I, or even you, Cameron!"

Leonora could not resist this barb. For Lord Cameron Rothwell, with houses and estates in London, Wiltshire, and Gloucestershire, was one of the richest men in all England. Leonora knew he would not take kindly to her suggestion that a mere Irish nobleman surpassed him in wealth and influence.

Lord Rothwell's mouth tightened. "There is something about Fitzarren that I do not trust. I cannot put my finger on it, but he does not quite ring true to me."

"Cameron's instinct is never wrong," asserted Melissa. "You should take his advice, Leonora, and discourage Sir Max."

Leonora gripped the arms of her carved chair. "I had hoped Paris had changed you," she accused Lord Rothwell, "but in fact I now see that it has merely exaggerated all your worst traits. You are still opinionated, arrogant and interfering. Well I give you fair warning that I will brook no one meddling with my life, and my choice of companions!"

Lord Rothwell sighed. "There is no cause to get on your high horse, Leonora. I have only your best interests at heart. And as for interfering, I would remind you that your own father asked me, on his death bed, to keep a brotherly eye on you, and to protect you."

"I still have no notion what my father meant by that," flared Leonora. "I am grown up now. I am capable of running my own affairs. What did he fear I needed protecting from?"

"The deserts of your own reckless nature, I imagine," replied Lord Cameron dryly. "And the fact remains that, although you and I are not related, as Melissa's brother and on the express wishes of your father I feel it my duty to look after you. Especially where your choice of marriage partner is concerned."

Leonora lapsed into silence. In truth, she had to admit that since the death of her father she had felt dismally alone in the world. Oh of course, it was a comfort living with Melissa. But there had been many occasions when she had found Cameron's masculine strength, humor and steadfastness most reassuring.

Nevertheless, she felt she could not allow him totally to take charge of her life. Especially where her beaux were concerned.

Why, she reasoned, if I bow to Cameron now and agree to cut Sir Max, it will mean that in future I shall practically have to obtain Cameron's written permission before I accept so much as an invitation to ride in the park with a gentleman!

Leonora was too spirited a girl to remain on the defensive for long. Accordingly, she changed the direction of the argument, and went straight into the attack:

"I do understand all that you are saying to me, Cameron," she said, with a smile of deceptive sweetness. "It is generous of you to think of me as one of the family, and take me under your protective wing. But I worry about you, too, in a sisterly way. You are a rich, eligible bachelor. There must be hundreds of quite unsuitable, grasping women hurling their caps at you. I should be quite distraught if you allowed yourself to fall into their clutches!"

Lord Rothwell threw back his dark head and roared with laughter. "Leonora, you are incorrigible! I assure you, I have every intention of remaining a bachelor until the end of my days. It is only twenty-seven years, you mind, since the law was repealed whereby women could legally be burned to death. I was only three at the time, but I distinctly remember asking my nurse to dress me in mourning black that day!"

"Cameron, really!" Melissa protested. "You cannot have *that* low an opinion of women?"

"On the contrary, I regard many women as delight-

21

ful, amusing creatures. I am happy to offer myself as their escort and companion. But what I have no intention of doing is giving my heart to any lady."

Leonora raised her eyebrows. "Come now, Cameron. Why all London knows," she declared, guessing wildly, "about the married woman you were seen escorting to every fashionable gathering in Paris."

Leonora had, in truth, never heard so much as a whisper about Cameron's activities in France. But she reasoned that he could not have spent all this time devoid of female company.

It was a shot into the blue. But it went home. "All London is wrong," snapped Lord Rothwell. "She was not married. She was a widow."

Melissa gasped. "Why Cameron! What is this? I had no notion that you were seriously involved with a Frenchwoman. Do you intend to marry her?"

His eyes darkened. "I do not wish to discuss the subject. All I will say is that I have no intention of marrying any woman—be she French, English, or Chinese!"

The tension in the Grosvenor Street drawing room was broken by a tap on the door.

"Excuse me, Lady Leonora," said a footman, "but Mrs. Harris asked me to inform you that young Daisy is now awake and refreshed."

"She will be anxious to know what is to become of her," said Leonora, rising. "I shall have her brought down to the Blue Saloon, where I shall ask her if she would like to become my personal maid. If she is content with the notion, she can start work immediately, pressing my new riding habit." Leonora cast a defiantly mischievous glance at Lord Rothwell and his sister. "I am riding in the park tomorrow with Sir Max Fitzarren. Naturally, I want to look my best!"

She swept from the room, her eyes bright with laughter at Lord Rothwell's furious expression.

Two

Leonora was delighted with Daisy's progress over the next few weeks. In her fresh blue dress, with her red hair pinned neatly under a crisply starched cap, Daisy proved an attentive, eager pupil as Mrs. Harris, aided by Melissa's maid Sarah, initiated her into the arts of a lady's maid.

She learnt that the secret of keeping Lady Leonora's chamois gloves beautifully soft and supple was to pour a few drops of olive oil into the rinsing water after she had washed them . . . that her ladyship's fine linen would retain its whiteness if wrapped in blue paper. She was taught how to press velvet without marking the pile, and to mend silk stockings invisibly by picking up the loops with a crochet hook.

"Between ourselves," the round-faced Sarah confessed to Daisy, "you'll have a much easier time of it working for Lady Leonora than I do with Lady Melissa. Lady Leonora is so nice and neat in her ways. When she takes off her dress she don't throw it down in a heap on the floor. It comes natural to her to be tidy and, well, considerate. But my Lady Melissa—"

Sarah waved to a plump arm to indicate the disarray of Melissa's dressing room. Discarded dresses, capes and muffs lay strewn on the floor. On the toilette table was an untidy profusion of silver-backed brushes, tortoiseshell combs, pins, and jeweled toothpicks. From velvet-lined jewel boxes dangled snarled strings of garnets and pearls. The lilac silk draped round the gilded mirror was covered in a fine film of powder. And the entire dressing room was permeated with the mingled scents of orange and lavender water from overturned perfume bottles.

"Phew! What a pen and ink!" laughed Daisy, wrinkling her nose and obligingly replacing the stoppers on bottles.

Sarah frowned. "Pen and ink? That's your way of saying *stink,* I suppose? We shall have to do something to improve your way of talking, Daisy. I am convinced Lady Leonora will soon lose patience with you for employing such colloquial speech."

"But the way I talk amuses her," grinned Daisy. "In fact, she's asked me to teach her some of the rhyming phrases."

"Mercy me," muttered Sarah, setting to work tidying Melissa's toilette, "there is no knowing what strange fancy will take Lady Leonora's interest." She sighed in exasperation. "Just look at this! Lady Melissa has spilt powder into her ring box. It will take me all morning to clean up her collection of rings."

"Let me help," offered Daisy, taking the precious rings from the box and laying them carefully on a folded piece of muslin. "I must confess, I don't know how you or Lady Melissa ever find anything in this dressing room if it is always in such a disorder."

"Not a day goes past without Lady Melissa raising the roof because something or other is lost," agreed Sarah, brushing powder from a brilliant sapphire ring. "Yesterday she could not find her favorite gold bracelet. I searched high and low. Finally the chambermaid discovered it under the bed. I imagine Lady Melissa must have wrenched off her dress with such impatience that the bracelet was torn off with it."

"Lady Leonora has set her heart on a new bracelet," confided Daisy. "I am to accompany her tomorrow to the goldsmiths."

More than any other aspect of her new life, Daisy most looked forward to a shopping expedition with her mistress. If Leonora had permitted it, Daisy would have stood in Bond Street for hours, admiring the fashionably dressed ladies and gentlemen parading by.

"Do not stare so, Daisy," instructed Leonora. "I declare, your eyes look ready to fall out of your head."

"I beg your pardon, my lady. But did you see that sight with the emerald green ostrich feathers stuck in her bonnet?" gasped Daisy. "And oh, just look at that carriage! Why, it is the most magnificent thing I have ever seen!"

She indicated a spectacular yellow coach, adorned with purple blinds, and drawn by superb prancing bays.

"You will never see a carriage like it in the whole length and breadth of England," smiled Leonora. "It belongs to the Prince Regent himself."

Daisy's eyes were bright. "I once caught a glimpse of him entering the theater at Drury Lane. Oh my lady, he looked so splendid, in a blue velvet cloak, and carrying a silver cane! I wonder where he is going now."

"Since it is nearly midday, he will be returning to Carlton House, probably to receive some foreign ambassadors," replied Leonora.

Daisy regarded Leonora with awe. "How can you be so sure, my lady?"

"Because I study the Court Circular," Leonora informed her. "It is published every day in the newspapers, and gives a full account of the Prince's official engagements."

"I wonder what the Prince does for the rest of the time. When he's not being official," Daisy murmured to herself.

The March wind flirted playfully with Leonora's golden curls. "I should imagine he reclines on a couch in his private apartments, and listens to the amusing tales of his gentlemen companions."

Daisy let out a peal of laughter. "From what I've

seen of the Prince, my lady, he's a little too portly to *recline* with any grace!"

"Daisy!" Leonora cast an anxious glance around. "You must not speak so of the Prince!"

A cheerful, "Hello there!" cut short her remonstrations. The call came from Sir Max Fitzarren, who had drawn level with them in his chaise. Daisy, who had been walking in the road, hastily jumped aside, but not before the chaise wheels had skinned the backs of her legs.

Sir Max stepped down from the chaise and bowed. "The top of the mornin' to you, my lovely Lady Leonora!"

The Irishman was a stockily built man of average height, with a shock of red hair, a fresh complexion and pale blue eyes which were fixed now admiringly on Leonora.

Daisy, rubbing the backs of her legs from their abrasive encounter with the chaise wheels, disliked Sir Max on sight. She was surprised that a lady of her mistress's good taste and discernment should find such enjoyment in the Irishman's company.

"Well, Sir Max," smiled Leonora. "You seem in fine spirits this morning. What brings you to Bond Street?"

"I've just been up to Lord Tressler's stables to inspect his new gray. Been giving him the benefit of my advice. It's a spirited animal, and in my opinion he's riding her above the bit."

Leonora shook her head. "He will never gain control of her that way. And he could ruin the horse's paces."

"Course he wouldn't listen to a word I said. He even intends entering her at Newmarket. I told him even my second best bay would beat this new nag any day of the week. We have a wager on it."

Leonora laughed. "You and your wagers! And you take them so seriously. Tell me, Sir Max, what was the most amusing wager you have ever heard of?"

He thought for a moment. Then his fleshy lips creased

26

into a smile. "This was before my time, of course. But I am told that one Christmas, the Duke of Queensbury raced his geese down to London against those of Lord Horford. But to ensure good speed, and win the wager, the Duke clad all his geese in boots!"

Leonora's eyes glimmered with mirth. "Sir Max, that is a cracker if ever I heard one!"

"I assure you, it is perfectly true." He tapped the door of the chaise with his whip. "Now how about coming for a short spin with me? You look so breathtakingly lovely. I shall be the proudest man in London with you seated beside me in the chaise."

"Such sweet talk! Methinks you must have been dipped in the Shannon at birth," murmured Leonora. She turned to Daisy. "You run along back to Grosvenor Street. And kindly inform Lady Melissa that I shall be home a little later. Now are you sure you have my new bracelet safe?"

"Yes, my lady. I have placed it in my reticule, and tied the ribbons twice round my wrist so no rogue can snatch it." Yet still Daisy made no move to go. She stood with drooping shoulders, her sulky face turned suspiciously toward Sir Max.

"What are you waiting for, girl?" he demanded, his voice raised. "Back to Grosvenor Street with you! Go, go!" Playfully, he raised his whip to her.

Daisy responded with a venomous glance, then turned and ran away down Bond Street.

"So that's the girl you've taken into your household," drawled Sir Max, helping Leonora into the chaise. "She seems a chitty-faced little thing. And insolent with it."

"She is intensely loyal to me," replied Leonora. "And I do believe you frighten her."

He smiled into her eyes. "I don't frighten you, do I?"

She laughed. "Oh no. You could never do that!"

As they bowled along Piccadilly towards Park Lane

27

on this bright March morning, Leonora reflected how furious Lord Rothwell would be if he knew she was once more in the company of the *unsuitable* Sir Max.

Leonora had been highly amused by the efforts of Melissa and her brother to try and dissuade her from considering Sir Max as a serious suitor for her hand. Indeed, never for one moment had Leonora contemplated marrying the Irish nobleman.

Cameron and Melissa must consider me soft in the head, she mused. *Just because I appear to find Sir Max lighthearted, entertaining company, that does not mean I would consider sealing the knot with him.*

It was as plain as a pikestaff to Leonora that he would prove most unreliable as a husband. He gambled too much, and drank to excess. He also possessed a quick temper which had led to many an unseemly brawl on the steps of Whites or Boodles. Of course, on the other side of the coin, he could be charming, articulate, and amusing at times. Yet Leonora was level headed enough to realize that eventually, and especially within a permanent relationship, these qualities would pall in any man.

As one of her beaux, she could forgive him if he arrived half an hour late for an engagement, with a tall story about saving Lady Pinsley from drowning in the Thames. But as a married woman, Leonora knew she would soon find his behavior irritating and irresponsible.

Lord Rothwell had, of course, pointed much of this out to Leonora. But his phrasing was so pompous, she thought. His attitude was too much like a schoolmaster reprimanding an errant pupil. Although she knew in her heart she was right, she would never have given him the satisfaction of saying so!

Something else Leonora could not bring herself to put into words—to Lord Rothwell or to any living soul— was the real reason for her surprising encouragement of Sir Max's attentions. This was a dark, dreadful secret which Leonora knew she could share with no one. She must bear the burden alone, until the time was ripe for her to turn on Sir Max Fitzarren, and gain a very personal revenge on this smooth-talking Irish charmer.

To her dismay, she found Lord Rothwell at the house when she returned from her ride with Sir Max. He strode out into the hall and said grimly,

"Would you kindly step into the drawing room for a moment, Leonora. I have something to say to you."

Leonora raised her eyes. Oh dear. Another slapped wrist for Leonora in punishment for associating once more with Sir Max!

"What is the use," Lord Rothwell demanded, "of taking your maid as a companion on your shopping expedition, if you then dismiss her the moment Sir Max hoves into view?"

"Be reasonable, Cameron. It would have been horribly cramped with three of us in that small chaise." Leonora took off her bonnet, and tidied her curls before the large oval mirror over the fireplace. "Besides, Daisy is so dour when Sir Max is about. I could never have laughed at any of his remarks with Daisy sitting lemon-faced beside me."

"Daisy is rapidly going up in my estimation," declared Lord Rothwell. "By the by, how did the infamous Uncle Jack react to the intelligence of her new employment?"

Leonora spread her hands. "I have sent a footman three times to his Covent Garden lodgings. But Uncle Jack is never there."

"Mmm," mused Lord Rothwell. "With any luck he'll have fallen down a coal hole and be picking St. Peter's pockets through the bars of the golden gates. Now, to return to what I was saying about Sir—"

"That reminds me of a wicked tale Daisy told me," laughed Leonora. "She says she knows of a woman who had a pair of fake arms made. Then she'd go to church, and sit with her 'arms' demurely folded, whilst her real ones were delving into her neighbors' pockets. Is that not shocking?"

But Lord Rothwell had no intention of allowing his pretty companion to send up a smoke screen.

"We are getting away from the point," he said sternly. "In all seriousness, I strongly advise you to see less of Sir Max Fitzarren. And in particular, do not consort with him without a chaperon."

"Oh, do not be so stuffy, Cameron!" flared Leonora. "I am twenty-one, an independent woman and quite capable of taking care of myself. Now if you will excuse me, I wish to change from my outdoor clothes."

He looked livid at her imperious termination of their interview. As he took an angry step toward her, she turned and quickly left the room. But she found no peace upstairs. Raised voices were issuing from Melissa's apartments.

"I tell you I left them last night on my toilette table!" Melissa was insisting.

"But my lady, I assure you the earrings were not there this morning," replied Sarah firmly. "Are you quite sure they are not in your reticule? Do you recall when you thought you had lost your gold earrings? After a long search you remembered that the earrings pinched you all through dinner, and you had taken them off and placed them—"

"Look for yourself!" shouted Melissa. "They are most certainly not in the reticule. Or on the dressing table. Which is where I most definitely left them."

Sarah said soothingly, "Do not fret, my lady. They will turn up eventually."

"There is to be no eventually about it! They are my favorite silver earrings. I want them found, now!"

Leonora sighed. Accustomed to these almost daily uproars over items Melissa had misplaced, Leonora knew that the wisest course she could take was to stay well out of the way. Accordingly, when she had changed her dress, she slipped down the side stairs. Hearing Lord Rothwell in the hall, asking the footman to advise Lady Melissa that he intended to visit Sir Roger Lamprey, who had unfortunately broken his arm, Leonora avoided him and sought sanctuary in the room they called the Blue Saloon.

This was Leonora's favorite room in the Grosvenor Street house. She loved the cool tranquility of the pale blue silk which covered the chairs and sofas. The carpet, soft underfoot, was of a deeper blue, as were the long window hangings, through which was revealed Melissa's formal, though pretty, long garden. A contrast to the blues in the saloon was provided by a white marble fireplace, and a silver bowl containing a mass of daffodils.

The first sign of spring, thought Leonora, smiling as she regarded the cheerful yellow blooms.

When Daisy, answering the call-bell, entered the saloon, she found her mistress seated before a walnut side table. Spread on the polished surface was a variety of different colored feathers.

Daisy bobbed a curtsy. "I'm so glad you rang, my lady. There is a fearful to-do going on upstairs over Lady Melissa's earrings. It's such a relief to be able to escape down here to this nice quiet room."

"Lady Melissa's jewelry will come to light soon enough," murmured Leonora absently, busy sorting the feathers into their varying sizes. "Poor Melissa is forever losing things. We are all quite accustomed to it. Now," she glanced up, "have you managed to clean those ostrich feathers for me?"

Daisy nodded her red head. "Mrs. Harris showed me how to do it. Lucky she did, too, or I'd have cleaned the ostrich feathers in limewater like I did those ordinary fowl ones. I didn't realize white ostrich were so special."

"They have to be handled carefully, or they look dingy instead of pure white," murmured Leonora.

Daisy left the room and returned a moment later with the beautiful feathers carefully wrapped in clean muslin.

"Mrs. Harris advised me to dip them in and out of soapy lather for five minutes, then rinse, and shake near the fire to dry. Don't they look lovely, my lady? Sarah was telling me your feather pictures are admired by all the ton."

"Anyone can do it. It is simply a matter of having enough patience, and a dash of imagination," replied Leonora modestly.

Leonora's feather pictures were indeed quite exquisite. Above her, on the wall of the Blue Saloon, was a glorious example of her work: a pair of pheasants set in maple frames. Leonora had caught to perfection their flamboyant, imperious attitude as they perched on the painted boughs, with their long protruding tail feathers sweeping majestically to the ground.

"May I ask what your new picture is to be, my lady?" enquired Daisy curiously, watching Leonora begin a rough sketch on the paper before her.

Leonora tilted her lovely head to one side. "I am still a little undecided. These ostrich feathers are so delightful. But I am a trifle tired of birds. Instead, I am considering a design depicting a fashionable lady, and using the feathers for her elaborate ball gown."

Daisy clapped her hands. "Oh yes! And perhaps she could have ostrich feathers in her bonnet, like that lady we saw in Bond Street this morning."

Leonora raised her eyes to heaven, and said with mock severity, "That was Lady Jersey, Daisy, and she was distinctly overdressed. One ostrich feather in a bonnet, or maybe two, is elegant. But *six* is vulgar. You must try to develop an eye, my dear, for what is good and what is bad taste."

"I do my best," replied Daisy mournfully, "but sometimes there seems to be such a thin dividing line between the two." She flashed Leonora an impish glance. "May I enquire, my lady, if you enjoyed your ride with Sir Max Fitzarren this morning?"

Leonora, busily engaged in recurling a feather with a

silver paper knife, smiled as she said, "There is no occasion to sound so arch, Daisy. Tell me, why do you disapprove of Sir Max?" When Daisy hesitated, Leonora urged, "Do not be afraid. You may speak plain to me."

Daisy muttered, "His looks displease me. His eyes are set too close together. And his mouth has a cruel twist to it."

Leonora sighed. "I fear you are being a little hard on the gentleman, Daisy. We cannot all have the good fortune to be blessed with perfectly regular features."

"Beggin' your pardon, but all my instincts tell me that Sir Max is no good for you, my lady," blurted Daisy anxiously. "I can't say why I feel like I do. He just makes me feel all cold and shivery inside."

"It may comfort you to know that you are in excellent company then," said Leonora coolly. "Lord Rothwell, also, all but comes out in a dangerous rash whenever the name of Sir Max is mentioned."

Daisy turned away, and muttered to herself, "With due cause! Lord Rothwell has known Lady Leonora since she was a little girl. It must cut him to the heart to have to stand by and hear Sir Max boasting of his conquest over her!"

But Leonora's sharp ears had caught a word or two of this. "What is this, Daisy? What are you saying about a conquest? Speak up, now!"

Daisy would not meet Leonora's eyes. She fiddled with the cord on her dress. "I . . . it was probably nothing my lady. I expect I misheard. They were talking very low."

"Who were speaking low?"

"Lord Rothwell and Lady Melissa," whispered Daisy.

"And what were you doing listening to a private conversation between brother and sister?" demanded Leonora hotly.

Daisy blushed poppy red. "I . . . I was just passing the morning room door and I heard raised voices. I couldn't help overhearing—"

Leonora threw down her paper knife. "Now, Daisy, you have just admitted that they were speaking very softly. How many times do I have to warn you that you must not listen at doors?"

Daisy hung her head. "I'm sorry, my lady. It won't happen again. And of course I wouldn't dream of repeating to a living soul—not even you, my lady—what I heard Lord Rothwell telling his sister about Sir Max and you."

Leonora cleared her throat. The little minx, she thought, smiling to herself. She has me helplessly cornered now!

She laughed good naturedly. "Come, Daisy. It would be cruel to leave me in suspense, having already admitted half the story to me. You must tell me everything."

Daisy required no further bidding.

"Lord Rothwell was furious," she began. "It is all over White's that Sir Max is boasting that you are already half in love with him. He says he only has to snap his fingers, and you come running. He'll have you at the altar, he declares, by the end of June at the latest!"

With a consummate effort, Leonora kept her voice light, and amused. "I am grateful for the advance intelligence, Daisy. I must order my trousseau immediately!"

"Lord Rothwell was beside himself with rage, my lady. He said the whole affair is degrading. *'How dare that jumped up Irish nobleman refer to Leonora in such a supercilious, cavalier fashion,'* he shouted. He was all for calling Sir Max out, but Lady Melissa prevailed upon him to desist."

Leonora shook her head in exasperation. "What business is it of Lord Rothwell's anyway? It is not Cameron whom Sir Max desires to marry, it is *me!* Lord Rothwell has no cause to go interfering in my affairs. I am perfectly capable of handling my own life, and that includes a proposal from Sir Max. I do not need Cameron acting as my spokesman, guardian, elder brother, and jailor every minute of thc day!"

Leonora arose and took a restless turn round the room. The trouble with Cameron, she thought, is that he has too much leisure. Too much time to concern himself with me. What a pity it is, she reasoned, that he does not have a wife and a parcel of children to be responsible for; he would not have a minute to spare, then, to meddle in my life!

She rested her long white fingers on the mantel shelf, and sighed. She believed Lord Rothwell would never marry—being so arrogant and so high principled. Where in the world would he find a woman who matched his exacting standards, and also possessed spirit enough to challenge his superior attitudes?

She turned to Daisy. "I imagine Lady Melissa's earrings must be found by now. All appears to be quiet upstairs. Will you go up and lay out my blue muslin for tonight? I seem to remember the lace at the hem is torn." Clumsy Lord Tressler had trodden on it when he escorted her to the opera.

When Daisy had gone, Leonora threw a shawl round her slender shoulders, and wandered out into the garden. She was careful to close the door softly behind her so any breeze would not disturb her fragile feathers on the table.

It was so pleasant, she reflected, to see the sun again after so many drab winter months. And how welcome were the first spring flowers . . . daffodils, sweet violets, and early primroses forming brave splashes of color beside the flagstoned path.

From the mews at the end of the garden, Leonora could hear the shouts of the stable boys as they groomed Melissa's horses. And the creak of the carriage wheels on the cobbles as the vehicle was turned toward the coach house.

The familiar sounds soothed Leonora, for in truth

she was seething with anger. In company, Leonora forced herself to keep her voice light and her countenance amused when Sir Max Fitzarren was mentioned. Not by so much as the flicker of an eyelash would she allow herself to reveal how much she loathed and despised the Irishman.

The first time Leonora had heard mention of the name Fitzarren was when a dear friend of hers, Clementina Westlake, returned from a visit to Bath. Clementina, a wide-eyed, innocent beauty of barely sixteen summers, had resided in Bath with her Aunt Prudence. Despite her name, prudence was the one quality the aunt had failed to display reflected Leonora grimly. The foolish woman had allowed young Clementina to associate with a distinctly raffish circle at the balls and assemblies.

When Clementina returned to Gloucestershire, she drew Leonora into her chamber, and in tremulous whispers confessed that she had fallen hopelessly in love. The object of her affections was a wealthy Irish nobleman. Leonora was horrified to discover that the young Clementina had succumbed totally to the charms of the sweet-talking Irishman. Utterly under his spell, Clementina had made him a gift of her youth, her beauty, her innocence, and her body.

"Do not scold me, Leonora," Clementina had murmured, her lovely eyes glistening at the memory of her lover. "I would not have surrendered to him had I not been totally convinced of his love for me. Oh, how he adores me, Leonora! He says it is writ large in the stars that we two are destined to find happiness together. He desires that we shall be married with all due speed!"

"He will be arriving shortly, then, to seek an interview with your father?" enquired an extremely worried Leonora.

Clementina's smile was joyous. "Oh yes! He has returned to Ireland to attend to certain tedious business matters. But as soon as they are settled, Max will come to me. I know he will! Oh, Leonora, just imagine! In only a few weeks' time, I shall be mistress of an Irish castle, greeting you as the Lady Clementina Fitzarren! Is that not a wonderful prospect?"

Yet day followed day, week followed week, but six months after Clementina's return from Bath, she had still heard no word from her Irish lover. With a heavy heart, Leonora watched her friend pine for the man she so foolishly loved, the man to whom she had so recklessly surrendered.

Every day, Leonora offered what comfort she could to the distraught girl. Yet never had Leonora felt so helpless. There was no other living soul to whom she could turn for advice for Clementina had sworn her to secrecy. And never in her life had Leonora reneged on her word.

As summer turned to autumn, Clementina grew pale, weak and listless. The physician diagnosed a bad chill. But when Clementina breathed her last, one misty November morn, only Leonora knew the terrible truth: that her beloved friend had died of a broken heart.

Leonora laid a bouquet of white flowers beside Clementina's headstone, and whispered, "Your secret is safe with me, dearest Clementina. But I give you this solemn promise. If ever I chance to meet Sir Max Fitzarren, then I shall not rest until I have taken revenge for the suffering he has caused you!"

Two months ago, that opportunity had presented itself, when Sir Max Fitzarren arrived in London. He devoted a week to a survey of all the prettiest and wealthiest young ladies in the capital. And then he set about paying court exclusively to the lovely (and rich) Lady Leonora Pagett.

Whenever she gazed on Sir Max, Leonora wished fervently that she had been born a man, equipped to fight with masculine weapons.

"If only I could call the scoundrel out to a duel," she thought, an angry fire raging in her blood. "Oh what pleasure it would give me to run the rogue through!"

But Leonora was a woman, and as such was compelled to deploy subtle, feminine tactics. When Sir Max first began to call on her, Leonora formulated her plan. It was simple. She resolved to encourage Sir Max in his attentions. She would laugh at all his jokes . . . look adoringly into his eyes . . . even flirt with him a little.

But oh, the effort it had cost her! Leonora picked up a fallen, rotted branch and flung it with all her might at the trellised wall, wishing with every fibre of her being that the splintering wood could have been Sir Max himself.

And yet, Daisy had confirmed that her plan was succeeding. Already, Sir Max was boasting all round London that Lady Leonora would be his bride by the end of June. All society would soon expect them to marry.

A slow smile illuminated Leonora's delicate face. "Well, my charming Sir Max," she murmured, "I shall keep you dangling until the very last moment in June. Then, when with blustering confidence you ask me to marry you, I shall gaze over your head with frigid disdain, and refuse you. I do believe I shall not even be polite, as a lady should, and couch my refusal in reluctant, regretful tones. I shall simply say no. Loudly, simply, and clearly. And you, Sir Max, will have to face the derision and scorn of the blades at White's, when they learn that in spite of your boasting, the most sought-after lady in London has turned you down flat!"

And, thought Lenora, her amber eyes dancing as she returned to the house, my plan will serve a second purpose. For by appearing to give every encouragement to Sir Max, she would be whirling the maddened Lord Rothwell into a cloud of blue smoke! *It is wicked of me, I know,* she thought, *but I do gain such fun from infuriating Cameron!*

But it was Lord Rothwell who was soon to leave Leonora gasping in amazement.

"Leonora, I have just received the most distressing intelligence!" cried Melissa, rushing into her dressing room one April afternoon.

38

Leonora, who was dressing for dinner, stared aghast at Melissa. Lord Rothwell's sister, usually so elegantly immaculate, was in the most unaccustomed disarray. Her straw bonnet was tilted at an absurd angle, with long strands of dark hair escaping to her shoulders. Her pelisse was unfastened, her dress and stockings spattered with mud.

"I ran all the way back from Park Lane," Melissa panted. "I could not wait for the carriage to be brought round. Oh, you will not believe what I have to tell you!"

"Daisy, kindly fetch Lady Melissa a glass of wine," Leonora ordered calmly, assisting her distraught friend to a chair. "Now take a few deep breaths, Melissa. Why, your face is ashen and your hands are like ice!"

"I was in such a hurry I left my gloves behind in Cameron's house," murmured Melissa, accepting the glass of wine from Daisy.

"Please leave us now," Leonora told her maid. "And do not listen at the door!"

Daisy obediently closed the door, and clomped loudly across the landing to prove she was well and truly out of earshot.

"Now," commanded Leonora, drawing up a velvet covered stool. "Tell me what has happened."

"It is Cameron!" wailed Melissa in despair. "He is going to be married!"

Leonora sat stunned for a moment. Then she broke into peals of laughter. "Come now, Melissa. You will have to get up much earlier than that to persuade me the moon is made of cheese! I am quite well aware that today is April Fool's Day. Cameron getting married, indeed! Why, if that is not the most amusing thinking . . ."

Her laughter faded away as she regarded Melissa's grave face. "You are not serious?"

"What I tell you is the truth," insisted Melissa. "I called on Cameron this afternoon, and waited for him in the drawing room whilst he attended to some business affairs with his attorney in the library. I was wandering idly round the room, when my eye fell on an unfinished letter on the writing table. Quite without intending to, I found I'd read the beginning of what was obviously the second page. And it said, quite plainly, *arrangements are now in hand for my marriage at the end of April to Miss Cecily Trantor. The wedding will take place at St. Margaret's, Westminster, and then my bride and I will be setting up home in Gloucestershire."*

Melissa raised the wineglass to her lips, the color gradually beginning to return to her face.

"What else did the letter reveal?" asked Leonora, quite taken aback by the news.

Melissa sighed. "I could not read another word, as an inkwell had fallen over the rest of the sheet and obliterated the remainder of the letter. I was so shocked, I did not wait to see Cameron. I left the house and rushed home immediately."

"Well who would believe it!" marveled Leonora, taking a brush and drawing it through her silken curls. "What a dark horse Cameron is! Why, only a few weeks ago he was insisting to me that he intended to remain a bachelor to the end of his days. No woman would ever capture *his* stony heart, he alleged. Yet here he is, planning to tie the knot! My, how I shall tease him about this!"

"How can you be so lighthearted?" protested Melissa. "It is the most dreadful thing to happen."

"I do not see why," asserted Leonora. "I feel total sympathy for Miss Cecily Trantor for I am convinced she cannot know what a terrible fate lies in store for her as the future Lady Rothwell. But speaking for myself, I shall be delighted to see Cameron married. And the happy pair will be making their home in Gloucestershire. Such a fine county! There is much to occupy one there. And it is hours and hours away from London! I wonder what they would like as a wedding present? A silver leash, perhaps, to fit round poor Cecily's neck? For of course she will never be allowed to leave the house without Cameron's permission. All her friends will be selected by him, and—"

"Leonora, this marriage cannot take place!" cried Melissa passionately. "We must stop them!"

Leonora's eyes widened in amazement. "But surely you are taking delight in your brother's happiness! Why, you will have a new sister in Cecily. It will all be quite charming."

Melissa shook her head. "Come, now, Leonora! Consider, for a moment, the character and disposition of Cecily Trantor."

Lenora pondered. "Now as I recall, she arrived in London just after Christmas, and has been staying with her aunt in Grosvenor Square. She has a thin, pale face, lank brown hair, and no conversation whatsoever."

"Just so! With the best will in the world I could never accept such a dowd as a sister. I dislike her intensely."

"But it would be unfair to allow your feelings to prejudice those of your brother," Leonora pointed out. "If he is in love with her—"

Melissa laughed hollowly. "He cannot love Cecily Trantor! The idea is preposterous. I have observed Cameron escorting many women round London. They are invariably sophisticated, elegant, witty, and beautiful."

Leonora nodded her agreement. "That is true. I have never seen Cameron with anyone insipid."

"Yet you yourself agree that insipid is exactly the word which describes Cecily," declared Melissa. She stood up and walked in an agitated manner round the dressing room as she continued, "She is absurdly young. Barely eighteen, I believe. She has mournful brown eyes and such a delicate—*I shall break if you so much as breathe on me*—air. As you know, in company, she sits with downcast eyes, hardly uttering a word. And her clothes!

My dear, I've seen my maid look more elegant when she's dressed for church on Sundays. How can Cameron possibly profess himself in love with such a creature?"

Leonora expertly pinned her hair into a circle of ringlets on top of her head. "Perhaps he is tired of sophisticated London ladies. No doubt he is captivated by Cecily's air of fragility."

"There is certainly nothing fragile about her wrists and ankles," said Melissa dismissively. "Why, she is positively pudding about the heels." She sighed. "It is merely that I dislike Cecily, Leonora. There is also the matter of them setting up home in the country."

"Since you have taken so against her, I should have thought you would have been pleased to have them living as far from you as possible," Leonora said reasonably.

"But I am fond of Cameron, and you know I like to visit him often," replied Melissa. "If they were living in Park Lane, I would suffer the odious Cecily in order to see my brother. But to journey all the way down to Gloucestershire would be the death of me. You know I simply cannot abide the countryside. It is far too noisy."

Leonora laughed. "Noisy? How can you say that, when here in London we live amidst constant clatter and bustle?"

"Country sounds are more sinister," insisted Melissa. "All that wind rustling in the trees, and timbers creaking, and those dreadful birds waking one up at five in the morning." She shuddered. "No, I could not abide it. Not all that and Cecily too! It is too much."

Leonora spoke to Melissa's reflection in the oval mirror. "I am sorry you are so distressed, Melissa. But if Cameron is set on marriage—and I confess I still find the notion quite unbelievable—then I do not see that you can do anything to prevent it."

Melissa seized Leonora's hand. "Alone, I cannot stop the marriage, Leonora. But you could help me!"

"I?" Leonora laughed carelessly. "But you are overlooking the fact that it matters not a spangle to me whom Cameron marries."

"I am aware of that," said Melissa slowly. "Yet you are always protesting that Cameron interferes too much in your life. I thought this might be an amusing opportunity for you to spike *his* guns for once."

A mischievous smile lit Leonora's face. "What wicked notions you have, Melissa! Yes, I must confess I am weary of your dear brother's attempts to order my affairs. Yet I still do not see how you propose to stop his wedding."

"I have not a single idea in my head," admitted Melissa. "After all, I only learned the news an hour ago. But you are so much more clever and inventive than I. You will surely hit on a plan."

"Mmm," Leonora rested her head in her hands, to concentrate her thoughts. "Tell me what you know about Cameron's relationship with Cecily Trantor. As you talk, something may occur to me."

"There is really very little to tell," said Melissa apologetically. "All I know is that Cameron has escorted her to the theater, and dinner, and rides in the Park. I paid scant attention to the matter as I did not for a moment believe that the acquaintanceship would blossom into romance."

"You mentioned that Cecily has been staying with her aunt. What do you know of her people?"

Melissa wrinkled her pretty nose. "Her parents are Sir Reginald and Lady Augusta Trantor. Such provincials, my dear! They reside all year in Norfolk, and regard London with horror. To them it is a city of smoke and sin. A stew. However, they are gracing the capital with their presence at the moment, no doubt to supervise the arrangements for their dear Cecily's nuptials. And, of course, to inspect the bridegroom. I quizzed Cameron's steward, and was informed that the Trantors will be dining at Park Lane this evening. Cameron has even ordered dinner to be served two hours earlier, to accommodate their rustic country ways!"

Leonora looked up, her face alight. "Indeed? How very interesting. Then I do believe I have devised a scheme, Melissa."

Melissa clasped her hands. "Oh, I knew I could rely on you! Heavens, just see the time. We are due at Lady Jersey's at six and I'm still in my afternoon dress. You shall tell me of your plan in the carriage on the way there." She hurried to the door, then paused. "Leonora, if you are not wearing your new gold bracelet tonight, may I borrow it?"

"Why, of course," Leonora said. She smiled and reached into her velvet-lined bracelet box. "But surely you have four perfectly good gold bracelets of your own?"

"Two Lady Jersey has already seen. I cannot possibly wear them to her house again. And another is with the goldsmith, having the clasp repaired. Whilst the fourth I appear to have mislaid," said Melissa ruefully.

Leonora shook her head. "You are impossible, Melissa. But no doubt Sarah will find the bracelet somewhere in your apartments."

"She has yet to discover my silver earrings," said Melissa. "Although she and Daisy have searched high and low, the earrings seem to have disappeared forever. But do not fret," she smiled, "I promise I will take great care of your bracelet."

When Melissa had gone, Leonora rang the bell for Daisy. The red-haired maid entered to find her mistress slipping off her evening gown.

"There has been a change in my arrangements for the evening," Leonora said, drawing on a light robe. "Now come and sit in this chair close to me. There is a little matter on which I wish the benefit of your advice."

Three

"Are you ready, Leonora?" called Melissa. "The carriage is at the door, and I should like to be there in good time. If one arrives late at Lady Jersey's, the crush in the lobby is quite unbearable. Thank you so much for the loan of your bracelet. It looks divi—why, Leonora!"

Melissa's eyes widened in horror as Leonora emerged from her dressing room. Smiling, Leonora executed a pretty pirouette.

"Do I look well, Melissa?"

Melissa struggled for words. Leonora was arrayed in a gown of bright pink, purple, green, and yellow striped silk, the neck of which was cut daringly low. Entwined in her curls were no less than six purple ostrich feathers. Her flawless complexion was rosy with rouge, while her long thick lashes were liberally brushed with eye black.

"My dear Leonora. Are you unwell? Have you a fever?" .

"I have never felt better in my life!" Leonora replied, laughing.

"But surely you do not propose to attend Lady Jersey's rout dressed in so, well, in such a—"

"Vulgar fashion," added Leonora. "Don't I look perfectly dreadful!" she exulted, admiring her reflection in the long mirror. She examined herself critically for a moment, and then murmured, "Just one finishing touch is required, I believe." And seizing the pot of rouge, she dusted the pink powder in the crease of her cleavage, to emphasise the gentle curve of her white breasts.

"Leonora!" said Melissa sharply. "If this is your idea of a joke, then I must advise you that I am not amused. And what is more, I absolutely refuse to allow you to accompany me to Lady Jersey's dressed like a common actress!"

Leonora clasped her hands in delight. "That is precisely how I desire to look, Melissa!" She turned to Daisy, who was standing in the doorway. "How gratifying that all our hard work has not been in vain, Daisy. But now we must put poor Lady Melissa out of her misery. You need have no fear, Melissa. I shall not be attending Lady Jersey's rout this evening. Instead, I intend to impose upon the hospitality of your brother."

"But he has invited the Trantors to dine! And you have not been invited," protested Melissa.

"So much the better," replied Leonora sweetly.

Melissa sank laughing into a chair as comprehension dawned. "My, how priceless! Cameron will be livid. And as for the Trantors . . . oh how I wish I could be there. And tell me, where in the world did you obtain such an appalling dress?"

"Daisy used to run errands for one of the actresses at Covent Garden," explained Leonora, puffing powder on to her face. "She went down to the Garden for me, and the actress kindly lent me the gown. Now, Daisy, give me your opinion. Do I look the part?"

Daisy grinned with amused approval as she regarded the gaudy spectacle of her mistress. "You could have walked straight out of Common Garden, my lady. Except for just one thing. You smell too nice and fresh. Tell you what—" she appealed to Melissa. "May I borrow some of your perfumes, Lady Melissa?"

"With pleasure," said the lady.

Daisy disappeared to Melissa's apartments, returning a moment later with bottles of spirit of ambergris, attar of roses, jasmine oil, and other scents. She emptied some of each into one bottle, shook it up then liberally sprinkled the contents over Leonora's hair, shoulders and bosom.

"Ugh!" gasped Melissa, recoiling as the sickly-sweet aroma filled the dressing room. "My, that odor is quite overpowering! Leonora, do you not feel this is carrying the joke a little too far?"

"One must be thorough," said Leonora firmly. "Besides, much of the pungency will have worn off by the time I reach Park Lane. Now, all that remains is my jewelry."

From her jewel box she took a matching diamond choker, bracelet, brooch, and earrings.

As Daisy fastened the clasps, Melissa said, "Talk about gilding the lily. Truly, Leonora, if I happened upon you in the street I would instantly cross to the other side."

Leonora laughed. "Well you will have to tolerate my company in the carriage, for I wish you to drop me at Park Lane on your way to Lady Jersey's." Her eyes danced. "Poor Cameron. Imagine, at this moment he is finishing his early dinner with the parents of his bride-to-be. He has enjoyed an excellent repast. He is in mellow mood as he lingers over the port. He is blissfully unaware that shortly I shall, so to speak, be driving a horse and cart straight through his elegant drawing room!"

Leonora timed to perfection her arrival at Lord Rothwell's Park Lane residence. Brockway, Lord Rothwell's steward, informed her that the gentlemen had just finished their port and had joined the ladies in the drawing room.

Staunch, imperturbable Brockway batted not an eyelid as he observed Lady Leonora's unusually flamboyant appearance. Having served the Rothwell family for over twenty years, nothing surprised or amazed Brockway any more. Accordingly, when Lady Leonora declared with a smile that she would prefer to announce herself to the party in the drawing room, Brockway merely nodded. Quietly, he withdrew to give orders for the master's best brandy to be laid ready on a silver tray. From the impish expression on Lady Leonora's face, Brockway surmised that Lord Rothwell would be in need, later on, of the strongest spirits the house had to offer.

Leonora's entrance into the drawing room would have been admired by Sarah Siddons herself. She flung open both doors and then simply stood, with arms outstretched, while the surprised Lord Rothwell and his guests stared at her with undisguised horror.

("It was only for about fifteen seconds that I stood there," Leonora told Melissa afterwards, "but believe me, it seemed like fifteen years!")

Lord Rothwell recovered first. He arose and hurried toward her, murmuring, "My dear Leonora. You are ill. Feverish. Let me call—"

Leonora gave him no time to continue, but flung herself into his startled arms, and planted a smacking kiss on his cheek. "Cameron, you dear sweet man! How divine to see you again!"

He glared down at her and whispered furiously, "I regret I cannot say the same for you! What the devil are you playing at, Leonora?"

"Dearest heart, please, please forgive me for intruding," trilled Leonora loudly, "but I have the most wonderful news, and I wanted you to be the first to hear." She smiled winningly at the trio of Trantors sitting in a frozen, immobile group near the fireplace. "And your delightful guests, too, must share in our celebration!"

At the mention of guests, "dearest heart" had no choice but to turn and effect the introductions. "Sir Reginald and Lady Augusta Trantor. May I present Lady Leonora Pagett, who resides with my sister in Grosvenor Street. Leonora, I believe you are already acquainted with Miss Cecily Trantor?"

Sir Reginald, a balding beanpole of a man, arose and bowed stiffly. The well upholstered Lady Augusta raised her eyeglass, peered in amazement at the colorful apparition before her, and inclined her head. The pale-faced Cecily, dressed in a drab, stone-colored dress, dipped a frightened curtsy and shrank out of sight behind her father.

"I am quite charmed to meet you," beamed Leonora. "Cameron and I are such old friends, don't you know. I am only too happy to clasp any acquaintance of his instantly to my bosom."

Lady Augusta gasped, casting an icy glance in the direction of Sir Reginald, who appeared to be mesmerised by Leonora's cleavage.

Appearing quite unperturbed by the hostile atmosphere, Leonora sank onto the sofa and patted the seat beside her. "Now you must come and sit by me, Cameron! Oh," she laughed conspiratorially, "my dear, I have rouged your cheek when I kissed you. Here, let me!"

Taking a scent-soaked handkerchief from her reticule, Leonora wiped the trace of rouge from her host's cheek. Impatiently, he dashed her hand away, and withdrew to the far end of the sofa.

His eyes were steely as he enquired, "Well, Leonora. You have kept us all in suspense long enough. Perhaps you would care to divulge the reason for your unexpected visit?"

Leonora spread her arms in a dramatic gesture. "My dear, I am to become an actress. I am to tread the boards at Covent Garden!"

"The intelligence does not surprise me in the least," sniffed Lady Augusta.

Lord Rothwell raised a dark eyebrow. "And how has this event come about?"

"As you know," said Leonora breathlessly, "it has long been an ambition of mine to become an actress. You will mind, Cameron, that you and I have discussed the notion often, and your encouragement has been a great support to me."

Lady Augusta bridled, and drew her daughter to the safety of a chair as far removed as was decently possible from the vulgar creature on the sofa.

Leonora went on, with sparkling eyes, "This afternoon, I had the good fortune to encounter Mr. Edmund Kean at Lady Pinsley's. I have long been an admirer of his work."

Sir Reginald coughed. "You must forgive us, Lady Leonora. We are but simple country people, unversed in sophisticated London ways. Am I to understand that this Mr. Kean is a strolling player?"

"An actor, yes indeed." Leonora flashed Sir Reginald a brilliant smile. "Why, when he made his debut at Drury Lane a few years ago he quite took London by storm. He has fierce black eyes and oh, such a tragic air! Even crusty Mr. Hazlitt, the drama critic, was overwhelmed. What were his exact words again, Cameron?"

"In his review in the *Morning Chronicle,* Mr. Hazlitt asserted that *no actor has come out for many years at all to equal Mr. Kean.*"

"Dearest Cameron, I knew you would remember. Cameron is *so* clever," Leonora informed the Trantors. "I cannot imagine what I should do without him. Well, to continue, Mr. Kean very sweetly gave me every encouragement and said he would make strenuous efforts to ensure that I was engaged for his next play. Oh, what a thrilling day that will be for me!"

Lord Rothwell smiled dryly, and commented, "I confess I am surprised that you found Mr. Kean so charming and agreeable. I distinctly recall Melissa being present when Lady Holland invited Kean to dine. Melissa reported that everyone was sorely disappointed in him, finding the man moody, arrogant, and awkward."

Leonora waved an airy hand. "The passing years have lent him social grace, Cameron."

"And what character, pray, does Mr. Kean intend you to portray?" enquired Lady Augusta coldly. "Nell Gwynne, perhaps?"

Leonora blithely ignored the barb, and chose the first role that came into her head. "Why, I am to be Rosalind, in Mr. Shakespeare's *As You Like It.*"

"As I recall," murmured Lord Rothwell acidly, "the part of Rosalind requires an actress with a talent for disguise. The role should suit you admirably, my dear."

Leonora regarded him from beneath her long lashes. So, Cameron had clearly recovered from his initial anger at her intrusion, and was now seeking to score points. Well, my interfering friend, this is one match you shall not win, Leonora resolved, the light of battle in her eyes. For once I am determined to turn the tables, and do a little meddling in *your* affairs!

For having scrutinized the terrified Cecily at close quarters, Leonora was in full agreement with Melissa. Under no circumstances could Cameron be permitted to marry such a soggy creature.

Leonora said lightly, "Why Cameron, are you not going to offer me a glass of wine so we may drink a toast to the success of my new venture?"

"I have no intention of offering you alcohol," he said firmly. "You seem in quite high enough spirits already. I shall be delighted, however, to ring for more tea to be brought."

"Tea! How delicious!" Leonora leaned across and touched Cecily's arm. Cecily started as if she had been stung, and shrank back into her chair.

"Miss Trantor, do you remember that silly, but really so amusing children's rhyme? As I recall, we used to sing it in the nursery at teatime:

> When I sat next the Duchess at tea
> It was just as I knew it would be.
> Her rumblings abdominal

51

Were something phenomenal
And everyone thought it was me!"

"Well really!" exclaimed the outraged Lady Augusta. "Of course my Cecily has never been taught such a crass rhyme. She was brought up, Lord Rothwell, to behave with decorum and propriety at all times!"

"Discipline, that's the answer with children," declared Sir Reginald. "They shouldn't be allowed to fritter away their time. As a matter of fact, I was talking to a very intelligent fellow about this, just the other day. Name of Bentham. He has a scheme whereby children's seasaws are connected to pumping machinery, thence turning their play to useful purposes. Sounds a capital notion to me!"

Lady Augusta nodded. "None of our children were permitted to be wayward. I recall Reginald striking terror into my sons, simply by striding through the schoolroom threatening, 'If you aren't good boys then Boney will catch you.' "

Leonora was quick to sense a Trantor flanking movement, whereby they hoped to draw the conversation away from herself, and into less controversial topics.

She sighed heavily. "Poor Mr. Bonaparte. One cannot help feeling some sympathy with him in his defeat." Leonora sensed relief among the party that they had diverted her from more audacious subjects. She continued thoughtfully, "And yet how heartened he would have been had he known of the Duke of Wellington's many downfalls."

Sir Reginald frowned. "What is this you say, Lady Leonora? To the best of my knowledge—and I consider myself something of an expert in martial affairs—the Duke of Wellington has never suffered a serious defeat."

"Not on the field of war, I grant you," smiled Leonora. "But surely you have heard of the time he turned home on leave from the Peninsula. It was a wet and windy night, and the Duke set out to visit Miss Harriette Wilson."

"Leonora, I suggest we talk about something else," cut in Lord Rothwell hastily. "As Sir Reginald and Lady Augusta are not acquainted with Miss Wilson, the tale can have no interest for them."

"Oh, Lady Augusta, have you not been introduced to dear Harriette?" enquired Leonora ingenuously. "But she is the most charming girl. She has lovely auburn curls, tiny hands and feet, and quite the most fetching demeanor. I am surprised you have not observed her driving in the park. Her carriage is quite distinctive. It is exquisitely lined with pale blue satin."

"Leonora, I strongly advise you not to pursue this topic of conversation," Lord Rothwell warned grimly.

"But I must finish the tale, Cameron, now I have aroused your guests' curiosity!" Leonora leaned forward and engaged Lady Augusta's eye. "Well, the Duke of Wellington came knocking at Harriette's door one night, but found to his dismay that she was . . . er . . . occupied. With the Duke of Argyll no less, who donned a nightcap and appeared at Harriette's boudoir window in the guise of an angry duenna, shouting at the Duke to be gone! The poor Duke of Wellington was furious, but had no choice but to beat an undignified retreat down the rain-lashed street. So you see, Sir Reginald, in the lists of love, the Duke was not always the victor!"

In the stunned silence that followed, Leonora crossed to the tea trolley and said blithely, "Naturally, you will be wondering how Harriette herself reacted to this drama. Well she was not at all put out. She laughed and laughed, and observed that it was all the Duke's own fault for not making a firm appointment with her in advance! Is that not priceless?"

"Kindly pour the tea, Leonora," ordered Lord Rothwell, in a voice that bode ill for her when his guests had departed.

Leonora fluttered prettily round the trolley. "With pleasure! You know how I adore acting as hostess for you, Cameron."

Lady Augusta said maliciously, "It will be a sad day for you, Lady Leonora, when Lord Rothwell brings home his bride to Park Lane."

Observing that Lord Rothwell had been engaged in conversation by Sir Reginald, Leonora took the opportunity to confide to Lady Augusta, "Oh, I assure you there is no danger of Cameron marrying for many years yet. If at all!"

Lady Augusta frowned. "Indeed? But Lord Rothwell is so handsome, so eligible in every degree. I am convinced any young girl would regard him as an excellent catch."

"Yes, dear Cameron takes the fancy of the ladies, I grant you that," smiled Leonora. "Why, believe me, he's had more women sitting in his lap than you or I have had dinner napkins!"

Cecily, still sitting with downcast eyes, blushed scarlet at this intelligence. Leonora continued, in the same low, intimate tone, "Strictly *entre nous,* Lady Augusta, the girl who marries Cameron will have nothing but my deepest sympathy. Lord Rothwell is a dear friend, but he does possess some quaint notions. Only the other day he was telling me how much he favors the Russian way of marriage."

"And what is that, pray?" enquired a nonplussed Lady Augusta.

"A Russian bride," Leonora informed her, "must present her husband with a whip which she has fashioned herself. He then strikes her with it three times, declaring, *'I love thee like my soul. But I beat thee like my fur cloak!'* "

"Why how dreadful!" Thoroughly alarmed, Lady Augusta rose to her feet. "Come, Cecily. We must leave immediately!"

Lord Rothwell glanced up. "What is this, Lady Augusta? You are not departing so early? You have not even finished your tea."

"I fear we must remove from your house forthwith, Lord Rothwell," said Lady Augusta firmly, flashing her bewildered husband a glance which brooked no denial of her intentions.

Lord Rothwell escorted the party into the hall, where they engaged in strained conversation until the carriage was brought round. Leonora stretched out on the drawing room sofa, taking deep calming breaths to armor herself against the full lacerating fury of Lord Rothwell's wrath.

She listened as the good-byes were said, the front door closed, the carriage drew away down Park Lane. Then she sat up, smoothed down her skirt, and mentally prepared her defense.

There was really no cause for Cameron to be unreasonably angry, she decided, reasoning that after all, he considered it his right to interfere in her affairs; it should do him no harm to have a taste of his own medicine. And Melissa was quite correct in her assessment of Cecily Trantor—a dull little milksop she is. How could Cameron even dream of marrying such an insipid creature? They do not suit at all, and Leonora vowed to have no hesitation in telling him so without allowing Cameron to cow her.

Nevertheless, she could not suppress a shudder of nervous apprehension as the drawing room doors opened. But it was only Brockway, bringing in the brandy, and two glasses.

When he had gone, Leonora leaped to her feet and studied her reflection in the glass above the fireplace.

"Heavens! How dreadful I look!" she gasped. The heat of the room had lent even more color to her already highly roughed cheeks. And the eye black on the lashes was smudged, giving her the ludicrous appearance of a clown!

"Before I demand an explanation for your outrageous behavior," said Lord Rothwell icily, holding open the drawing room doors, "I should be obliged if you would remove yourself from my sight and clean every speck of that muck from your face!"

Leonora whirled round, ready to challenge him. But one glance at his grim expression was enough to send her scurrying to the dressing room. Now the drama of the evening was over, she was experiencing an acute feeling of anticlimax. And not a few pangs of remorse.

Oh, how livid Cameron looked, she thought fearfully, as she scrubbed off the rouge, and reasoned: *He will never forgive me! How I wish I could slip quietly out through the back door and run away home. But in his present mood he would be bound to follow me, and then the recriminations would be even worse. No, there is nothing for it but to face him, and brazen it out. And I shall not tolerate any attempt on his part to browbeat me. In fact I shall make a point of emphasizing that what I did to-night was only in his own best interests!*

With her pretty face cleansed, and her head held high, Leonora reentered the drawing room, fully prepared to do battle. Determined to seize the initiative by speaking first, Leonora declared boldly,

"There is a maxim, Cameron, that the end justifies the means—"

She trailed away, surprised to see that he was offering her a glass of brandy. "I think you deserve it," he said sardonically, "after such a brilliant performance. Congratulations."

Confused, Leonora sat down near the fire. "But aren't you angry with me?" she faltered.

"Bewildered more than angry," he replied, warming the brandy glass between his hands. "Clearly, your objective was to turn the Trantors firmly against me. What I do not understand is *why* you were so set on blackening my character so thoroughly."

"Because you have proposed to that whey-faced Cecily!" cried Leonora. "I could not allow you to marry her. She is unspeakably boring!"

"*Unspeakably* is an apt description," observed Lord Rothwell dryly, "considering she uttered barely a single word during the entire evening."

"That is exactly my point," said Leonora earnestly. "You cannot wed such a drab creature. You would be utterly miserable."

"I couldn't agree more," he replied, sitting back and crossing his long, lithe legs. "Which is why I have never troubled myself to propose marriage to the lady."

Leonora nearly dropped her glass. "But Melissa saw your letter!" She broke off, and dropped her eyes. There was nothing to be gained by incriminating Melissa, and making Cameron angry with her, too.

"Ah!" exclaimed Lord Rothwell with a wry smile. "I am beginning to comprehend. Brockway informed me this afternoon that Melissa was waiting in the drawing room. But when I came through from the library, she had hurriedly departed. I assume she saw the letter, then, on the writing table."

Leonora sprang to Melissa's defense. "She did not mean to pry! And she did not read all the letter."

"That was impossible, as one of my dogs jumped up and caused me to spill ink all over the second page," murmured Lord Rothwell, with an amused gleam in his gray eyes. "How galling for dear Melissa! But she read enough, I gather, to jump to the conclusion that I was about to tie the knot with Miss Trantor."

"But the declaration was quite plain!" protested Leonora. "And written in your own hand."

Lord Rothwell sipped his brandy, and said calmly, "But for that idiot dog, Melissa could have gone on to learn that I was in fact writing that letter on behalf of Sir Roger Lamprey, who has had the misfortune to break his right arm. The letter was to his sister, advising her of the marriage arrangements. Sir Roger could, of course, have dictated the letter to one of his clerks, but as this is such a confidential, delicate matter, he did not want it gossiped about below stairs. Thus I agreed to write the letter for him."

A blush stained Leonora's cheeks. "Oh heavens! I had no idea! . . . I . . . we naturally assumed . . ." She thought for a moment and then exclaimed, "But you cannot entirely blame us for imagining that you held Cecily in high esteem. Melissa says you have been seen with her at the opera, and riding in the park."

"Sir Roger has been in a great deal of pain with his arm. I was merely acting as Miss Trantor's escort whilst he was incapacitated," explained Lord Rothwell. "And a very tedious time I had of it, too!"

The full horror of the situation was just beginning to dawn on Leonora. "Oh, Cameron," she wailed in distress. "I hope my behavior here tonight has not soured Cecily's feelings for Sir Roger. If the Trantors now regard you as beyond the pale for being acquainted with such a vulgar lady as me, I fear that they will also now regard your friend Sir Roger with grave suspicion. It does not bode well for him, does it?"

"It most certainly does not," agreed Lord Rothwell. "In fact Sir Reginald informed me as he was leaving that he intends taking his daughter back to Norfolk forthwith. The marriage will most definitely not take place."

"Cameron, what have I done? Oh, why am I so impulsive, so hotheaded! Sir Roger will be beside himself with rage!"

Cameron slapped his thigh, and laughed. "On the contrary. I assure you, he will throw himself at your feet. You see, the truth is that his engagement to Miss Trantor has all been the most regrettable mistake. It is in fact her aunt who is the object of his affections."

"The same aunt with whom Miss Trantor has been residing in London?" asked Leonora, feeling quite dizzy with relief that her blunder was not to have disastrous consequences.

Lord Rothwell nodded. "She is, so I gather, an extremely attractive young widow. Unfortunately, on three separate occasions when Sir Roger called upon her, the aunt was not at home. But Miss Trantor was. She swiftly gained the mistaken impression that Sir Roger was paying court to her, and wrote to her parents informing them of this. Before Sir Roger knew what was happening, Sir Reginald and Lady Augusta had arrived in London, and were greeting Sir Roger as their son-to-be."

"Poor Sir Roger!" Leonora said, laughing. "What a terrible situation. But why did he not immediately make the situation clear to them?"

"He was too gallant. Or too fainthearted, depending on your point of view," replied Lord Rothwell. "Lady Augusta is a formidable woman. She hurled herself into action, ordering her daughter's trousseau and drawing up guest lists for the wedding. It would have taken a stronger man than Sir Roger to explain that it was all a dreadful misunderstanding. So you see, Sir Roger has every reason to be grateful to you."

An impish smile played round Leonora's mouth. "How I wish I had known all this from the start! Then I would really have pulled out all the stops to shock Lady Augusta within an inch of her life! I was so sorry she decided to depart early. I was about to tell her the story of the lady of ill repute who outraged her gentleman caller by inserting a thousand-pound bank note between two slices of bread—and eating it!"

"Hold it!" exclaimed Lord Rothwell in amazement. "When I first heard that tale, years ago, the bank note in question was a mere hundred pounder. It just shows how the cost of living—or loving—has soared!" He hesitated. "Would you object if I smoked a cigar, Leonora?"

"Not at all," she smiled, pouring him more brandy. "I love the aroma."

As he lit the cigar, Lord Rothwell commented, "I assure you, even without the bank note anecdote, you managed to persuade Lady Augusta of your total undesirability. Before she left, she told me in no uncertain terms what she thought of you."

"Oh, what did she say? Do tell, Cameron!"

"I would not dream of repeating any of it. A less

well-traveled man than I would have been shocked that a lady of her breeding should be acquainted with such low expressions. But I will tell you that she was particularly scandalized by the liberal amount of rouge you were sporting."

"I was somewhat heavy-handed with it," confessed Leonora.

"I quite agree! But I was not going to give Lady Augusta the satisfaction of knowing that. Instead, I quashed her with the inimitable Dr. Johnson's words: *better she should be reddening her own cheeks, madam, than blackening other people's characters!*"

Leonora gasped. "Did you really tell her that? Cameron, how gallant of you!"

He said gravely, "I am aware that you do, on occasions, regard me as over-critical of you, Leonora. But I would never, under any circumstances, allow anyone to say a word against you."

Leonora bit her lip, feeling suddenly confused and awkward at his unexpected kindness. She stood up. "I have taken up enough of your evening. I must go home—"

Quite without warning, the room seemed to whirl around her. She felt dizzy, and lightheaded. It was difficult to breathe.

Instantly, Lord Rothwell was at her side, his strong arms supporting her.

"Sit down," he ordered gently.

"She gazed up at him from the chair, and murmured faintly, "I am so sorry. I cannot imagine what is the matter."

"When did you last eat?" he enquired quietly.

"Oh . . . I suppose at breakfast. I was intending to dine at Lady Jersey's, but then I changed my plans and came here . . . and you had finished dinner."

"And you have been drinking brandy on an empty stomach," observed Lord Rothwell, pulling the bell and issuing instructions to Brockway.

Within ten minutes, Leonora was served with a tempting supper of cold meats, savory biscuits, and fruit pie. She ate in silence for a while, then laid down her fork with a sigh of content.

"Thank you, Cameron. I had not realized how ravenous I was!" She laughed. "It is surprising I was not really enacting that absurd poem I told Miss Trantor about the Duchess and her rumbling tummy!"

Lord Rothwell shook his head in mock exasperation. "Wherever did you learn such a rhyme? I know for a fact you did not know it as a schoolgirl. Or for sure, you would have repeated it to me, and I should have been obliged to pretend that I disapproved!"

"Daisy told it to me," smiled Leonora. "She knows all manner of shocking rhymes. I must confess, she has been most helpful in preparing me for this particular escapade. Without her I should never have been able to lay hands on such an appalling dress."

Lord Rothwell sighed in distaste as he regarded the multi-colored creation adorning Leonora's slender frame. "I have not set eyes on anything so vulgar since the days when I consorted with certain actresses in Paris."

Leonora pushed away her plate. "Oh Cameron, do tell me about Paris! Is it really so glamorous, and exciting, and gay?"

"Yes, every bit so," he smiled.

"And what adventures did you have there?" she pressed. "Were you really in love with a beautiful widow? Was it it a tragic, doomed affair?"

He stood up, and said abruptly, "If you have finished your repast, then I shall escort you home."

Rebuffed, Leonora said with dignity, "Naturally, I do not wish to pry into your private life. If you do not wish to discuss Paris—"

"No I do not!" he thundered. "I should be obliged if you would remember that and not mention the subject again!"

What a contradictory man he is, mused Leonora, as they rode back to Grosvenor Street in the carriage. One moment he is kindness and consideration itself. And the next, he is as cold and unapproachable as an iceberg.

She realized that she had touched a raw nerve when she mentioned Paris, but wondered what did befall him there. Did he fall passionately, hopelessly in love? Did he wander with her through scented gardens, and declare his love in the moonlight as he and the woman he desired gazed on the waters of the Seine?

The notion of the cynical, rugged Lord Rothwell losing his heart made Leonora smile. How impossible. Cameron was far too much in control of himself and his emotions ever to fall in love.

"What is amusing you?" he enquired. "You seem lost in thought."

"Oh, I was just contemplating that I shall not now have to go to the bother of choosing you a wedding present," she replied lightly.

He riposted, "I confess I was flattered by your alarm and concern for me. Why, I wonder, should you put yourself to so much inconvenience to prevent my nuptials?"

"It was Melissa who was upset by the notion, not I!" Leonora protested hotly. "She loathed Cecily, and could not abide the thought of you burying yourself in the Gloucestershire countryside. As for myself," she went on scornfully, as he assisted her from the carriage, "I assure you I do not give a button whom you marry!"

He left her at the door. But his mocking laugh echoed in her ears as she ascended the stairs.

"Such conceit!" she muttered furiously. "Imagining that I would care about an event so insignificant as his marriage! He can wed whom he chooses. It is nothing to me. It is his wretched bride I feel sorry for!"

Hearing Melissa's raised voice echoing from her apartments, Leonora hurried to tell her of the dramatic events in Park Lane that evening. Just as she reached

Melissa's bedchamber, the door was flung open, Melissa stood before her, with tears streaming down her face.

"Leonora! I don't know how to tell you! The most dreadful thing! Your bracelet. Your beautiful new gold bracelet has been stolen!"

Four

Leonora threw off her cloak, and commented in an unconcerned tone, "You mean you have mislaid the bracelet, Melissa."

"Not at all!" declared Melissa indignantly. "I know you think me careless, and there have, I admit, been many occasions when I raised a false alarm. But this time I know I am not in error."

Leonora followed Melissa into her dressing room as she continued, in an agitated tone, "I returned home early from Lady Jersey's rout as I was developing a headache. Sarah mixed me a powder, and I lay down on the sofa there to rest. But before doing so, I distinctly remember taking off your bracelet and putting it safely in my jewel case. Then I fell asleep. When I woke up, I crossed to my toilette table to brush my hair, and saw to my horror that the jewelry case was lying open, and the bracelet was gone!"

"Perhaps Sarah remembered that it was my bracelet, and took it along to my apartments," suggested Leonora.

Wearily, Melissa rested her head on her hands. "I have already questioned Sarah. She did not touch the bracelet, or indeed enter the room again after she had given me the powder. "No," Melissa sighed, "I am afraid the unpleasant fact has to be faced. I am harboring a thief in my household."

"But your servants are so loyal, so faithful! Who . . ."

"Why, the culprit is quite obviously Daisy," Melissa said sorrowfully.

"I refuse to believe it!" protested Leonora.

"But consider the number of mysterious happenings in this house since Daisy's arrival." Melissa counted on her fingers. "First my best silver earrings disappear. Then my gold bangle. And now your bracelet is gone."

"You still have no evidence against Daisy," flared Leonora. "Why, she herself carried my bracelet home from the goldsmiths in Bond Street. Had she been intent on stealing it, she could easily have kept it then, and invented a story about a rogue attacking her in the street. No, I simply cannot believe that Daisy is dishonest. I shall call her here immediately and we shall have the entire matter out in the open!"

"I am afraid that is impossible," said Melissa quietly. "You see, Daisy has gone."

"Gone?" echoed Leonora. "Where? When?"

"About half an hour ago, after speaking to Sarah about the bracelet's disappearance, I asked her to fetch Daisy from her quarters. Sarah returned to inform me that Daisy had departed, and in something of a hurry. Sarah found this strange, as just before I rang for her, she and Daisy had been enjoying their supper together and Daisy had shown no sign that she intended to leave."

"I see." Leonora absently fingered her diamond necklace. "You believe that Daisy took the bracelet whilst you were asleep, hoping that you would not discover its disappearance until the morning. But when you suddenly rang for Sarah, she feared that all had been discovered, and ran away."

Melissa nodded. "I am afraid that sounds the most feasible explanation. I am so very sorry about your bracelet! It is all my fault for not taking more care."

"Do not fret," soothed Leonora. "We have yet to get to the bottom of the matter. I am still quite unconvinced that Daisy is the culprit."

66

Melissa soaked a handkerchief in lavender water and pressed it against her brow. "What a dreadful day this has been. First I learn that my beloved brother is to marry a simpering idiot, and then—"

"But Melissa! cried Leonora. "In all the commotion over the bracelet, I have forgotten to give you the news about Cameron." She sat down near Melissa. "I had the most fascinating evening," she began. "My entrance at Park Lane was superb . . ."

When she had finished her tale, Melissa's gray eyes were shining. "So he is not to marry Cecily Trantor after all!"

"No, it was all an unfortunate misunderstanding."

"What a relief!" sighed Melissa. "And what a dear friend you are, Leonora, to come so swiftly to my aid. Oh dear, it makes me feel even worse about your bracelet. I shall call on Cameron first thing in the morning and ask him to come and investigate the whole affair."

"No!" Leonora's tone was vehement. "There is no need to trouble him. He will regard us as a couple of blockheads if we are constantly running to him for advice. I am convinced we can resolve this matter ourselves."

"But how?" queried Melissa doubtfully. "The first essential is to interview Daisy. But she has disappeared."

"I have a strong suspicion that she will have returned to Covent Garden," mused Leonora. "If I set off now, I have a good chance of catching up with her."

"But it is half past ten at night!" cried Melissa. "You cannot leave the house at this hour!"

"Of course I can," laughed Leonora. "Everyone will be pouring out of the Covent Garden theatres. I shall mingle with the crowd and be perfectly safe."

Melissa was aghast. "You are not contemplating going alone? Leonora, I forbid it! You must at least take a footman!"

"If I am to find Daisy, then I must make myself as inconspicuous as possible," said Leonora. "And if I have a footman plodding behind me, then Daisy's sharp little eyes will soon seek me out. I do not believe for one moment that she stole any of the jewelry. There has clearly been some misunderstanding. My plan is simply to follow her, and see who she speaks to. I have a notion that she may be in trouble, and require my help. Now, there is no time to be lost. I must hurry away and change."

It was with considerable relief that Leonora discarded the gaudy multi-colored dress in which she had shocked the Trantors. She removed, too, all her jewelry and ornaments, and selected a simple gown of pink muslin. Over this she threw a light cloak of navy colored wool.

"Leonora, this is a foolhardy scheme!" wailed Melissa, as Leonora was about to depart. "I do wish you would not go. I shall feel so responsible if any ill befalls you!"

"Do not fuss, Melissa," laughed Leonora, as she stepped out into the porch. "Where is your spirit of adventure?"

"I have none," admitted Melissa. "I would rather be tucked up safely in bed than roaming the streets of London by night."

Leonora's hair gleamed bright as molten gold in the lamplight. "Go to bed, Melissa. And I will tell you all about it in the morning!"

Leonora took the carriage to Drury Lane. Once there, she wrapped a shawl lightly round her head, and dismissed the driver. Her search for Daisy was, she knew, better carried out on foot. A smartly painted carriage venturing down the dark back lanes of Covent Garden would be absurdly conspicuous. And the last thing Leonora desired was to draw attention to herself.

Her amber eyes were alight with expectation as she glanced around the bustling area of Covent Garden. It is almost as busy now, by night, as it is during the day, she mused.

Fashionably dressed society people were emerging from the theatres, laughing and gesticulating as they discussed the merits of the plays they had seen. In a corner, a ballad vendor shouted his wares, and on the theatre steps sat a flowergirl, selling violets, primroses, and oranges. Above the hubbub of voices rose the screech of iron-rimmed wheels as the carriages lined up, ready to take the theatregoers to select midnight supper parties.

A tremor of excitement fluttered through Leonora as she mingled with the crowd. She felt not a bit afraid at being out this late on her own. How furious Cameron would be if he knew, she smiled, imagining his handsome face darkening with anger.

But Cameron simply did not understand that, unlike most girls, she could not abide to feel cosseted and cocooned for every minute of the day. Cameron maintained that he was anxious to protect her, but she felt smothered when he set down rules and regulations about where she might go and the people she met. He did not appreciate that occasionally she saw the need to break free, to travel unchaperoned, to go where she wanted.

Otherwise she felt caged—oh, with pretty golden bars at the windows, to be sure, but confined nevertheless. Most women, she believed, did not seem to mind restrictions being placed on their liberty. But, as Cameron often pointed out so caustically, the Lady Leonora was unlike any other woman he had ever encountered!

As she sauntered midst the cream of London society, Leonora pondered anew the problem of Daisy. The more she considered the matter, the more convinced she became that Daisy was not guilty of theft.

After all, reasoned Leonora, she could easily have pocketed the gold brooch that night at the theater. But she was honest, and returned it. And as Leonora had explained to Melissa, it would have been simplicity itself for Daisy to have stolen the bracelet on the morning she carried it home from Bond Street.

It was not as if Melissa had any direct evidence against Daisy concerning her missing earrings and bangle.

No one had observed Daisy either taking anything, or even behaving in a suspicious, underhand manner.

If only, Leonora cried to herself, she hadn't run away from Grosvenor Street tonight! By acting thus, she appeared to have incriminated herself. But Leonora was sure that Daisy must have had a good reason for leaving, and her every instinct warned her that the girl might be walking into danger.

As it was Leonora who urged Daisy to enter her employment, then she must assume total responsibility for her. She would not leave Daisy to fend for herself and, at all costs, must find her quickly.

But how? As she roamed through Covent Garden, Leonora had been searching everywhere for a flash of red hair, the gleam of bright blue eyes. Already, the crowd was beginning to thin, making Leonora's task easier. Yet still Daisy's pert little face was nowhere to be seen.

Leonora pondered that perhaps she was mistaken in thinking Daisy would have come to Covent Garden. Yet she could have run in quite the opposite direction. To Islington, perhaps, or Clerkenwell Green.

"Lovely violets!" called the flowergirl. "Pretty primroses! Only a penny a bunch, my lady. They'd look a treat pinned to your cloak."

Smiling, Leonora bought some violets. Then, noticing that the girl had only a few bunches of primroses left in her basket, Leonora handed her another three coins. "There. Now you have sold all your flowers, and your work is over for the night."

"Thank you, my lady," beamed the girl. "It ain't often I get the chance of an early night." She stood up, knotting the ribbons of her battered black straw bonnet, and pulling her shawl close around her thin shoulders.

Leonora hesitated. "I wonder . . . it occurs to me that you may be in a position to assist me. I am looking for a girl called Daisy. She would be about your age, I suppose, with red hair and blue eyes. Have you seen her?"

70

The flowergirl's eyes were suddenly wary. "I see a lot of people, my lady. Can't remember them all."

"I assure you," said Leonora quietly, "I only wish to help Daisy. I fear she may be in trouble. If you do know where she is, and you fail to tell me, then you will be doing her a grave disservice."

The flowergirl stared into Leonora's face for a moment. Then she nodded. "You look a kind lady. Not like some folk I meet in the Garden. But I trust you. Daisy was here not long ago. She didn't stop. We just had a few words together. But I'll tell you this: she really had her dander up! I've never seen her so riled!"

"Did you notice which direction she took when she left you?"

The girl flicked her thumb. "Back of Henrietta Street. I think she was trying to find her Uncle Jack. Right villain he is, too."

Leonora pressed sixpence into the girl's hand. "Thank you. I am most grateful."

As she set off toward Henrietta Street, the flowergirl called after her in alarm, "My lady, you must not venture there alone! It ain't safe!"

Leonora paid no heed. She slipped between the few remaining carriages and disappeared into the dark back streets of Covent Garden. As she made her way along the unlit roads, the warnings of Melissa and the flowergirl were soon ringing in her head. By day, Leonora had always found Covent Garden a delightful place, with its bustling good-humored crowds jostling round the colorful stalls laden with fruit and flowers.

But by night the streets took on a more sinister complexion. She hurried past gin shops, and rowdy taverns, while from gloomy blind alleys came the sound of scuffles and drunken brawls.

As she rounded a corner into a narrow cobbled street, a man lurched into her path, his breath smelling foully of alcohol.

Before he could speak, Leonora declared imperiously, "Kindly stand aside!"

Shocked, he instinctively obeyed the authority in her tone, and Leonora hurried on, unmolested, but with her previous high confidence now considerably chipped.

In truth, she was beginning to grow desperate, wondering how, in this mysterious maze of alleys, she was ever going to locate Daisy. And if she did not find the girl, how was Leonora to make her way home again? For it had dawned on her with chilling clarity, that in these dark, unfamiliar lanes, she was now hopelessly lost.

What was she to do? The night was growing cold and Leonora shivered inside her light cloak. Tiredness, too, was creeping over her limbs, causing her more than once to miss her footing and stumble across the cobbles.

Perhaps Melissa was right after all, and this is a foolhardy venture, she thought. And yet she would never have forgiven herself if she had not come after Daisy whose name would be blackened at Grosvenor Street with no opportunity to defend herself.

Straightening her back, Leonora walked on with renewed vigor, resolving she must find her. Concentrating all her thoughts, Leonora now believed Daisy has gone in search of that odious Uncle Jack. But she had no idea at all—no clue—to his whereabouts.

Leonora's mind was a blank. Then she stopped quite suddenly in the middle of the road, and beat her fist against her brow.

Of course! Why didn't she think of that before!

On three occasions she had sent a footman to Uncle Jack's lodgings, to advise him of Daisy's whereabouts. All she had to do now, thought Leonora feverishly, is remember the address. She recalled that it was a lane named after a singing bird. Nightingale Lane? No! Skylark Lane? That didn't sound right either. Lark . . . that's closer, but it isn't correct. But she believed it began with an L. A songbird . . . Linnet! That was it! Linnet Lane!

Desperately, Leonora gazed round her in the gloom. But how was she to find Linnet Lane? All these streets and lanes looked depressingly alike.

At that moment she espied a gnarled old woman scuttling out of a gin shop. Leonora seized hold of her arm.

"One moment, if you please! I wonder if I may trouble you for directions to Linnet Lane?"

The woman peered up at her suspiciously. "A lady like yourself shouldn't go wandering down there by herself. They're all rogues and villains down Linnet Lane."

Leonora pressed a coin into her hand. "Please. The matter is most urgent!"

The woman shrugged. "On your own head be it, then. Go down to the end of this street, and Linnet Lane's the third on your right. But take care!"

Murmuring her thanks, Leonora hurried off into the night. When she arrived at Linnet Lane, she found that it was in fact little more than a wide, blind alley. From the end came the sound of raised voices. For a moment, she believed it to be just another drunken affray, but then she realized that one of the voices was familiar to her. It was high-pitched, shrill, and female. It was Daisy!

She saw that Daisy was standing outside a crumbling lodging house, arguing with a large man whom Leonora recognized as the odious Uncle Jack. As the flowergirl had remarked, Daisy was indeed in a towering rage.

"Don't try and cod me! You stole my lady's bracelet!" she accused.

"That I did not!" shouted Uncle Jack.

"You did, you hammerheaded thief! One of your queer-diver friends recognized the Lady Melissa's carriage, didn't they, that morning in Covent Garden. You found out where I'd gone, and now you've stolen the Lady Melissa's earrings, and her gold bangle, and my lady's bracelet!"

He roared: "Aye, I'd have taken them if I'd had the chance. And more too. But if you want the truth—"

"The truth!" spat Daisy. "Coming from you that would be a rare treat!"

"The fact is I had no notion where you'd gone until this afternoon when I saw you talking to that actress in the Garden. Surprised I was, to see how a filthy lass like you was suddenly so neat, with your hair washed and a clean dress on. Well, well, I thought. Young Daisy has gone up in the world. So I followed you. I admit it. But I stole nothing."

"You lie!" shrieked Daisy. "As soon as I heard that bracelet had gone, I knew it was you. Well I want it back. Now!"

He swung his fist at her. "Watch how you talk to me! I'll give you a milling, you cheeky brat!"

Daisy ducked and caught him a sharp blow in the shin with her boot. Howling with pain, he grabbed her hair, and slapped her face. "I'll teach you respect for your elders. I'll teach you to run away. A lady's maid, are you? Not no more. All that's finished. From now on, *I'm* your master—"

"Unhand that girl immediately," ordered Leonora, stepping out of the shadows.

Uncle Jack was so surprised, his fingers automatically uncurled from Daisy's hair. "And . . . who might you be?" he stuttered.

"I am the Lady Leonora Pagett. I have taken Daisy into my household as my personal maid," Leonora informed him haughtily.

He raised an eyebrow. "Have you now? And why was I not advised?"

"My footman called three times at your lodgings, but you were never at home," Leonora said. Daisy had crept away from Uncle Jack and was standing beside her mistress.

The man's face assumed a crafty expression. "But as Daisy's legal guardian, I think I'm owed some sort of payment if you want to take her away from me."

"I shall be delighted to reimburse you for your loss. I am sure we can come to some arrangement. Providing, of course, you can produce documents proving that you *are* Daisy's legal guardian."

Daisy laughed. "He can't do that, my lady. I've never seen no such papers. And in any case, it was his late wife who took me in and cared for me. All I've ever got from him is beatings."

"Shut your mouth!" shouted Uncle Jack. He whirled on Leonora. "I tell you I want payment. And if you won't give it, then I must take it!"

His grimy hand closed on Leonora's cloak. Daisy screamed, and lunged forward to claw his face. He swept her aside, then seized her by the shoulder and with a vicious shove sent her hurtling into the darkness of the alley. Daisy raised her voice and began to scream:

"Help! Help! Call the Law! My mistress is being attacked! *Help!*"

Uncle Jack grinned evilly. "Let her shriek all she likes. This is *my* home ground, you see. It's amazing how deaf people round here can be when they choose. Now, my pretty lady, how about you and me getting better acquainted?"

"Don't you dare touch me!" cried Leonora frantically. She struggled furiously but in vain as his hands groped beneath her cloak., Terrified, she squirmed this way and that as his greasy hands tore at her bodice, and her head was pressed back against the hard wall.

"Let's start with a little kiss," rasped Uncle Jack, his thin lips moist with desire.

"On the contrary!" declared an icy, authoritative voice. "*I* shall start by giving you a good thrashing!"

Leonora could not believe her eyes. Cameron! Just when she had given up all hope, Cameron had come to her rescue, here in this remote Covent Garden backstreet!

There was a crack of a whip and a scream of agony

from Uncle Jack. With terror now in his eyes he backed away from the furious nobleman bearing down on him with such venom. Lord Rothwell paused, the point of his whip poised against the villain's neck as he cringed against the wall.

"How did you find me?" whispered Leonora, feeling almost dizzy with relief at the reassuring sight of Lord Rothwell.

He replied grimly, "Melissa was most concerned about you. Quite properly, she sent a message to Park Lane telling me where you had gone. Naturally, I came straight down to Covent Garden. But of course by that time there was no sign of you. I was beside myself with anxiety . . . oh no you don't, my lad!"

Uncle Jack had taken advantage of Lord Rothwell's momentary distraction to try and make a break for it. But a lash from Lord Rothwell's whip sent him cowering back to the wall.

Lord Rothwell continued, "I plunged down into this maze of alleyways, searching this way and that for you. There was no sign. I was in despair! Then, thank God, I heard Daisy shrieking for help . . ."

"Oh Cameron, thank heavens you came when you did! I was in quite desperate straits!"

"I would have torn every brick and house down with my bare hands to find you," he informed her gravely. "But Leonora, when will you learn not to engage in such foolhardy escapades? You have no idea how worried I was about you!"

"I must confess I was somewhat fearful myself!" confessed Leonora. "But where is Daisy now?"

"With my footmen at the end of the lane." He snapped his fingers, and immediately two burly footmen attired in the Rothwell livery came running down the alley. "My men will escort you home."

"But what about you?" said Leonora in alarm. "Are you not to accompany us?"

Lord Rothwell turned a cold, lethal eye in the direction of the shivering Uncle Jack. "No. First there is a little matter to settle concerning the whereabouts of some jewelry . . ."

"Daisy, would you kindly refresh my memory on something," said Leonora, as she sat at home in the room they named the Blue Saloon working on her feather picture. "Just what, exactly, is a queer diver? Last night you declared to Uncle Jack that one of his queer diver friends must have seen Lady Melissa's carriage in Covent Garden, and so ascertained where you were living."

Daisy was shaking ostrich feathers free of dust. "Queer diver means a bungling pickpocket, my lady. They're all rogues. Every one of 'em."

"But how did your uncle first take up this, er, occupation?"

"As a young lad, I believe," replied Daisy. "He'd go to the Bartholomew Fair at Smithfield. It was easy pickings there. Later on, he started taking the job seriously, and got himself a proper coat."

"To keep him warm, you mean, whilst working outside in inclement weather?" queried Leonora.

Daisy giggled. "Bless you, no my lady. Uncle Jack's coat had nothing to do with warmth! He'd wear two, you see. Each very thin. The outside one would look torn and tattered, But in fact each rent was cunningly positioned so he could make a snatch, slip it through one of the slits, and into the pockets of the inside coat."

"That is really quite ingenious."

Daisy shook her red head. "It's bad, my lady. Real bad."

"But Uncle Jack must be very rich by now."

"Oh no. He gambles it all away. In truth, my dearest wish is never to set eyes on him again."

"There is no reason in the world why you should," said Leonora soothingly. "It was very brave of you to ven-

77

ture out last night to confront him. What still puzzles me is how you knew my bracelet was missing. For when Lady Melissa discovered it had gone, it was Sarah she called to her apartments."

"I had a notion that something was up," muttered Daisy. She reddened and would not meet Leonora's eye. "So I . . . er . . . well, that is . . ."

"You followed Sarah and listened outside Lady Melissa's door," sighed Leonora. "Oh Daisy!"

"I know it was wrong but I'm not sorry I did it," said Daisy defiantly. "I was positive it was Uncle Jack who'd taken it and I was sure I'd never rest until I got the bracelet back. But now of course he's swearing black and blue that he was not guilty of taking it."

She leaped forward to hold down the delicate feathers on the table as the door opened, causing a draft.

In swept Melissa, accompanied by her brother. Daisy curtseyed, and was about to withdraw, when Melissa detained her.

"No, stay a moment, Daisy. Lord Rothwell has some disturbing news which it is only right that you should hear. And for my part I wish to beg your pardon for thinking ill of you over the disappearance of the bracelet."

That was handsome of Melissa, reflected Leonora. She turned to Lord Rothwell who was immaculately dressed in a chocolate brown morning coat, with fawn breeches and boots glossed to a high shine.

"What is the intelligence you have for us, Cameron?"

"I have to inform you, Leonora, that Daisy's Uncle Jack most definitely did not steal either your bracelet or Melissa's jewelry."

"How can you be so sure?" queried Leonora.

Lord Rothwell replied briefly, "We engaged in a lengthy physical altercation, which settled the matter."

"Excuse me, my Lord," blurted Daisy. "But does that mean you laid into my Uncle Jack?"

"That is a more graphic description of the incident, yes."

"But Cameron, what danger you were in! Did not his rough cronies come down and set upon you?" cried Leonora.

Lord Rothwell brushed a speck of dust from his lapel. "Two of them did attempt to intercede. When last seen, they were lying flat on their faces in the gutter."

Daisy stared up at him, wide-eyed with admiration.

Smiling, Leonora said, "Very well, Daisy. You may leave us now."

As the door closed behind her, Melissa said anxiously to her brother, "You remain convinced that Uncle Jack is not the culprit?"

"I am positive. I spared him nothing. But he steadfastly refused to admit his guilt."

"Poor Uncle Jack," murmured Leonora. "To suffer a beating from you—yet to be innocent all the while!"

"Innocent indeed!" snapped Lord Rothwell. "Have you forgotten that he was on the point of attacking you? And in any event, what I handed out to him will in small measure compensate for all the thrashings he has inflicted on Daisy." He drummed his fingers on the side table, and went on slowly, "The perplexing thing is . . . if Uncle Jack did not take the jewelry . . . then who did?"

The trio sat in silence for a while, pondering the problem.

"I am mystified," confessed Melissa at last. "As you know, all my servants have been with me for years. I trust them implicitly."

"And it is not as if you have had any strangers about the house," said Leonora. "Workmen, decorators or suchlike."

Melissa shuddered. "No, I always arrange for renovations to be undertaken in August, whilst I am out of London. I cannot abide being present during all that upheaval. It is bad enough putting up with the noise from the house

79

next door. Workmen are forever coming and going in there. The banging and thumping is quite intolerable. I was only saying to Lady Jersey last night, 'In a fashionable neighborhood like Mayfair one simply does not expect—' "

"This is getting us nowhere," cut in Lord Rothwell. "Have either of you any further suggestions or thoughts on the robberies?"

The two girls shook their heads.

"Well I shall not allow the matter to rest," declared Lord Rothwell. "There must be an explanation. Somehow, I shall discover the truth of the matter."

As he spoke, Leonora rearranged the bowl of violets on the bureau. "I think as long as I live," she murmured, "when I look on violets I shall recall the events of last night."

Lord Rothwell smiled at his sister. "Your house looks quite charmingly fresh, my dear. And it is the flowers which make it so. Violets here in the Blue Saloon, and I noted an enormous bowl of roses on the hall mantelpiece."

"They must be hothouse blooms," said Melissa. "Aren't they delightful? They are a gift from an admirer of Leonora's." Melissa bit her lip, realizing she had made a slip.

"Yes, Sir Max Fitzarren sent the roses," said Leonora gaily, watching Lord Rothwell's mouth tighten. "Wasn't it sweet of him?"

"I thought I advised you not to encourage his attentions?" glowered Lord Rothwell.

"But what was I to do when his footman called with the flowers? Throw them out into the street and stamp on them?" enquired Leonora innocently.

She decided that it would be unwise to mention to Cameron that she had accepted an invitation from Sir Max to join a party of his friends in an excursion to the Vauxhall Gardens.

Lord Rothwell bade the two girls a curt farewell. He had obviously decided to say no more (on this occasion) about the Irishman he despised. But as he strode out into the large square hall, his elbow knocked against the bowl of red roses on the mantelpiece.

Whether it was by accident or design Leonora never knew. But the bowl tipped over, and the fragile blooms dropped *en masse* into the flames of the fire below.

Five

Leonora decided it would be prudent to have Daisy accompany her on the visit to Vauxhall Gardens. Although Sir Max had invited her to join a party of his friends—which in theory should have meant safety and respectability in numbers—Leonora wanted to make doubly sure that her suitor had no opportunity to be alone with her. She had not forgotten his celebrated boast that he would have a wedding ring on her finger by the end of June.

Very well, my red-haired Irish friend, thought Leonora as she slipped on a gown of pale green silk. I'll show you that we English girls are not as dimwitted as you clearly believe us to be. I shall flirt with you. I shall listen attentively to your every word. I shall laugh at all your jokes. But throughout it all, I shall keep Daisy doggedly by my side. And that is how we shall proceed throughout the spring. Until at last, in a frenzy of impatience as the end of June looms, you seize a few precious moments alone with me to propose.

And then what a shock will befall you! How London society will laugh when they hear of my icily sarcastic rejection of your suit! I give you my word, Sir Max. Their scorn will be so great, you will not dare show your face again in any of London's fashionable drawing rooms.

Gloomily, Daisy fastened a simple gold locket around her mistress's neck.

"Why the long face?" smiled Leonora. "Are you not pleased to be paying your first visit to Vauxhall? I assure you, it is the most delightful place. I am convinced you will enjoy your outing." Seeing the girl clamp tight her lips and lower her eyes respectfully, Leonora urged, "Come now. You may speak plain with me. Why are you not looking forward to our excursion?"

Daisy mumbled hesitantly, "You asked me to speak plain, my lady. Well, the truth is, I wish we were going to Vauxhall in different company."

"Oh dear," sighed Leonora. "I had forgotten your unreasonable antagonism toward Sir Max. Can you see nothing good in him at all, Daisy?"

"No, my lady. He's a chunk of wood if ever I saw one," replied Daisy, picking up the silver-backed hairbrush and drawing it through Leonora's shining hair.

"A chunk of wood?" echoed Leonora. "Do you mean to assert that Sir Max is thick in the head?"

"Not at all, my lady. It's rhyming. Chunk of wood —no good!"

"Heavens, however do you remember all these quaint rhyming expressions?" laughed Leonora.

"It's easy when you use them every day," said Daisy. "But since I came to Grosvenor Square I've forgotten a lot. Sarah says its no great loss, either!"

Leonora smiled to herself. Chunk of wood indeed! Sir Max would tear poor Daisy's hair out if he heard about that!

Leonora was sorry she could not reveal to Daisy her plans for the downfall of Sir Max Fitzarren. The girl would have made a useful, quick-witted ally. But after the incident with Uncle Jack, Daisy now regarded Lord Rothwell as her hero. She gazed at him with shining eyes. She spoke of him in the Servants' Hall in hushed tones, and with the utmost reverence.

Leonora felt she could not risk Daisy letting slip to Lord Rothwell the truth of the situation between herself and Sir Max. Part of the fun, after all, was watching Cameron's fury whenever her name was coupled with the Irishman's!

When Leonora entered Sir Max's commodious carriage, she was surprised to observe that she was the only passenger.

"I understood you to say that there would be a party of us, Sir Max," she enquired of the stocky Irishman.

He grinned. "Did I really say that? Perhaps I did. Unfortunately, my friends have been detained. So it will be just the two of us visiting Vauxhall."

"Just the *three* of us," Leonora corrected him sweetly, beckoning Daisy from the Grosvenor Street house.

Even Daisy's sullen expression brightened as they entered Vauxhall. The Gardens were illuminated by a thousand lamps, shining like stars from the trees.

"Why, it's so bright it's like daylight!" Daisy marveled. "And just look at all the people. The whole world is here tonight!"

Sir Max frowned, and murmured disapprovingly, "Do you always allow your maid to join in your conversation in public, Lady Leonora?"

"I find Daisy's comments most refreshing," replied Leonora coolly. "Shall we wander down that avenue? I believe the fountains are quite the most splendid sight. Tell me, Sir Max, do you have anything like this in Ireland?"

He smiled, and when he spoke his voice was lyrical. "I hail from Galway, Lady Leonora, where there are no formal gardens. No avenues of beech trees. There, the glory lies in lush rolling hills, green against the brilliant blue of the sea."

"It sounds delightful. Can you observe the sea from your house?" asked Leonora.

"To be sure. Although my home is more accurately

85

described as a castle, rather than a house," he said with a careless laugh.

"A castle! How romantic! Does it have turrets, and a moat, and a drawbridge?"

Leonora's eyes were alight with amusement. *Here is your cue, Sir Max, to tell me that one day you will carry me over the threshold of your castle!*

But Sir Max decided on more subtle tactics. "Indeed it is a fine place. But," he sighed heavily, "I confess it is lonely there. It is so remote, you see."

"Oh dear. Are there no other castles nearby? No friendly neighbors?" enquired Leonora impishly.

He smiled sadly. "My castle stands on its own in five thousand acres."

"How convenient," murmured Leonora. "It is so tiresome being overlooked."

"You are fond of the country, then?" he enquired. "The wildness and loneliness do not disturb you?"

"Indeed not. I have a house and estate of my own in Gloucestershire." *As you well know, Sir Max. As you know also the size of my fortune, my age and, no doubt, how many teeth I have in my head. If your story is true about owning a castle in Galway, I am convinced the place must be in a sad state of decay. For all London knows, Sir Max, that having gambled your fortune away, you are desperately in need of a wealthy bride.*

Sir Max's next remark was drowned by Daisy, who was thumping her chest and coughing violently. Leonora was about to suggest that they pause at one of the drinking fountains, in order that Daisy might ease her throat, when she realized that her faithful maid was, in fact, merely trying to signal a warning.

Leonora had been so engrossed in her conversation with Sir Max, that she had not realized he was leading her straight toward the notorious Dark Walk. Here, the branches of the trees arched and met, excluding the moonlight. And no pretty lamps were hung to guide the walkers' way. Even now, Leonora could hear high-pitched squeals emitting from the Walk as rascally young men pursued the ladies into the shaded arbors.

It was not difficult for Leonora to affect a little shiver. "The night air is colder than I had anticipated. Shall we retreat to the music room? I understand that it is quite enchanting."

Sir Max masked his disappointment with effusive concern. "My dear Lady Leonora. How inconsiderate of me. I should never forgive myself if you caught a chill. Come, let us hurry to the music room."

Leonora heard Daisy breathe an audible sigh of relief as they approached the safety of the brilliantly lit music room, where the orchestra was playing all the merry, popular tunes of the day.

As they were about to enter, Daisy said to Sir Max, "I beg your pardon. But I believe there is a person nearby who wishes to speak with you."

She pointed in the direction of one of the famous Vauxhall Garden statues. Lolling against it was a roughly dressed lad, with a sharp face and foxy eyes. He was indeed beckoning to Sir Max.

The Irishman shrugged. "You are mistaken, girl. I am most certainly not acquainted with such a ruffian."

Turning his back on the lad, he began to usher Leonora before him into the music pavilion.

"Sir! The lad is following us!" blurted Daisy.

Sir Max scowled. Leonora had never before seen him so out of countenance. The boy dashed up and grasped the red-haired man by the arm.

"Must speak to you. It's a matter of business. Most urgent."

Leonora waited for Sir Max to reprimand the ruffian for daring to address him in such a familiar manner. To her surprise, her companion said, tight-lipped:

"Would you excuse me for one moment, Lady Leonora? I shall return directly."

Grim faced, he strode off, followed by the lad. Once out of earshot, they stood under the beech trees engaging in a heated conversation.

"How very odd," murmured Leonora, as she waited in the doorway of the music room. "I must confess, Daisy, I would dearly love to know what they have to say to one another! I have never seen such an ill-matched pair!"

Daisy's blue eyes were fixed on the couple under the beech trees. "It's something to do with the Great North Road, my lady."

Leonora said in amazement, "Mercy, you must possess sharp ears, Daisy. I cannot hear a word!"

Daisy gave a hesitant smile. "Neither can I. I'm lip reading, my lady!"

"Oh Daisy!" laughed Leonora. "Is there no end to your talents?"

Daisy frowned. "Now there's a rum thing. That young ruffian keeps calling Sir Max by the name of Harry. That doesn't sound quite right, does it?"

Leonora was convinced that Daisy was in error. After all, to a lip reader, the movement of the mouth required for Harry was very similar to Arren. And quite apart from the fact that the Irishman's christian name was not Harry, it was out of the question for a nobleman to be spoken to so familiarly by such a lowly person.

There was no time for further speculation. The boy suddenly ran off into the night, and Sir Max came hurrying to join Leonora.

He was smiling. His voice was bland, and well controlled. "Forgive me, Lady Leonora. That young lad had simply been sent by one of the bucks at White's to tell me the result of a little wager I had on a horse."

"Indeed?" said Leonora coolly. "From the boy's agitated manner I had assumed that your castle was on fire!"

Sir Max smiled indulgently, "He is but a simple stable lad. To him, anything connected with horseflesh is of vital importance. And he had not the wit to understand that he should not come rushing up and interrupt our pleasure."

They entered the music pavilion, where Sir Max found them seats with a good view of the orchestra and the crowd of laughing people. After they had listened to the music for a few minutes, Leonora enquired,

"And did you win your wager, Sir Max?"

He started. "What . . . oh, the wager. Yes to be sure. Most satisfactory."

"These wagers will be the ruination of you, Sir Max! What with that and your gambling as well!"

He laughed. "But my small skirmishes with Lady Luck are but trivial affairs. Most of the great men of our age have flirted with fortune, Lady Leonora."

"Ah. Now tell me whom it is you are seeking to emulate," she smiled.

"I confess, I am a great admirer of the late Charles James Fox," said Sir Max. "You will mind that he was not only a valued companion of the Prince Regent. He was also a great statesman. But it was nothing to him to play the tables at Brooks without a break from eight in the evening until three the following afternoon. Then, clear headed despite his lack of sleep, he would deliver a brilliant speech in the House of Commons before returning to Brooks to dine. The night would be devoted to gambling at White's, and after a short nap he set off for the races at Newmarket. His—"

"Stop, stop!" cried Leonora. "I feel quite fatigued just listening to your account. Yet I cannot believe that Mr. Fox died a wealthy man."

Sir Max shrugged. "That I do not know. He was a true gambler, in the sense that whether he won or lost, he showed not a trace of emotion. He could be ten thousand pounds up in the morning, and thirty thousand down by midnight, yet he never turned a hair."

"It seems to me," commented Leonora, tapping her

foot in time to the music, "that the only people who win at gambling are the proprietors!"

Sir Max fell silent, and Leonora surmised that he was reluctant to pursue the topic.

She stood up. "I fear it is growing late, Sir Max. Melissa will be concerned about me."

When they were settled in the carriage, he remarked, "Lady Melissa, I mind, is the sister of Lord Rothwell. No doubt he visits you often?"

"Indeed, yes." *To warn me against associating with you!*

As if reading her thoughts, Sir Max said with a chuckle, "I'm sure you don't pay too much attention to what *he* has to say, do you?"

Leonora replied demurely, "Naturally, as he is Melissa's brother I rely on him to advise me. There are so many matters in which a young lady like myself feels totally ignorant. Lord Rothwell's maturity and experience are a great comfort to me."

Sir Max patted her hand. "Lord Rothwell is a fine enough man. Do not misunderstand me. But he does tend to be a little pompous in his manner."

Leonora ignored Daisy's outraged intake of breath. "I must confess, he does have strong words to say about those who indulge in excessive gambling," murmured Leonora, enjoying herself enormously.

"That's exactly my point!" exclaimed the Irishman. "As I have already explained to you, there is really no harm in gambling! No, what I really want to impress upon you, Lady Leonora, is that if I were you, I should not allow Lord Rothwell to have too much influence in your life."

"You wouldn't?" asked Leonora, wide-eyed and innocent.

He shook his head. "You strike me as a spirited, independent young woman. Perfectly capable of thinking and acting on your own account. Now wouldn't it be a pity if all that spirit were crushed by someone who happened to think in a straight-laced fashion?"

The carriage came to a halt in Grosvenor Street. "Thank you so much for a truly pleasant evening, Sir Max," said Leonora as he assisted her down the steps. "You have certainly given me much to ponder on!"

"Your company has been enchanting," he smiled. "May I call on you again, soon?"

"That would be delightful," said Leonora, favoring Sir Max with the warmest, most brilliant of smiles.

Leonora was well pleased with the outcome of her visit to the Vauxhall Gardens. As she returned from an afternoon call on Lady Jersey (to express her deepest regrets at being unable to attend Lady Jersey's recent reception), Leonora pondered on the progress of her relationship with Sir Max.

From Max's point of view, she mused, *everything is developing splendidly. It is now April, which gives him two clear months to persuade me to tie the knot. He will not, of course, be anxious to arouse my suspicions—or worse, those of Lord Rothwell—by appearing in undue haste to marry me. No, it must all be made to appear as if, with the coming of spring, he gradually found himself falling in love with me. How touching! He cannot resist, it seems, my spirited, independent nature. Naturally, the depth of his affection is in no way related to the size of my fortune!*

More red roses had arrived for Leonora that morning, accompanied by a note from Sir Max thanking her for such a delightful evening. And at this early stage in the budding romance, roses are quite the proper gift to send, Leonora decided.

Later, as mutual affection deepens, he may present me with a small, tasteful piece of jewelry, she thought, *and a gold brooch fashioned like a rose would be a meaningful gift.* Leonora further mused:

91

By that time, of course, we should be so much in one another's company that an engagement would almost be taken for granted by our acquaintances. His proposal will come as no sudden shock to me. But how surprised will be Sir Max when he hears my reply!

It is interesting that he is so wary of Cameron. And with due cause! Why if Cameron knew of my true plans for Sir Max, he would be furious. He would tell me I was playing with fire—and he might well be right. But of course, I'd die rather than admit Cameron was right, and this would lead to another of our violent quarrels. He'd probably silence me by putting me over his knee and spanking me.

Leonora flushed, remembering the time when Melissa's brother had done just that. In a fit of schoolgirl temper, she had thrown an inkpot at her tutor and run off, refusing to apologize. Cameron had relentlessly sought her out in the shrubbery and without a word tipped her over his breeches, tanning Leonora until her eyes watered. The indignity of it still made her squirm.

Leonora realized that Daisy, sitting opposite her in the carriage, was muttering sullenly to herself.

"Is anything wrong, Daisy?"

"Great North Road," said Daisy, a frown creasing her brow. "It was one of the things I made out in that conversation between Sir Max and that ruffian last night. Then Sir Max came back and said they'd been discussing a wager on a horse."

"That's right. You know Sir Max is forever having wagers on one thing or another." *No doubt he has been tempted to take a wager on his certainty that I will wed him. But he must realize the foolishness of that. For I should be bound to hear of the wager and be so insulted that I would refuse to set eyes on him again.*

"But my lady, there *is* no race course on the Great North Road!"

"How you do fuss!" said Leonora impatiently. "No

doubt the horse in question was merely stabled some-where along the road. There are countless reasonable ex-planations. I know you do not like Sir Max, but you must not be so suspicious of his every word and gesture!"

"No, my lady."

Daisy subsided into silence, and said not another word until they reached Grosvenor Street.

As the carriage drew up outside Melissa's house, the front door opened and out swept a dark-haired woman whom Leonora did not recognize. She was, Leonora judged, in her late twenties—handsome rather than pretty, and elegantly dressed in the height of fashion. She looked neither to right nor left, but quickly entered her carriage and was borne away.

Although Leonora had been able to catch only a brief glimpse of her, there was something about the woman's de-meanor—an air of superiority, an arrogant tilt to the head —to which Leonora took an instant dislike. Curious to know more about her, Leonora hurried into the drawing room where she found Melissa reclining on a sofa, leafing through the latest issue of the *Lady's Magazine.*

As Leonora entered, Melissa threw down her peri-odical and exclaimed animatedly, "Oh, thank heavens you are come! Did you see her? Did you set eyes on my visitor on her way out?"

"If you are speaking of the dark-haired woman in the velvet-trimmed pelisse, then yes I did catch a glimpse," replied Leonora. "But who is she? Her face was not at all familiar to me."

Melissa's gray eyes were sparkling with excitement. "Her name is Madame Bettine Valbois. She and her broth-er have just arrived in London from Paris. And Cameron, of all people, asked me to receive her!"

Leonora sat down. "She is acquainted with Camer-on?"

"He sent me a note this morning," said Melissa breathlessly, "saying that Madame Valbois unfortunately knew no one in London society. It would greatly oblige him, he said, if I would be so gracious as to be at home when she called this afternoon."

"Naturally, if *you* receive her, then the rest of the ton will follow suit," remarked Leonora. "But tell me, how did your brother come to make her acquaintance?"

"When he was in Paris!" cried Melissa. "Do you not recall the rumor that he was involved with a French widow? An affair of the heart! A grand passion! I am certain, Leonora, that the widow is none other than Madame Valbois!"

"But what is she doing in London?" asked Leonora, quite taken aback by the news.

"Ah, now that is a matter for speculation," smiled Melissa. "Madame Valbois maintains that she is here on a short excursion with her brother. Yet she clearly took care to advice Cameron of her arrival."

"Surely Cameron would not be so foolish as to take up with a woman like that again!" protested Leonora hotly.

Melissa's eyes widened. "Why Leonora, whatever can you mean? Truly, I found Madame Valbois to be the most charming person. She comes from a highly respected French family. Her brother is the Comte de Selvigny. I found her manners and demeanor most agreeable. And oh, the cut of her gown, Leonora! So French! And the quality of the lace. Quite superb. And you must own that she is an attractive woman. Far in a class above that moon-faced Cecily Trantor."

Leonora struggled for words. "Yes . . . indeed everything you say is correct. Yet there is something about her . . . an air of superiority which I found disagreeable."

Melissa laughed. "It is most unlike you to be so unreasonably prejudiced, Leonora. Why you have not even been introduced to the lady."

"I confess I have no urge to make her acquaintance," replied Leonora distantly.

"Oh but you must!" cried Melissa. "I have arranged that we shall call on her on Thursday afternoon."

"Then I regret that on Thursday morning I shall develop a severe headache!"

"You will do no such thing!" scolded Melissa. "Madame Valbois is quite well aware that you are living here with me. She longs to meet you. For you not to call would be an unforgivable slight. No," said Melissa with unaccustomed firmness, "I must insist, Leonora, that you accompany me on Thursday!"

As the ladies made their departure on Thursday, Daisy flopped on to a stool beside the large kitchen range.

"My," she sighed to the housekeeper, Mrs. Harris. "I'm fair worn out. It took two whole hours to get Lady Leonora dressed this afternoon." She smiled her thanks as Cook handed her a buttered muffin. "I've never known Lady Leonora so persnickety about her dress."

Sarah commented, "It's usually my mistress who discards six dresses as unsuitable before deciding on the seventh. Mind you, Lady Leonora is so beautiful she looks lovely in any fabric, any color."

Daisy shook her red head. "I couldn't agree more. But today, for some reason, nothing was right for her. The pink mull was too limp. The waist of the green sarcenet was too high. The tamboured muslin was too elaborate. I tell you, I was at my wit's end."

Sarah nodded. "I heard Lady Melissa chiding her —quite gently mind—for taking so long to dress. *If you do not make haste, Leonora,* she said, *we shall be late, and Madame Valbois will be most insulted.*"

"That's right," agreed Daisy. "Then Lady Leonora muttered something I could not catch. But I guessed from the steely glint in her eyes that it was not a complimentary remark!"

"No," went on Sarah, "because then Lady Melissa pointed out that Lord Rothwell had been so good and kind to them both: *He rarely asks for any favors, Leonora. And look how brave he was, coming to your rescue against that vile Uncle Jack person. The least we can do is*

95

oblige Cameron by being polite to his Parisian friend."

"Is she the French lady who was here the other day?" enquired the cook.

Sarah's eyes were huge with admiration. "Yes. Oh, how elegant she looked."

Daisy wiped the last piece of muffin in the butter on her plate. "Can't say I took to her myself."

"You only caught a glimpse of her," challenged Sarah.

Daisy shrugged. "I know. But I'm funny like that. Some people I warm to straight away. Like Lady Leonora, for instance. I knew immediately that she was kind and honest. But with some folk, I get a strange prickly feeling down my spine. That person means danger, the prickle tells me. Watch out! And I'm never wrong. What's more," she continued, "Lady Leonora wasn't too impressed with Madame Valbois either!"

"Perhaps that's why she was so reluctant to call on her?" suggested Sarah.

Mrs. Harris, who from her lofty position as housekeeper would not have deigned to criticize or comment on her employers, could not resist the enquiry, "And what, then, did Lady Leonora finally choose to wear this afternoon?"

"A very simple muslin, of forget-me-not blue," replied Daisy. "With the prettiest lilac bonnet, pearl-buttoned lilac kid gloves and a parasol of fluted blue silk. She looked unbelievably lovely."

Leonora was quite well aware that her behavior had been most unreasonable. *Whatever is the matter with me,* she asked herself as she and Melissa were admitted to the Hanover Square house which Madame Valbois had rented.

It is most unlike me to be so short-tempered. I have argued with Melissa, and snapped at poor Daisy. And as for the ridiculous fuss this afternoon over which dress I should wear! Really, I feel most ashamed. I vow I shall do my utmost to make amends by being as charming and pleasant as I can to Madame Valbois.

Leonora and Melissa were ushered into a drawing room tastefully decorated in shades of green and gold. Madame Valbois came forward to greet them, her finely boned face alight with pleasure.

"Lady Melissa, how delightful to see you again! And this must be the enchanting Lady Leonora, cousin of your late husband. Please excuse me for not waiting to be introduced formally, Lady Leonora, but I freely confess I have been longing to make your acquaintance!"

Madame Valbois was soberly dressed in dark gray pin-tucked silk, the neck edged with delicate white lace. Her hair was loosely coiled on top of her small head, and her bright brown eyes rested on Leonora with animated interest.

To her dismay, Leonora felt all her good resolutions ebbing away. For some strange reason, the atmosphere in the drawing room seemed oddly tense. Leonora was conscious that she felt very much on guard. But why? Madame Valbois was being charming. The afternoon promised to be a delightful experience. Why, then, did Leonora feel so strongly that Madame Valbois was not her friend, but her enemy?

As Leonora deliberated on these matters, Madame Valbois beckoned forward a tall, fair haired gentleman.

"May I introduce my brother Edouard, Comte de Selvigny."

He took Melissa's outstretched hand and bowed. Leonora was surprised to see Melissa blush. She was relieved, however, to discover, at least, she felt no hostility toward him. Indeed, she found herself warmly drawn toward his kindly eyes, and noble, upright bearing.

As they sat down, Leonora, deciding that the time had come for her to make some contribution to the conversation, enquired civilly, "Is this your first visit to London, Madame Valbois?"

The Frenchwoman flashed her a brilliant smile. *"Mais oui!* And I am so enchanted with what I have seen. The serenity of St. Paul's. The beauty of the River Thames by night. And the gaiety of the park when everyone gathers to ride at five o'clock. I assure you, Paris is dull in comparison."

Leonora viewed Madame Valbois through narrowed eyes. This gushing praise of London sounded suspect to Leonora's ears. True, London was a delightful city. But Paris, too, was equal in splendor. What of the soaring majesty of Notre Dame? The mystery and enchantment of the Seine by night? Why, wondered Leonora, is Madame Valbois so eager to ingratiate herself with Melissa and myself?

The Count was smiling at Melissa. "My sister is, of course, quite fascinated by the sights of London. But I believe she is also anxious to know about the shops."

Again that glowing smile, which did not quite reach Madame Valbois's brown eyes. "That is so, Edouard," his sister said, "Lady Melissa will appreciate that in the spring, every woman becomes dissatisfied with her wardrobe. She desires fresher, more novel modes . . . new jewelry, and parasols too! But I have no notion where to go for my purchases in London. For a stranger like myself, the city is so bewildering." She leaned forward. "I should be most grateful for your help and advice."

A footman entered, bearing a tray of wine and sugared cakes.

Melissa accepted a glass of wine, and informed Madame Valbois, "As I am sure you will have surmised by now, Madame, London is rather unique. Each particular area of the city has its own character, and you will find that different trades, too, are centered in certain parts of the capital."

Although Melissa's remark was directed at the Frenchwoman, Leonora was intrigued to observe that her eyes were drawn time and time again to the handsome Count.

He murmured, "That is an interesting point, Lady Melissa. I have already ascertained that St. Paul's churchyard is rich in bookshops."

Melissa nodded. "That is certainly so. Whilst Whitechapel is celebrated for tailoring, and Clerkenwell for watchmakers."

"Though of course for fashions," Madame Valbois said, smiling, "I understand that Bond Street and Regent Street are the only places to be seen in. I have been admiring that unusual shade of blue muslin from which your dress is styled, Lady Leonora. Do please tell me which establishment you patronize."

"I rely on Messrs. Clerk and Debenham of Wigmore Street," replied Leonora.

"And Mr. Swan and Mr. Edgar, in Regent Street, are also establishing an excellent reputation," added Melissa.

Leonora set down her wineglass on the walnut side table. "I am surprised, Madame, that you are so interested in our English modes. Here in London, we all envy your Parisian designs. No lady of the ton is without a copy of *La Belle Assemblée*. Any style, however outlandish, has only to be described as Parisian to be greeted with cries of approval."

Madame Valbois gave a slight, depreciating shrug. "You English regard our Parisian fashions as chic. We in France admire *la mode Anglais*. Both, no doubt, are equally excellent. Yet because we women are perverse creatures, is it not true that we always covet that which is unfamiliar to us?"

Her brown eyes held Leonora's, and in them she detected the glimmer of a challenge. It was as if her words held a deeper meaning. As if, thought Leonora, Madame Valbois was not talking about mere dresses at all!

Leonora repressed an inward shiver. *Really, the wine must have gone to your head,* she admonished herself. *Whatever ails you today? Why do you persist in seeking hidden meanings in every simple remark of Madame's?*

Leonora forced herself to concentrate her thoughts on clothes. It was interesting, she reflected, that on first sight Madame's gray dress appeared somber—even dull. Yet Melissa, beside her, in sprigged muslin, with violets decorating her straw bonnet, seemed fussily overdressed. Leonora was glad that she herself had chosen the simple blue muslin, accentuated by flawless accessories. She had observed Madame Valbois's eyes resting appreciatively on her lilac kid gloves.

Fortunately, the count seemed to find nothing amiss in Melissa's appearance. He was, in fact, most attentive to her, refilling her glass the moment it was empty, and ordering a screen to be brought to shield her from the drafty window.

Madame Valbois sipped her wine, and continued, "I confess I find it fascinating that the person with the greatest reputation for elegance in London should be a man. Your Beau Brummel is celebrated throughout Europe, you know."

Her brother added, "I do hope we set eyes upon the gentleman whilst we are in London."

"He is easy to recognize," Leonora informed them. "Mr. Brummel drives about in high style, in a glossy black tilbury drawn by a spirited black horse."

Madame Valbois's businesslike brain had been at work. "No doubt," she said, "Mr. Brummel is a great favorite with all the tailors, hatters, and shirtmakers?"

"Indeed, he has quite made the reputation of Weston's, his tailor in Old Bond Street," exclaimed Melissa. "And Hoby, the bootmaker at Piccadilly, is said to be worth a fortune."

The count smiled. "With Bettine satisfied with regard to the shops, I confess my main interest in coming to London is to visit the theaters. We were fortunate enough to see a production of *Measure for Measure* at the King's Theater last week. It was quite excellent. And such an enormous audience!"

Melissa nodded. "I believe the King's seats over three thousand people. We usually take a box for the season."

Madame Valbois said quickly, "But is that not rather expensive?"

Melissa colored. She was unaccustomed to discussing money-matters with anyone outside her own family.

"But tell me, Lady Melissa," Madame Valbois persisted. "How much does it cost to buy a box?"

Leonora came to Melissa's aid. "It is twenty-five-hundred pounds for the season," she said crisply. "Alternatively, you may obtain admission to the pit for only ten shillings and sixpence."

The Frenchwoman laughed, impervious to Leonora's barb. "Ah yes, during *Measure for Measure* the pit was filled with young dandies. I do not agree with my brother in his opinion of the play. I found it excessively tedious. But the evening was enlivened for me by the amusing antics of those young men in the pit. They swaggered back and forth, showing off their new clothes, and canes, and snuff boxes. They were not in the least put out when people from the gallery shouted to them to be quiet!"

Leonora said frostily, "My sympathy is entirely with the actors. Sometimes the noise from the pit is so loud they can hardly make themselves heard."

The count said quietly, "I agree absolutely, Lady Leonora."

His sister made a dismissive gesture. "Pouf! All artistic people are themselves notoriously unstable. The Green Room in any theater is always filled with ladies of ill-repute. Even the famous Mr. Kean was, I hear, extraordinarily eccentric and rude."

"That at least is true," nodded Melissa. "It was utterly impossible to entertain him socially. And Lord Byron, you know, is quite as bad. Why, I heard of him being invited to dinner and refusing every dish that was placed in front of him, insisting instead that he desired only biscuits and soda water. It happened that there were none

101

in the house, so he sourly made do with mashed potatoes and vinegar!"

"How very embarrassing for the poor host!" trilled Madame Valbois. "Such a thing could never happen in Paris. All Frenchmen are connoisseurs of good food. In fact, I believe that we French have an instinctive regard for all that is finest and best in life."

"Come, now, Bettine," her brother reproached. "Surely you are not asserting that the French are superior to the English?"

"Naturally not, but I do maintain that we are, perhaps, just that little bit more civilized, or sophisticated, call it what you will."

Leonora caught Melissa's eye, and signaled. "I cannot abide five minutes more of this woman's company! May we leave now. *Please?*"

Melissa rose to her feet. "My, how the time has flown, Madame Valbois. It has been so pleasant conversing with you and the count. I had not realized the hour was so late. It will soon be time for the lamps to be lit."

Leonora said sweetly, "Is not the gas lighting in this part of London so pretty, Madame? Have you anything comparable in the streets of Paris?" Leonora knew full well that the new London lighting was far in advance of anything to be seen in Europe.

"I fear not," said Madame Valbois curtly.

Leonora continued blithely, "The very lamps themselves are a marvel to behold, are they not? Some of them have been forged, you know, from French cannon made obsolete by the Battle of Waterloo."

No one, least of all Madame Valbois, needed to be reminded that this had been a resounding English victory. That will teach you, though Leonora, to allege so smugly that the French are the superior race!

Madame Valbois rallied. "Indeed, I too had not realized the hour was so late. It has been quite delightful seeing you both. I shall have much to tell dear Lord Rothwell over dinner this evening."

"My brother is dining with you?" enquired Melissa.

"We are to have that honor," smiled Madame Valbois. "I know he is looking forward to talking over old times . . ."

Leonora could not comprehend the flood of fury that swept through her. *After all, what is it to me,* she pondered, *with whom Cameron chooses to dine?*

Yet as the farewells were said, and Madame Valbois said, "It has been a pleasure to make your acquaintance, Lady Leonora. I do hope we shall meet again soon," Leonora found herself hard put to return the compliment.

Six

Melissa settled back in the carriage with a sigh of satisfaction. "My, what a diverting afternoon! Were you not quite fascinated by the Frenchwoman, Leonora?"

"Indeed I was not," replied Leonora coolly.

Melissa's eyebrows rose beneath her straw bonnet. "But she is so amusing. So elegant. So informed! I am surprised that a lady of your taste and discernment, Leonora, should take against her so unreasonably."

"And I, for my part, am surprised at you, Melissa, for extending the hand of friendship to such an affected woman. You say she is informed. But she has much to learn about the rudiments of social etiquette. Blatantly to enquire of you the price of a box at the theater! You were put to the blush there, Melissa, and do not attempt to deny it!"

Melissa shook her head with an indulgent, dismissive smile. "But Madame Valbois is French, my dear, and unaccustomed to our English ways. She had no intention of embarrassing me. No doubt in Europe it is perfectly the thing to discuss money matters so freely in public. I shall quiz Cameron on the matter. He will know." She pressed Leonora's arm, and continued in a conspiratorial tone, "Now confess, Leonora. Were you not positively intrigued to set eyes on Cameron's celebrated French widow?"

"Intrigued, yes. That I freely admit. After all, I have

a healthy curiosity just like everyone else," laughed Leonora. "But I was in no manner impressed by the lady. I find it impossible to imagine Cameron being desperately in love with her."

"Nonsense!" protested Melissa. "I can envisage the pair of them only too clearly. She is attractive, well-dressed, and possesses a lively style. And she has, too, that indefinable, singularly French quality—such a bright way of regarding one, that makes it impossible to tell what she is really thinking."

Yes, you are right on that last point, mused Leonora. *But unlike Melissa, Leonora was sure that she could read Madame Valbois's mind. All the time, Leonora realized, it is as if she is constantly reviewing the situation, assessing how to turn the conversation to her best advantage. Oh, on the surface she is all charm. So very agreeable. But in my view, beneath that well-cut French bodice beats a very stony heart indeed!*

"I wonder," Leonora said finally, "how she and your brother became acquainted in Paris."

"Cameron never would tell. You mind how he clams up whenever the subject is mentioned," said Melissa. "However, I shall in due course winkle the truth from Madame. I confess, she is quite different to the person I had originally imagined. Cameron mixed with quite a raffish crowd in Paris, and I had assumed that his lady-love was an actress."

Leonora laughed. "Beware mentioning that to Madame! From her conversation this afternoon I gather that she believes all actresses to be fallen women."

"So how did she meet Cameron?" pondered Melissa. "Yes, I must definitely coax the facts out of her!"

"You intend to continue the relationship, then?" enquired Leonora stiffly.

"But of course! You will grow to like her in time, Leonora."

Leonora lapsed into a sad silence. She had known Melissa for a long time, and they had always been such good companions. But now Leonora was at a loss to understand why Melissa should be fostering this friendship with such an unsuitable French widow. Knowing Madame Valbois, thought Leonora gloomily, she will need little encouragement to be constantly at the house in Grosvenor Street. She will accompany us to the theater, on our rides round the park, on shopping expeditions. We will never be free of her.

For Melissa's sake, it would be churlish to reveal her true feelings about Madame's presence. She will be compelled to smile, and pretend that her company is oh, so agreeable!

The prospect was not a happy one. Leonora shifted restlessly in her seat. Unwilling to dwell any further on Madame Valbois, Leonora remarked as the carriage turned into Grosvenor Street, "Madame's brother, le Comte de Selvigny, seemed a most amiable person."

"Did you think so? Yes ... he appeared extremely agreeable."

Something in Melissa's tone made Leonora turn and stare at her. "Why Melissa, you are blushing!"

"Indeed, you are mistaken!" Melissa dropped her glove. "Oh ... oh see, the workmen are back at the house next door! It is too vexing! They will be banging and hammering and I shall not be allowed a moment's rest before dinner!"

Melissa's evasive tactics were in vain. It was soon impossible for her to pretend that she did not find the count a most attractive gentleman. He, too, seemed enchanted by Melissa. Over the coming weeks, the count was a constant caller at Grosvenor Street, taking Melissa for rides in the clement spring air, to the opera, and out to dine.

When he was not present himself, the count's footman would be at the door, bearing bouquets of fragrant blooms for Melissa. Indeed, the saloons of the house were filled with flowers that April, for Sir Max Fitzarren, too, was continuing his courtship of Leonora, and the red roses continued to arrive daily, on the stroke of ten o'clock.

With Melissa happily occupied for much of the time with the count, Leonora found herself increasingly glad of the attentions of Sir Max. She permitted him to act as her escort to the numerous balls, receptions, and assemblies of the London season. He was amusing company, and had she not been aware of his true, lecherous and deceitful nature, she might have allowed herself to be romantically swayed by his considerable charm.

But the memory of poor Clementina's suffering was constantly there, like a warning cold edge of steel pressed against Leonora's throat. So throughout April, she laughed and danced and dined with Sir Max. But she was careful always to have the faithful Daisy in lynx-eyed attendance. And never did she allow Sir Max the chance to be alone with her, lest he should seize the opportunity to ask her to marry him. April was far too soon for that, Leonora decided. I want to watch you become desperate, Sir Max, with the end of June approaching and all London goading you to fulfill your boast about our nuptials. Oh fear not, dear Clementina. I shall take revenge on Sir Max Fitzarren for the dreadful pain he caused you!

Occasionally, in a ride through the park, or in the crush at the theater, Leonora would encounter Lord Rothwell escorting Madame Valbois. Impeccably dressed, she clung to his arm like an exotic little bird. Her bright brown eyes, Leonora observed, were everywhere—darting glances across the crowd, noting who was present, what they were wearing, and whom they accompanied. Oh yes, thought Leonora dryly, there is not much that escapes the sharp attention of our French widow!

What *does* Cameron see in her, pondered Leonora for the hundredth time. He appeared to be constantly in her company. Normally, Leonora could have relied on Melissa gently to quiz her brother on the matter. But now all Melissa's thoughts and energies were concentrated on the count. And Leonora, naturally, would have expired rather than admit to Cameron that she had any interest in his relationship with Madame. So the Frenchwoman's attraction remained a mystery to Leonora.

All I can think of, Leonora decided in exasperation, *is that she must possess considerable charms which remain quite invisible to me!*

Another issue which remained unsolved was that of Melissa's disappearing jewelry. The silver earrings, gold pin and Leonora's bracelet had still not come to light. Then during the weeks of April, a sapphire brooch and a diamond necklace were missing as well.

Madame Valbois had no doubts about where to seek the culprit. "You must interrogate your own household," she advised Melissa, as they all gathered for a conference on the matter. "For my part, I confess I have never felt entirely easy about that pert red-haired maid. There is something a little too shrewd, too knowing in her eyes. I do not trust her."

Daisy, reprehensibly listening at the drawing-room door, pulled a face, and muttered, "I might say exactly the same of you, your Froggy Hagship!"

In the drawing room, Melissa said firmly, "I assure you, Madame, Daisy is completely loyal, as are all my servants."

The count fingered his fair moustache, and murmured, "Lady Melissa, may I enquire . . . where, exactly, is your dressing room situated in the house?"

"Why, overlooking the rear garden," smiled Melissa.

"And in this fine weather, it is likely that you would have had the window open during the day?"

Melissa nodded. "Of course. The warm spring breeze is so welcome after the rigors of winter."

"Monsieur le Comte," said Leonora. "If you are suggesting that perhaps the thief climbed up to Melissa's window, then I must advise you that this would be impossible."

"Quite correct," agreed Lord Rothwell, crossing his long legs. "That was one of the first aspects I checked when Melissa's jewelry started to disappear."

The Count held up his hand. "Ah. With respect, you misunderstand me, Lord Rothwell. I was thinking along different lines. I understand there is a bird—I do not know what you call it in English—but it is quite large, and bold. It is colored white, with very dark blue markings—"

"A magpie!" cried Leonora.

"Ah yes!" smiled the Count. "Now the magpie is renowned for its attraction to bright, shiny objects. Could not one have flown into your room and stolen your jewels, Lady Melissa?"

Melissa sighed. "That is a wondrously inventive notion, Count. But you see, the first items of jewery disappeared during very cold March weather, when I never had the window open."

The party was sunk into gloom once more. A small smile, however, glimmered on Leonora's lovely face. A magpie, she thought, gazing at Madame Valbois's pointed face and sharp brown eyes. An acquisitive little magpie, forever searching for all that glitters! Yes, that describes Madame exactly!

Madame Valbois said thoughtfully, "It is strange, is it not, that all the thefts have been from the Lady Melissa's apartments. None of Lady Leonora's jewelry has disappeared, apart from her bracelet—"

"Which of course was in my care at the time," said Melissa sadly.

Madame shrugged. "You see, it is quite evident that the culprit must be someone intensely loyal to Lady Leonora. Which brings me back to that girl—"

"Madame!" said Leonora sharply. "I have already made it plain that Daisy has my complete trust. And that of the Lady Melissa also." Melissa nodded her agreement. "I should be glad, therefore, if whilst you are under this roof, you would refrain from criticizing my personal maid!"

The Frenchwoman nodded, and lowered her eyes. Daisy, outside the door, gave a silent whoop of delight, which was observed by Mrs. Harris as she swept through the hall. A moment later, Daisy found herself in the kitchen, with her ears singing where the housekeeper had boxed them in punishment for eavesdropping.

Unaware of the below-stairs drama, Lord Rothwell turned to his sister. "You may rest assured, Melissa, that I am determined to get to the bottom of this matter. In the meantime, I think it would be advisable for you to lodge all your jewels in my safe at Park Lane."

Melissa fidgeted with her lace handkerchief. "But Cameron, I am fond of my jewelry. I like to wear it, not have it hidden away in a gloomy safe."

He sighed. "All you have to do is decide which items you wish to wear each day, and send round your footman for them."

Leonora laughed. "Come, Cameron. That would never do. You know Melissa can never make up her mind if the gold earrings look better than the silver—or should she wear the diamond pendants instead?"

"It is quite true, Cameron," confessed Melissa. "It sometimes takes me two hours to choose my jewelry. Why, the lanes between Grosvenor Street and Park Lane would be jammed with running footmen, racing back and forth whilst I sat in my dressing room in an agony of indecision."

Leonora saw the count catch Melissa's eye, and a warm, loving smile passed between them.

Lord Rothwell arose. "I still maintain that the safe is the most secure place for your jewels, Melissa. I hope you will reconsider. Meanwhile, I can only repeat that the matter will have my full attention. Now, if you will excuse me, I am due at my club. Will you accompany me, Count?"

The fair-haired Frenchman replied, "Another day, I should be delighted, Lord Rothwell. But this afternoon your charming sister has agreed to ride with me in the park."

Lord Rothwell nodded pleasantly, and turned to Madame Valbois. "Until later, then, Bettine. Are you still set on attending Lady Pinsley's rout?"

"Mais oui!" She gazed up at him imploringly. "Everyone will be there! I would not miss it for the world!"

"I find such occasions tedious myself," he confessed. "But if you desire to go, then naturally I shall be delighted to escort you."

Leonora and Melissa exchanged a brief, amazed glance. *Can this really be the cynical, irascible Lord Rothwell who is speaking?* wondered Leonora. *My, how he has mellowed of late. I have never before known him dance attendance on a lady in this manner. What can it be about Madame that affects him so?*

But although Leonora pondered the question far into a sleepless night, she was no nearer a solution as dawn broke over Grosvenor Street.

It came as no surprise when one beautiful May day, Melissa entered the Blue Saloon and declared, "Oh Leonora, I am so happy! You must be the first to know . . . Edouard, le Comte de Selvigny and I . . . we are engaged to be married!"

Heedless of the feathers from her picture flying to the floor all around her, Leonora jumped up and ran to embrace the radiant Melissa.

"My dear, I am delighted for you! We have all grown so fond of the count, you know. I am sure you will be divinely happy together!"

Seeing that Melissa was trembling, Leonora drew her on to the sofa.

Melissa said hesitantly, "I was a little nervous of telling you, Leonora."

"But why? I am full of joy for you!"

Melissa smiled. "Well ... it is just that having been married to your dear cousin Julian, I feared that you would condemn me for not respecting his memory in marrying again. And then, Edouard and I have known each other for such a short time ... little more than a month! I thought you might counsel me to take longer to decide."

Leonora hugged her. "Oh Melissa, anyone can see that you and the Count are blissfully content in one another's company. And I am sure no one, least of all I, would expect you to remain a widow forever. You have been offered the chance of happiness, and you would be foolish not to take it. And as for the matter of how long you have known Edouard, why that is quite irrelevant. I believe you fell in love with him right at first sight, did you not?"

Melissa nodded. "I cannot describe the feeling, Leonora, when we walked into Madame Valbois's drawing room that day, and my eyes met Edouard's. It was as if everything, all the world, was suddenly brighter. I felt I wanted to laugh and sing and dance!"

"And instead you were compelled to sit and make social conversation with Madame Valbos!" laughed Leonora. She could not resist adding, "Though were I in your shoes, I should certainly not rejoice in the prospect of having her as a sister!"

Madame Valbois was the first caller that afternoon. She swept into the drawing room, and kissed Melissa on both cheeks. "My dear! I am quite overwhelmed at your news! You are everything I have ever wished for in a sister. I know Edouard is going to be blissfully content with you. And I promise you, Lord Rothwell and I are quite delighted!"

Lord Rothwell and I! How dare she, fumed Leonora.

Madame went on, with a teasing note in her voice, "I must tell you what Cameron said when Edouard called on him. Cameron's eyes were bright with laughter, as he remarked: *'Is it not amazing? Melissa can send her en-*

tire household into disarray whilst she vacillates over which necklace to wear to a ball. Yet when it comes to the matter of choosing a husband, she makes up her mind with breathtaking speed!' "

Melissa smiled. "Dear Cameron. I am so glad he approves. As you know, there will be a family celebration dinner here tonight. I hope you are free to attend, Madame?"

"Indeed, I look forward to it with great pleasure. And please, as we are to be sisters, you must call me Bettine!"

Melissa smiled. "I confess, I still cannot believe that events have come to pass so rapidly. Though of course, the wedding will not be until the autumn. There will be so much to arrange."

"Naturally, you will sell your London house and come to live in France," instructed Madame. "Edouard's chateau is quite magnificent. You will adore it!"

"I am sure I shall, Bettine. Edouard has told me so much about it. But he has also fallen in love with London. So we shall keep on this house, and spend six months of the year in France, and six in London."

"That sounds a perfect arrangement," Leonora said, smiling.

Madame Valbois then engaged Melissa in a discussion about her trousseau and the honeymoon tour. Leonora's thoughts drifted in another direction. It occurred to her that with Melissa married, and presumably continuing to live in Grosvenor Street for the London Season, then she, Leonora, would be well advised to find somewhere else to reside.

Naturally, she suspected that Melissa would never urge her to leave. And the count, too, was far too gallant even to hint at such a move.

But were I in their situation, thought Leonora, *I should not really desire a third person living under my roof. It is only natural for newly married couples to yearn for privacy. No, the correct course of action is for me to effect a tactful withdrawal.*

Accordingly, when all the visitors had left, Leonora voiced her views to Melissa.

As she had anticipated, Melissa protested vehemently at the idea of Leonora departing. "I would not hear of it! And neither would Edouard. You are most welcome here, Leonora. And it is not as if we shall be in the house for all the year. Whilst we are away in France the house will be yours!"

Leonora smiled. "It is most kind of you, Melissa. But remember, I have a home of my own on the estate down in Gloucestershire. I should like to spend some of the summer there. But during the London Season we shall all be in the capital, and I feel most strongly that the time has come for me to set up my own household. My mind is quite made up on the matter."

"But I shall miss you dreadfully!"

"Nonsense. You will have your new life with Edouard," said Leonora sensibly. "And that is how it should be. Now, the important thing is for me to find myself a house."

"I feel wretched!" wailed Melissa. "I really cannot bear to see you go! I know I shall have a new husband for company, but I need you too! I shall be miserable if I cannot talk to you every single day!"

Leonora thought for a moment, and then remarked, "Of course, the house next door is empty. If I bought it, we should still be in a position daily to enjoy one another's company, Melissa."

Melissa's face brightened. "Oh yes! That is a capital solution. You shall buy the house next door!"

"Wait, wait," laughed Leonora. "I shall first have to inspect it, to see if it is suitable. I wonder who holds the keys?"

Melissa shook her dark head impatiently. "You need not bother with keys. Workmen are forever there. The door is sure to be open. Come, let us go now and have a look round!"

Infected by Melissa's enthusiasm, Leonora agreed. But in the hall, the two ladies were detained by Mrs. Harris.

"Lady Melissa, I should be so grateful if you could spare me a moment. There is the seating plan for tonight's dinner to be decided. And you usually prefer to supervise the table decoration yourself ... and may I, my lady, express the best wishes of your household on your engagement. We hope sincerely that you and the count will find great joy together."

Melissa smiled. "Why, thank you, Mrs. Harris. How very kind. I shall be speaking to you all personally, of course, but meanwhile I'd like to make plain that staff arrangements here at Grosvenor Street will remain quite unaffected by my marriage. And I know you will all serve the count as loyally and faithfully as you have served me."

"You may depend on that, my lady," Mrs. Harris assured her.

"Now," said Melissa, "there is the seating plan and the table decoration. Oh, so much to do before dinner!"

Leonora laid a hand on her arm. "Go and attend to the preparations, Melissa. I can perfectly well view the house by myself."

"Why not wait until tomorrow?" suggested Melissa. "Then Cameron could accompany you."

And the interfering Madame Valbois as well, no doubt, thought Leonora. *Thank you, but no! Choosing somewhere to live is a very personal matter, and I do not feel inclined to suffer Madame's opinions on the subject.*

"There is no cause to trouble Cameron," smiled Leonora. "I shall have the whole matter over and done with in fifteen minutes."

As Melissa had predicted, the front door to Number Eleven Grosvenor Street was open. The only guards were the two stone griffins placed on either side of the door columns. Leonora stepped into the hall, which was similar in size to that in Melissa's house. Instinctively, Leonora immediately started to plan the decor. A welcoming bowl of flowers on the mantel . . . a jewel-colored rug thrown over the hard brown tiles on the floor . . .

Leonora was about to go and inspect the downstairs apartments, when she heard voices echoing from above. Clearly the workmen were still there. I had best make my presence known to them, she decided. Else if they come upon me unawares, one or other of us is going to receive a dreadful fright!

Softly, she made her way upstairs, noting the fine carving on the oak banister. Leonora was about to enter the room from whence the voices issued, when she felt a large, strong hand seize her by the shoulder.

She gasped in fright. With pounding heart she whirled round and found herself face to face with Sir Max Fitzarren.

"Why, Sir Max! How you startled me!"

He looked pale, and ill at ease. He tried to smile but his pale blue eyes were clouded with anxiety.

"What are you doing here, Lady Leonora?"

"Why, I was searching for a house to buy, and Melissa and I hoped this residence would be suitable, as it is next door to her home."

Sir Max nodded. "What a strange coincidence. It seems as if we are both bound on the same quest. For I, too, am desirous of purchasing an establishment for myself. To own the truth, I am weary of my lodgings. And after all, a gentleman in my position should have his own London house, should he not? It is only right and proper."

"Indeed so," agreed Leonora. "Well, since we are both here, why do we not look around the property together? In fact, I was just coming upstairs to advise the workmen of my presence in the house."

"Workmen?" frowned the Irishman.

"They are the bane of Melissa's life," said Leonora. "Forever in and out, making the most appalling noise all

117

day long." And they do not appear to have been working very efficiently, she thought, observing the peeling plaster, and broken window frames. Her hand reached out to turn the handle of the door which would admit her to the workmen's room.

Sir Max took her arm and hurried her back toward the stairs.

"No cause to bother about them, Lady Leonora. They are probably enjoying a quiet game of cards. They will be sorely embarrassed if you disturb them."

"As you like," said Leonora lightly. "Now, which floor shall we view first, Sir Max?"

He shook his head. "My lady, I must advise you that you are wasting your time looking at this house."

"Oh!" smiled Leonora. "You are determined to purchase it yourself, then!"

"Not at all. Quite the contrary. I have inspected it from top to bottom, and it is really a most unsound investment. Particularly for a lady like yourself. It is damp—"

"Damp?" echoed Leonora. "But how can that be? We are not close to the river. And Melissa's house next door has certainly never suffered from wet rot."

Sir Max waved a hand and declared airily, "There is probably an underground spring. I assure you, the building is most unstable. I would not dream of purchasing it myself. And besides that, I do not observe in the house the elegance, the beauty of line necessary to provide the perfect setting for one as lovely as yourself."

Are all the Irish born with the gift of beguiling words, wondered Leonora. Aloud, she murmured, "I confess, Sir Max, there are certain aspects of this house which I find rather pleasing. That exquisitely carved hand-rail on the stairs, for instance."

But as she spoke she found she was being urged gently, but firmly, down the stairs.

"A thought has just struck me," said Sir Max, guiding Leonora toward the front door. "There is another house vacant, within a stone's throw from here, in Brook Street. I am sure it would be more to your liking. Allow me to escort you there."

Leonora hesitated on the doorstep. "It is growing late. And I have to change for dinner."

"I assure you it will take only a minute," smiled the red-haired man. "And consider how your mind will be set at rest, knowing you have found yourself a truly desirable residence."

There seemed no harm in accompanying Sir Max. Brook Street was indeed only a few minutes' walk away. And now she had determined to set up her own household, Leonora was anxious to have the matter settled as speedily as possible. If she waited until the morning to view the Brook Street house, then Cameron and his bright-eyed magpie would be sure to insist on accompanying her. Leonora knew she could not abide any interference in her plans from that loathsome Frenchwoman.

The house to which Sir Max directed her was indeed attractive, with bow fronted windows and a good-sized drawing room overlooking a pretty garden.

"How fortunate that we met today, Sir Max, and that you chanced to have the keys to this house in your possession," Leonora remarked, making a mental note that the dining room was far too small.

"Ah. Yes. The keys . . . well, as I informed you, I have been inspecting various houses in the area today," he replied blandly.

When she had completed her tour of the property, Leonora rejoined Sir Max in the drawing room, and commented, "I fear it is not at all suitable for my requirements. On the one hand, the dining room is cramped. I like to entertain, you know, and I really desire a spacious dining room. Yet the rest of the house contains far too many rooms for my purposes. It seems absurd for me to buy a house suited to a family, when there will be only myself and my servants residing here."

As she spoke, Leonora felt a chill creep over her. She

was gripped by a strong sense of foreboding. It stemmed, she realized, from the fact that she and Sir Max were totally alone together in this empty, echoing house. And no one in the world knew she was here!

How could I be so foolish, Leonora accused herself, as the panic rose within her. For all these weeks I have been so careful to keep Daisy with me on my outings with Sir Max. I have never allowed him to be alone with me. But now here we are together. What is worse, by remarking that I intend to reside here as a single woman, I have just given him the perfect opportunity to propose to me! And that, at the moment, is the last thing I desire.

She froze as Sir Max took a step toward her. His voice was low and persuasive. "My dear Lady Leonora. What a dreary future you paint for yourself, living alone in solitary splendor! I will not hear of such a thing. We have been acquainted for some time, now. You must be aware that my feelings for you are more than—"

He was going to propose! There was no doubt about it. Horrified, Leonora did the only thing possible. She closed her eyes, uttered a small groan, and sank to the floor in an excellent imitation of a dead faint.

Melissa laid down her fork. "Such a shock you gave us, Leonora! Sir Max was most concerned about you when he escorted you home. Are you sure you are quite recovered now?"

Leonora almost wilted under the concerned regard of the party assembled round the dining table. Melissa and her new fiancé gazed upon her with anxiety. Madame Valbois's brown eyes were sharp with suspicion. And Lord Rothwell was looking extremely angry.

"I still do not understand," he said, "what you were doing in a house in Brook Street. *Alone* with Sir Max Fitzarren! If you really feel the desire to set up your own establishment in London, then surely I am the proper person to assist you in a search for a house."

Leonora lowered her eyes. Cameron would be even more furious if he knew how close Sir Max had come to proposing, she reflected wryly. Fortunately, her ruse at Brook Street had succeeded. By the time she had "revived" sufficiently for Sir Max to escort her home, the suitable moment for his proposal had passed. Fully aware that she had escaped by only the barest whisper, Leonora had no intention of enduring an interrogation from Cameron over the incident.

She asked, "Shall we discuss the matter at some future date, Cameron? After all, this is supposed to be a celebration dinner. Are we not to have a toast to the newly engaged couple?"

"Yes of course." Lord Rothwell cleared his throat. "To Melissa and Edouard. We offer you our sincere congratulations, and heartfelt good wishes for a long and happy marriage!"

Glasses were raised to the smiling pair. "To dear Melissa and Edouard!"

Naturally enough, the remainder of the dinner was devoted to a discussion of Melissa and Edouard's future plans. Melissa was anxious to spend some time in Florence on her wedding trip ... Madame Valbois could recommend an excellent Parisian modiste for her traveling clothes ... Edouard was so looking forward to entertaining them all at his chateau. "There is fine hunting here, Cameron. And the fishing is magnificent."

It was only as they were finishing the excellent lemon sorbet that Lord Rothwell remarked, almost casually, "Whilst we are all gathered together, this seems an opportune moment for me to mention a dinner of my own to which I should like to invite you all."

"At Park Lane?" enquired Madame Valbois. "How delightful!"

"Is it to be a family affair?" asked Melissa. "Or will anyone else be present?"

"There will be one other guest," said Lord Rothwell,

the glimmer of a smile lighting his gray eyes. "We shall be honored by the presence of the Prince Regent himself."

Madame Valbois was so overwhelmed she forgot herself sufficiently to utter a piercing shriek. "The Prince! *Mon Dieu!*"

"Cameron, how exciting!" smiled Leonora. "How did this come about?"

"I recently attended a small reception at Carlton House," explained Lord Rothwell, "and the Prince very civilly expressed an interest in my Rowlandson watercolors."

"Lord Rothwell's collection is one of the finest in all England," Madame informed her brother.

Lord Rothwell continued, "Naturally, I invited the Prince to view the painting at his leisure, and he indicated that he would be pleased to dine at Park Lane."

Melissa's face was radiant. "Oh, I am so glad you waited until the end of our dinner to inform us of this news, Cameron. Otherwise I should not have been able to eat a morsel of food for excitement! Now, would you like me to act as your hostess for the evening?"

Before Lord Rothwell could reply, Madame Valbois said smoothly, "My dear Melissa, I am sure your brother would not dream of imposing such a burden on you. Why, with all the details of your marriage to arrange, your days will be fully occupied. The strain of the occasion will be far too great for you. If Lord Rothwell will permit, I should be delighted to take on the responsibilities of hostess."

Leonora's fine eyes glittered with anger. Really, she fumed, it's obscene the way that Frenchwoman never misses an opportunity to link herself with Cameron!

Melissa smiled. "That is most thoughtful of you, Bettine. I am sure Cameron will be glad—"

Lord Rothwell interrupted with a discreet cough. "Your kindness and consideration quite overwhelm me, ladies. But in fact, I had it in mind to ask Leonora if she would do me the honor of acting as my hostess for the dinner with the Prince Regent."

Leonora flushed with pleasure and surprise. "Why, Cameron!"

Madame Valbois uttered a lilting, indulgent laugh. "It is a sweet thought, Cameron. No doubt Leonora is flattered that you should ask her. But I am convinced that, on reflection, you will agree that she is far too young to undertake such a task. It will be no ordinary evening. Entertaining royalty is a special event, one beset with pitfalls of etiquette—one demanding, surely, the more experienced touch of a more mature woman. A girl of Leonora's tender years could not be expected to appreciate the delicate nuances involved in acting as hostess when a Prince is present."

"On the contrary," said Melissa a trifle coldly, "you are unaware, Bettine, but Leonora has in fact entertained the Prince before. And then when she was only seventeen."

Madame's eyebrows rose in disbelief.

"When my father was alive," Leonora explained, "the Prince honored us with a visit at our home in Gloucestershire. As my mother had died many years previously, naturally it fell to me to act as hostess during the Prince's stay."

"And she acquitted herself admirably," Lord Rothwell informed the sullen Madame Valbois. "Well, Leonora, will you stand by my side and receive the Prince with me next week?"

"I should be delighted, Cameron," she replied, her eyes sparkling.

Melissa arose. "Then with that matter decided, we shall leave you gentlemen to your port and brandy."

"Do not expect us to join you yet awhile," warned Lord Rothwell. "I have no doubt you ladies will require at least an hour to debate what you are to wear for the Prince!"

Laughing, Melissa led the way from the dining room.

But Madame Valbois, Leonora observed, was not even smiling. On the contrary, the glance she bestowed on Leonora as she swept through the doorway was one of pure, chilling malice.

Seven

Melissa was apparently quite unaware that Madame Valbois was still smarting from Lord Rothwell's snub over his dinner party.

As she poured tea into the delicate Dresden cups, Melissa commented, "My, I am still overcome at the notion of dining with the Prince. But it is you to whom we shall turn for advice on the occasion, Leonora. You are the only one amongst us who has previously entertained royalty."

"It was only for a few days," Leonora said.

Madame Valbois, stiffly sipping her tea, said nothing.

"Only a few days!" exclaimed Melissa. "My dear, from the point of view of the anxious hostess, having an important guest to stay overnight is far more fraught than merely entertaining him to a single dinner! And you were so young at the time. However did you cope?"

"I wrote to Lady Jersey and asked her advice," Leonora replied.

"Ah, that was wise," Melissa said. "No doubt she was able to turn your attention to all sorts of matters that would not otherwise have occurred to you."

Leonora nodded. "I was extremely worried about the Prince's private apartments. I had no notion how many rooms I should set aside for his personal use. But Lady

Jersey soon set my mind at rest. She told me that his valet, Dupaquier, must have a bed in a room as near to the Prince as possible. But the Prince himself never uses a dressing room, preferring instead to robe in his bedroom which he likes to be well heated. He takes his own sheets everywhere, and Lady Jersey indicated that there was no cause for the housekeeper to pile the bed with blankets. Even in the winter the Prince can tolerate only two, and no quilt."

Lenora was amused to notice that Madame Valbois was finding it impossible to maintain her mask of polite indifference at these revelations. She was leaning forward, listening attentively to every word. No doubt, thought Leonora, when she returns to Paris she will captivate salon society with her intimate knowledge of the Prince Regent's domestic habits.

Madame fingered the pearls at her throat and said thoughtfully, "I hear that the entertainment at Carlton House is on the most lavish scale. How I should love to be invited there!"

"You would be overwhelmed by the Prince's collection of pictures and ornaments," remarked Leonora. "His taste is justly celebrated. I was not at all surprised to learn that he expressed a desire to see Cameron's watercolors."

"The only trouble is," Melissa said, "the Prince is so fond of acquiring new objects—be it furniture, paintings or china—that he is forever unhappy at the arrangements in the saloons. Lady Sarah Spencer is ever complaining that she can scarcely find time to catch a glimpse of each transient arrangement at Carlton House before it is all turned out to make way for a new display!"

Madame Valbois raised an eyebrow, and whispered, "Lady Sarah Spencer? Is she one of the Prince's mistresses?"

"Not to my knowledge," replied Melissa with a smile. "Although in truth, so many ladies have caught the

Prince's eye, it is often difficult establishing what their relationship may be!"

Leonora remarked dryly, "The Prince appears to collect pretty women in much the same spirit that he acquires new works of art! First there was Mary Hamilton, do you recall, and then Mary Robinson, the actress."

Madame's nose wrinkled with disapproval. "But what of Mrs. Fitzherbert? All Paris was abuzz with talk of her and the Prince a few years past."

"They were lovers for many years," agreed Leonora. "But then they began to quarrel. I understand that she disapproved of some of the Prince's more raffish companions. And matters were not improved when one of them rode his horse into Mrs. Fitzherbert's house, and all the way up the stairs!"

"Mrs. Fitzherbert is out of favor now," said Melissa. "It is Lady Hertford who currently holds the key to the Prince's heart." She smoothed down the skirt of her silk dress. "For my part, I believe the Prince would be wise to act with more discretion. It is not seemly for a married man to be observed flaunting his mistresses all over the capital!"

Madame laughed. "Oh, you English! You are so naive! Why, in France, most men have mistresses. It is all totally discreet, and quite understood between man and wife. Pouf! Why make such a fuss? What does it matter?"

"It matters a great deal," flared Leonora. "I can assure you, Madame, no husband of mine would have a mistress! If he did I'd tear her limb from limb. And then I'd leave my mark on him, too, in no uncertain fashion!"

"Bravo!" applauded Lord Rothwell from the drawing room door. "How I admire your fighting spirit, Leonora! I pity any errant husband returning sheepishly home to face *your* wrath!" He turned to Madame. "Leonora is quite, quite magnificent when she is angry!"

"Indeed?" the Frenchwoman remarked, affecting an

expression of disinterest. She murmured sweetly, "But do you not agree, my lord, that Lady Leonora is expecting too much in demanding that her future husband be faithful only unto her. In time, I am convinced she will learn to be more accommodating, and adopt a more sophisticated attitude toward these matters."

Lord Rothwell rested an arm on the mantel, and replied gravely, "Certainly, if the marriage is one purely of convenience, then it is quite the accepted thing for both parties to go their separate ways. But if one professes to marry for love, then there should be no cause to succumb to temptation. Though in Leonora's case the whole question is academic. Any man lucky enough to win her for his bride would never need to look elsewhere for lively female company."

Leonora could not believe her ears. Whatever had come over Cameron this evening? First he made a point of asking her to act as his hostess at his dinner for the Prince Regent. And now this compliment had fallen so unexpectedly from his lips!

Lord Rothwell laughed. "Besides, as I have already said, Leonora is a fearsome adversary. She would never sit meekly by and watch her husband paying court to another lady!"

Madame Valbois shrugged, and realizing that she was gaining no advantage from pursuing this line of conversation, arose and poured tea for the gentlemen.

The count, meanwhile, stood with his hand resting lightly on Melissa's shoulder, as if to reassure her that his sister's talk of all Frenchmen having mistresses was pure nonsense. Melissa smiled up at him, and remarked to her brother, "We have been discussing the amours of the Prince Regent!"

Lord Rothwell nodded. "In that respect, I agree with Mr. Sheridan. He once asserted that the Prince is *too much every lady's man to be the man of any lady.*"

"What is so strange," commented Leonora, "is that the Prince admires grace and femininity in a woman. Yet his own daughter, the Princess Charlotte, is considered to be something of a hoyden."

"Is she not married now to Prince Leopold of Saxe-Coburg?" enquired Madame. "I can only assume that she was passionately in love with him. For he was certainly one of the most impoverished princes in Europe."

Melissa smiled. "Why yes. I recall his first visit to London. We were all so shocked, because he found himself in such reduced circumstances that he was compelled to rent lodgings over a grocer's shop in Marylebone High Street!"

The count smiled fondly at her. "Did you attend the wedding, my dear?"

"It was quite magnificent," Melissa replied. "The ceremony was conducted at Carlton House. The couple knelt side by side on red velvet cushions, framed by candlesticks six feet high." She laughed. "But there was one most amusing incident. At the point in the ceremony when Prince Leopold declared, 'with all my wordly goods I thee endow,' Princess Charlotte stifled a most un-bridal giggle. She was obviously thinking of those sordid lodgings above the grocer's!"

A little while later, Madame Valbois rose to take her leave. After thanking Melissa for a delightful evening, she turned to Lord Rothwell. "You have not forgotten your promise to take me for a ride in your new gig tomorrow?"

He hesitated. "It will be a pleasure, of course, Bettine. But I feel it my duty to make myself available to assist Leonora in a search for a house."

"But of course!" cried Madame. "I shall be glad to help you, Lady Leonora. I assure you, I have an excellent eye for a sound property investment!"

Leonora said hastily, "It is most kind of you both. I am deeply grateful for your concern. But I feel that for the coming week my time will be fully occupied with the arrangements for Cameron's important dinner."

"Quite so," agreed Melissa. "There will be much to do, and you must not overtax your strength, Leonora.

There is plenty of time for you to search for a house later in the summer."

Lord Rothwell nodded. "So be it. But I shall be most annoyed, Leonora, if I discover you viewing houses with Sir Max Fitzarren. As I have told you before, he is a most disreputable character, and I wish you would have nothing more to do with him!"

"I agree absolutely!" said Madame Valbois. "It makes me most unhappy to observe you in his company, Lady Leonora!"

Leonora's eyes were stormy as she bade the guests good night. She hurried upstairs to her chamber and flung herself on the bed.

How dare they, she fumed. It had been bad enough when Lord Rothwell had criticized her for consorting with Sir Max. But now the magpie Madame was presuming to voice her opinion as well!

Why can't they leave me alone, Leonora muttered angrily. *Do they think I am a total fool? Why, I am more aware than anyone in London of the dark, evil side to Sir Max's nature! And if my plans are allowed to proceed, I shall have the pleasure of tumbling him in the dust of his own smashed ego!*

But what I cannot abide is being told—nay ordered —not to associate with him. Lord Rothwell and Madame conspire to make me feel as if I am back in the schoolroom once more—instead of twenty-one years old, with my own fortune, my own life at my command!

What really irritated Leonora was that Madame Valbois should make such a point of siding with Lord Rothwell in the matter. She loses no opportunity, thought Leonora resentfully, to align herself with him. And was it her imagination, or was Madame also making great display of confirming her engagements with him?

You have not forgotten your promise to take me for a ride in your new gig . . .

It seemed as if she was anxious to impress upon

Leonora most particularly, that she and Cameron were the very closest of companions. Leonora wondered *why should she especially desire to inform me of this? It is almost as if Madame regards me as a rival.*

Leonora laughed out loud at the thought of her having any romantic thoughts for Cameron—or he having any toward her! Why, the idea was preposterous!

True, Lord Rothwell was ruggedly handsome, dashing and rich, amusing too when he chose to be. But the notion of falling in love with him had never crossed Leonora's mind. They had known one another for so long, and argued so much, it seemed quite absurd to imagine him murmuring sweet words of romance to her.

And he seemed to have had some relationship with Madame Valbois. How could he! A hot tide of fury flooded through Leonora. What did he find attractive about her? Where had they met, and how had their relationship developed?

This was a mystery which even Melissa had been unable to unravel. She had questioned Madame Valbois about Paris, but the Frenchwoman was most evasive on the subject of what had happened there between Cameron and herself. And Lord Rothwell, of course, remained as tight-lipped as ever over the matter. He would quite cheerfully talk about the sights of Paris, the shops, the theaters, the restaurants. But never, ever, would he be drawn into any discussion of the women he had known there.

Which is perfectly correct and gallant of him, mused Leonora. But how infuriating, too!

It amazed Leonora that a man of Cameron's discernment should fail to recognize the acquisitive, calculating streak in Madame's nature. It was obvious that her bright brown eyes were set firmly on the title of Lady Rothwell —and becoming mistress of Cameron's handsome London house and vast country estates. Leonora further reasoned:

How can Cameron be so blind to the trap Madame is setting for him? By escorting her so frequently, he is in grave danger of their relationship being accepted by

131

society as a permanent arrangement. He will discover that everyone (most of all Madame!) naturally expects wedding bells to ring out. And faced with such social pressure, it will require a very strong character indeed to refuse to escort the lady up the aisle!

Leonora sighed. *If only I could talk more freely to Melissa about the matter. But of course, with Madame destined to become Melissa's sister by marriage, it would be tactless of me to utter a word against her. Indeed, even if Melissa were not engaged to the count, it would still be difficult for me to speak adversely of the Frenchwoman to Melissa. Right from the beginning, Melissa has looked kindly upon her, and defended her against all my criticisms. Surely Cameron could not be in love with Madame Valbois! He had far too much good sense.*

Yet Leonora was compelled to admit that where romance was concerned, sound judgment was often cast to the winds. It happened frequently that the ton was agog with news of a rich heiress eloping with a penniless rake. Or a Duke scandalizing his family by marrying a lowly laundry maid. *There appears to be no rhyme or reason where affairs of the heart are concerned,* realized Leonora.

It had to be confessed that love was not a subject on which Leonora felt qualified to speak. Having escaped the sting of Cupid's dart for twenty-one years, she had been beginning to believe that what people called love was, in truth, a purely imaginary state. That it did not exist at all!

But of late, she had changed her opinion. Watching Melissa and the count together—the manner in which their eyes lit up when the other entered the room . . . their delight in one another's company . . . their tender concern for one another—all this had aroused a restless envy in Leonora. It occurred to her that there was something important missing from her life.

Could it be love she craved? She had never before desired it or searched for it. She had been content amusing herself with her many beaux, dancing till the early hours with one, dining with a second, riding in the park with a third. And of late there had been the diversion of Sir Max, and the necessity to take her revenge for his abuse of poor Clementina.

But when the Season is over, and I have sent Sir Max back to Ireland with his tail between his legs, what will be left for me then, pondered Leonora. Melissa will be married, and occupied with her new husband. I shall spend a few months on my country estate, and then return to London to set up my own household. Naturally, Cameron will protest that it is unseemly for a single lady to reside by herself. And for once, he will be right. I shall ask dear Aunt Harriet to come and be my companion.

Leonora was perfectly well aware that she had no reason to feel despondent. She was young, beautiful, and wealthy. The pleasures of London were hers to enjoy. Why then, was she conscious of a growing emptiness in her life?

Madame Valbois is unsettling me, Leonora decided as she blew out her candle. There is something about the woman which makes me feel wary, and forever on guard. But I must not allow her to affect me so. It is absurd. I shall put her out of my mind, and concentrate on my duties as Cameron's hostess for the dinner with the Prince Regent. And the first matter to be decided is what I should wear!

The question of their appearance was one, which, naturally, preoccupied all three of the ladies who would be present at the dinner. Leonora declared that she intended to wear a white silk gown, simply cut, and frosted with diamonds. Melissa chose an elegant style in pale apricot, fringed with exquisite lace, which perfectly complimented her dark coloring.

Madame Valbois, however, when quizzed on her choice of gown, murmured that she had not made a decision. When Melissa pressed her further, Madame smiled enigmatically and declared that she would prefer to keep her dress a secret until the evening.

Melissa would not entertain such a notion. "Nonsense, Bettine! There is no cause to be so mysterious. We are none of us in competition!"

Reluctantly, Madame admitted that her gown was of deep red silk, adorned with rubies.

"She is clearly quite determined to catch the Prince's eye!" Melissa informed Leonora.

No, not the Prince's eye, but Lord Rothwell's, Leonora silently corrected her. The more Leonora pondered on the matter, the more positive was she that Madame Valbois did indeed regard her as a rival for Cameron's affections. This secrecy over the dress only served to prove her point.

Why Madame should have formed this mistaken impression about her relationship with Cameron, Leonora had no idea. The kindest thing, she knew, would be for her tactfully to disabuse Madame of the notion. But Leonora rebelled against that solution.

I cannot abide the woman, she thought. *Why should I leave the field clear for her to ensnare Cameron? I should not mind if I believe that she and Cameron were ideally suited. In that case, I should be happy to give them my blessing. But Cameron would be miserable married to Madame! I am convinced of it. So I shall do my utmost to make life as difficult for her as I possibly can!*

A mischievous smile flirted across Leonora's pretty face. It occurred to her that it would be most amusing to pretend that, as Madame suspected, she and Cameron were deeply attached to one another. That would most certainly spike the Frenchwoman's guns!

Then Leonora sighed. It would not do. Diverting though it might be, to play that particular game one required two players. And Leonora had no doubt that if she attempted a coquettish conversation with Cameron, instead of his responding to her in a like manner, to annoy Madame, he would merely throw back his dark head and laugh!

"Leonora! Is the lace lying flat on the neck of my dress? I have a horror that it will curl in the heat of the lamps!"

Leonora said soothingly, "You look quite charming, Melissa. Do not fret. The lace is perfect, and I am sure it will curl neither in the heat of the lamps nor the warmth of the Prince's smile!"

Madame Valbois anxiously studied her complexion in the mirror over the drawing-room fireplace at Park Lane. "Oh, I am so pale!" she mourned. "I wonder if there is time for me to apply a little rouge before the Prince arrives?"

"I should stay where you are," advised the count. "It would not look well for you to come rushing from the dressing room just as the Prince makes his entrance."

"Why not pinch your cheeks to encourage a little color into them?" suggested Melissa.

Madame's dress, Melissa had earlier murmured to Leonora, was a mistake. "I confess I am quite surprised, Leonora. Normally Bettine displays such exquisite taste."

"Exquisite!" echoed Leonora dryly.

"But frankly, that deep crimson simply does not suit her. A lighter tone of red would flatter her complexion. But that strong hue simply drains all the color from her skin. And it adds years to her appearance!"

"Leonora!" called Lord Rothwell, resplendent in an immaculately cut black evening coat, with an emerald green waistcoat, "Come! The Prince's carriage is at the door."

Leonora hurried into the large front hall, and took up her position with Lord Rothwell at the foot of the sweeping oak staircase. He must have sensed her flutter of nerves, for he laid a reassuring hand on her arm, and said, "There is nothing to worry about, Leonora. You look quite enchanting. And you have supervised all the arrangements quite perfectly. I am most grateful to you."

As the Prince swept past the bowing Brockway and

through the double doors, he smiled with pleasure as he regarded the handsome couple waiting to greet him. Lord Cameron Rothwell, tall, athletically built, a man the Prince held in high regard for his wit, charm, and sophistication. And beside him, the beautiful Lady Leonora Pagett, with her golden hair shining under the lamplight, and her elegant white dress spangled with diamonds.

"Good evening, Lord Rothwell. What a great pleasure it is to be once more in your company."

Lord Rothwell bowed.

"The honor is ours, Sir." He guided Leonora forward. "The Lady Leonora Pagett, who has kindly agreed to act as my hostess for the evening."

As Leonora arose from her curtsy, she saw that the Prince was smiling warmly upon her. "But of course I remember the delightful Lady Leonora! As I recall, I spent a most relaxing few days at your late father's home in Gloucestershire. I have such pleasant memories of that time, and your charming hospitality."

How civil he is, thought Leonora, as Lord Rothwell ushered their royal guest into the drawing room. While Lord Rothwell effected the introductions, Leonora noticed Madame's sharp eyes observing every detail of the Prince's appearance. She could well imagine Madame at some future date regaling her Paris salon companions with the intelligence that:

"When one is near to the Prince one realizes that he is in fact above the common size. Well-proportioned, though perhaps just a little inclined to fat. He has a noble countenance, and the most beautiful glossy hair. On the evening when he dined with me, he was most finely dressed in a dark blue evening coat with a silk waistcoat of a lighter blue."

The Prince, always well informed, was aware of Melissa's engagement to the Comte de Selvigny. At the earliest opportunity he made a special point of wishing them both every happiness in their forthcoming marriage.

Leonora made little contribution to the conversation at this stage, as she was understandably anxious about the dinner. Her main concern was the seating arrangements.

She recalled being beset by the same anxiety when the Prince had come to stay in Gloucestershire, and there had been twelve guests at table. Leonora had been in a quandary. Etiquette dictated that the guest of honor sat on the right hand of his hostess. But when that guest was the Prince Regent, was it correct for her to indicate his seat, or would he prefer to choose for himself? Lady Jersey had not made this point clear in her advisory letters.

The Prince, however, had solved her dilemma by offering Leonora his arm, and asking her where she usually sat for dinner. When Leonora told him, he had immediately taken the chair to her right.

But will he do the same this evening? wondered Leonora. *Or should I place Madame Valbois next to him, in deference to her position as the most senior lady present?*

Dinner was announced. Leonora bit her lip, and looked desperately across at Lord Rothwell. The Prince, however, came swiftly to her aid.

"I do hope, Lady Leonora, that I am to have the privilege of sitting next to you as we dine."

Almost dizzy with relief, Leonora offered him her arm, and the party progressed into the oak-paneled dining room. The chandeliers cast a soft light over the guests as they seated themselves around the table, where a snowy damask cloth formed a perfect setting for sparkling crystal and shining silver.

Behind the Prince's chair stood two of his own liveried pages. It was their duty to receive from Lord Rothwell's footmen all dishes intended for the Prince, and lay each one before him. Leonora had already quietly advised Madame that it was the custom for the Prince to be served before any ladies present.

The Prince took the lead in opening the conversation. Pausing over his dish of salmon with fennel sauce,

137

he remarked, "I have heard, Lady Leonora, that you and I share an interest in common. Namely the poetry of Sir Walter Scott."

Lord Rothwell laughed. "I suspect, Leonora, that His Highness is referring to a certain incident at a ball, when you sold copies of Sir Walter's loyal poem in order to raise money for soldiers' widows and children."

"Exactly so," nodded the Prince. "I am only sorry I was not present at the ball. I should have been proud to contribute to the cause."

Madame Valbois enquired, "May I ask, Sir, which of Sir Walter's poems you favor most?"

"Without doubt, 'The Lay of the Last Minstrel,' " replied the Prince. "I know it by heart. It humbles me to think that such a great work should come from the head of one man."

"With respect, Sir," said Leonora, an impish twinkle in her amber eyes, "I believe that you were indirectly responsible for almost causing severe injury to that poetic head!"

The Prince laughed. Observing Comte de Selvigny's puzzled expression, he explained, "As you may be aware, I am much interested in the arts. Some years ago it was my pleasure to present the Royal Academy with a handsome bronze lantern, which they hung in the Great Room of Somerset House. Unfortunately, at the annual dinner of the Academy, the lantern fell, and two tons of bronze came crashing down, missing Sir Walter Scott's head by the merest whisper! I was so alarmed, I invited him round the next day to a private dinner with me at Carlton House."

Madame Valbois sipped her chilled white wine and gushed, "The glorious Carlton House is the talk of all Europe, Your Highness. Everyone remarks on your exquisite taste in the furnishings and decor."

Gallantly, the Prince responded, "The magnificence of Carlton House owes much, Madame, to the work of your compatriots. Many of the cabinetmakers, woodcarvers and metal-workers were brought over especially from France to work on the house. And as you may know, I am extremely proud of my Gobelin tapestries, Sèvres china, and many more French *objets d'art!*"

The Comte de Selvigny fingered his fair moustache. "It is strange, but in France we have the totally mistaken impression that English royal princes receive a most austere education, and are not encouraged to patronize the arts. Clearly, Sir, that was not true in your case."

The Prince shook his head. "Indeed no. I was extremely fortunate. I enjoyed the most varied education. Naturally, I was well versed in the classics. But I also learned to play the cello, to appreciate the fine arts, to fence, and to draw. And in my garden at Kew, I even learned to sow and harvest my own crops. What is more, I have another hidden talent. I know how to bake bread!"

Leonora had one eye on the entry of the magnificent sirloin of beef, perfectly cooked, and running with succulent juices. Satisfied that everything appeared to be well under control in the kitchens, she turned to the Prince, "I confess, your education puts me to shame, Sir. As Lord Rothwell will bear out, I spent most of my schooldays playing practical jokes on my poor tutor!"

"Then that is something else we have in common, Lady Leonora. On one occasion, knowing an extremely greedy musician had been invited to dinner, I told him that something especially delicious had been prepared for him. He sat down eagerly to eat. The cover was lifted from the dish, and out jumped a live rabbit!"

"You were fortunate in having an enlightened father, Sir," said the count. "My own papa maintained that all the education a boy required was to be proficient at reading and riding!"

"You are an expert horseman?" enquired the Prince eagerly. "We must race some day. I should enjoy that!"

"Before you take up the challenge, Count," laughed Lord Rothwell, draining his glass of red wine, "I should advise you that the Prince has been known to ride from

London to Brighton and back in one day. That is, in just ten hours!"

"Ten hours!" exclaimed Melissa. "But it is over a hundred miles from London to Brighton and back. Mercy me!"

"But the exercise gave me great pleasure," smiled the Prince. "I assure you, I was not over-fatigued."'

"Such stamina!" cried Madame Valbois admiringly.

As the meal progressed, it became apparent to Leonora that Madame was resolved to make her mark upon every aspect of the conversation. During the dessert, a frothy confection laced with the Prince's favorite cherry brandy liqueur, the discussion turned once more to horse-flesh. This was a topic on which the Frenchwoman was scarcely expert, but determined not to be excluded, she announced brightly:

"I declare, one of the finest sights in the world is that of a gentleman of breeding astride a fine horse. Why, only yesterday afternoon I observed the most dashing gentleman in the park. His cravat, his riding coat, his breeches, his boots, all were immaculate beyond belief. Such style! Such assurance!" She smiled confidently at the Prince. "Indeed, I believe the gentleman to be a special acquaintance of yours, Sir. His name is Beau Brummel!"

The Prince's eyes were suddenly icy. Lord Rothwell, Melissa, and Leonora sat frozen with horror.

Oh Madame, thought Leonora desperately. *What have you done! What have you said! Have you no notion of the dreadful social blunder you have just committed?*

Eight

With all the poise at her command, Leonora rose to her feet and said quietly, "Shall we withdraw, ladies, and leave the gentlemen to their port?"

"Thank you, Leonora," Lord Rothwell said, his gray eyes signaling to her the real reason for his gratitude. He turned to the Prince. "And then, Sir, perhaps you would care to accompany me to the West Gallery, where my watercolors are on display?"

The Prince nodded. "I shall look forward to that, Lord Rothwell."

It was with an overwhelming sense of relief that Leonora led Melissa and Madame into the seclusion of the drawing room.

Madame Valbois threw herself down on the sofa, her face drawn. "What did I say? What was wrong? Oh, the disdain on the Prince's face when I mentioned Beau Brummel. It will haunt me forever!"

Melissa sat down beside her. "You were not to know, Bettine," she said soothingly. "You are a visitor to England. On reflection, the Prince will realize that you cannot be expected to be au fait with the ups and downs of his friendship with Mr. Brummel."

"But I do not understand!" protested Madame. "In Paris everyone talked of Beau Brummel as a close companion of the Prince."

"That was indeed so," said Leonora. "For many years they were seen constantly together, although their friendship was not based on any true appreciation of each other's character. In truth, I hear that the Prince was somewhat jealous of Mr. Brummel's elegance, and sarcastic turn of phrase."

"Whilst Mr. Brummel was quite naturally flattered by the Prince's attention," explained Melissa. "All would have been well, however, if Mr. Brummel had not been so foolish as to presume to be familiar with the Prince when in public."

Leonora nodded. "There were several unfortunate incidents, when Beau Brummel rose too far above himself. There were quarrels. Then one day the Prince arrived at a ball at the Argyle Rooms, and spoke to Lord Alvanley but ignored Mr. Brummel. At which Mr. Brummel puffed out his chest and called loudly, 'Alvanley, who is your fat friend?' "

Madame Valbois gasped. "Oh, how unforgivable! I imagine that must have been the end of their relationship?"

"Almost," said Melissa. "But the Prince was determined to seek revenge for Mr. Brummel's obnoxious ridicule of his appearance. He asked Mr. Brummel to a dinner at Carlton House. Mr. Brummel, imagining that he was basking once more in the Prince's favor, forgot himself and drank too much wine at dinner. The Prince bided his time, and then said in ringing tones to the Duke of York, 'It would be as well to ring for Mr. Brummel's carriage before he becomes quite drunk.' Beau Brummel stood up, left the room, and they have never spoke to one another again!"

Madame Valbois raised a weary hand to her brow. "No wonder the Prince looked so angry. I am mortified!"

Melissa handed her some tea to calm her nerves, but Madame's fingers were trembling so much, she could scarcely hold the cup.

Leonora thought it kinder not to point out that Madame had, in fact, committed another faux pas in her remarks about Beau. She had referred to him as a gentleman of good breeding. But all London was aware that Mr. Brummel was in truth the grandson of a humble valet.

It was nearly an hour before the gentlemen entered the drawing room. Leonora surmised that Lord Rothwell was wisely using the time to divert the Prince's attention to more pleasing matters than soured friendships.

When at last the drawing room doors opened, she glanced nervously at the Prince's face. To her relief, he was smiling, and seemed restored to his former good humor. Leonora caught Lord Rothwell's eye, and he gave a slight nod as if to reassure her that Madame's folly was well and truly forgotten.

The Prince did indeed seem in excellent spirits, and talked warmly of Lord Rothwell's watercolors. "I declare myself quite envious. Lord Rothwell has excellent taste."

Leonora hastened to offer the Prince some coffee. He smiled his thanks. "How thoughtful of you, Lady Leonora, to remember my aversion to tea."

Madame Valbois, clearly anxious to make amends and restore herself to the Prince's favor, slid her tea cup out of sight behind a bowl of lilac.

"Sir," she trilled, "I could not agree with you more. In fact, I share the views of your eminent writer, Mr. William Cobbett. Did he not declare, 'I view the tea drinking as a destroyer of health, an enfeebler of the frame, an engenderer of effeminacy and laziness, a debaucher of youth, and a maker of misery for old age.' "

The Prince nodded. "I am most impressed to find you familiar with one of our English writers, Madame."

"When Lord Rothwell was in Paris," she confided, "he was generous enough to lend me one of Mr. Cobbett's works. I keep it with me constantly."

Leonora and Melissa exchanged a surprised glance at this rare reference to Lord Rothwell's activities in Paris.

Lord Rothwell, looking unusually ill at ease, remarked quickly, "It is true to say, is it not, Sir, that although you dislike the beverage, you are an avid collector of teapots?"

The Prince smiled, and accepted from his host a glass of cherry brandy. "Many would regard collecting teapots as a somewhat eccentric interest. But I find them fascinating. Only today, I was pleased to receive a new design from Mr. Wedgwood."

The count enquired, "Is that the same Mr. Wedgwood with a showroom in York Street? I believe his pieces are quite unique."

"I value his work highly," said the Prince, "though I must confess that the Empress Catherine of Russia does not exhibit the same respect. Mr. Wedgwood was good enough to make her an entire dinner service, which was transported to Russia with great care, and at enormous expense." He sighed. "But I hear that the lady is prone to extravagant rages, during which she throws the exquisite dinner service piece by piece at the servants!"

When the laughter had died away, Lord Rothwell asked Leonora if she would play for them on the pianoforte. An apprehensive Leonora agreed, on condition that Melissa added a vocal accompaniment.

After the first few minutes at the instrument, Leonora's tense fingers relaxed and she began to enjoy her playing, and the beauty of the music. Melissa was gifted with a true, sweet voice and the musical entertainment they provided proved a melodic end to what had been, with one glaring exception, a highly successful evening.

As the Prince bade his farewell, he complimented Lord Rothwell and Leonora on an excellent dinner, and delightful company. "I hope to have the pleasure of seeing you soon at Carlton House."

Leonora dipped a curtsy. The door closed behind him, and the royal carriage departed. Observing that Leonora was looking fatigued, the count immediately offered to escort her and Melissa back to Grosvenor Street.

Madame Valbois, however, shook her head when the

footman enquired if he should fetch her cloak. "Not yet awhile, thank you. I confess I am still quite overcome from the honor of being in the Prince's company. Cameron, let us sit quietly in your drawing room for a while, and sip a brandy together."

Lord Rothwell escorted the count, Melissa, and Leonora to the door. As they said their good nights, Leonora glanced back, through the hall and into the drawing room.

The lamps had been turned down low. Madame Valbois had poured two brandies and was stretched out on the sofa, smiling as she waited for Lord Rothwell to return to her.

Leonora breakfasted alone the following morning, as Melissa was fatigued and wished to sleep late. As the sun streamed in to the breakfast parlor, Daisy hovered at her mistress's elbow. Leonora knew the girl would not rest until she had been told every detail of the dinner party with the Prince Regent.

Daisy listened enraptured as Leonora good-naturedly gave an account of the evening.

"Oooh, my lady, how agreeable he was toward you! But I'm not surprised, as you looked so lovely in that white dress, with all those diamonds! I'll wager that put Madame Valbois's sharp little nose right out of joint!"

"Daisy! You must not speak of the Lady Melissa's future sister in that impertinent manner!"

The red-haired girl hung her head. "I don't mean any disrespect, my lady. But try as I might, I can't take to that French lady. And she don't like me, neither. I can tell. Her brown mince pies are always peering at me suspiciously."

Leonora was by now sufficiently acquainted with Daisy's singular rhyming expressions to be aware that *mince pies* was a term for eyes. Although she perfectly agreed with Daisy about Madame, she would not have dreamed of admitting so.

Buttering a piece of toast, she remarked, "Well, it

was a highly successful evening. Lord Rothwell is to be congratulated. He was the most perfect host."

Gazing from the window, Daisy cried, "Why, here is Lord Rothwell now, my lady!"

"Heavens, at this early hour!" commented Leonora. "Whatever can he want? Lady Melissa is still asleep."

It occurred to her to wonder if Madame Valbois was sleeping late this morning. What time had she left the house in Park Lane last night?

Lord Rothwell, however, as he strode into the breakfast parlor, showed no sign of lack of sleep. He looked fit, energetic, and in excellent spirits.

"Daisy, be so good as to ask for some coffee to be sent in for Lord Rothwell," instructed Leonora.

Reluctantly, Daisy retreated from the parlor, though not before she had bestowed an adoring glance on Lord Rothwell.

Observing this, he exchanged a smile with Leonora. "My goodness! What have I done to deserve that?"

"She regards you as the most exalted being on this planet," said Leonora, adding wryly, "It appears that your circle of female admirers grows ever wider every day!"

As the coffee was brought in, he remarked, "Melissa, I suspect, is still tucked up in bed?"

Leonora nodded, hoping he was not intending to linger too long over his coffee. The reason she herself was up bright and early this morning was that she had an engagement with Sir Max Fitzarren. He would be calling for her shortly, and the last thing she desired was for the two gentlemen to come face to face in Melissa's breakfast parlor.

She smiled. "What brings you here so early, Cameron?"

He replied, his gray eyes holding hers, "I felt I must come round first thing to thank you most sincerely for being the perfect hostess last night."

"That is sweet of you, Cameron. But I enjoyed every moment of it. Truly."

He nodded. "It was a highly successful evening. Thanks to you. The Prince was most impressed, Leonora, with your beauty, your poise, your total command of the situation. In fact, he told me that he had not enjoyed such a relaxing evening for many a long month."

Leonora flushed. "I am delighted."

Lord Rothwell felt in his pocket and drew out a long, slim leather box. "I felt it would be fitting if you had some memento of the occasion."

He handed her the box. With her fingers trembling from surprise, she opened it and gazed on the most exquisite filigree gold necklace.

"Why, Cameron, it is quite magnificent!" she gasped.

"A small token of my gratitude," he replied with a smile. He moved to the back of her chair, and fastened the delicate necklace round her white throat. Leonora sat very still, acutely conscious of the touch of his sensitive fingers on her skin.

She turned her head and looked up into his gray eyes. "Thank you, Cameron. I shall treasure it always!"

Still with his hand resting on her shoulder, he murmured, "And I too shall treasure the memory of the way you looked last night. Why, I must confess, that when the Prince took your arm to escort you in to dinner, I felt—"

"Sir Max Fitzarren has arrived, my lady," intoned a footman at the door.

It was only then that Leonora realized she had been holding her breath, waiting for Cameron's next words. What had he felt when the Prince took her arm? What had he been about to tell her?

Now she would never know. The moment was lost. Just a few seconds ago, there had sprung into life a tender rapport between herself and Lord Rothwell. But with the arrival of Sir Max, that empathy had evaporated into the bright spring air.

Sir Max strode jauntily into the room. He seemed not at all put out to find Lord Rothwell there. After greeting Leonora, Sir Max rasped, "Ah, 'morning, Rothwell. Visiting your sister, no doubt?"

"No doubt," replied Lord Rothwell icily, his steely gray eyes raking incredulously over Sir Max's appearance. Indeed, Sir Max was hardly dressed for a morning engagement in town. His coat was of an excessively loud tweed, accompanied by riding breeches, and a garish yellow and green cravat. Lord Rothwell, who always dressed in the most impeccable taste, was observed to wince as he regarded the cravat.

Leonora, frantically attempting to restore normality to the situation, declared gaily, "Did you see, Sir Max, that Melissa's engagement to the Comte de Selvigny is announced in *The Times* today?"

The Irishman grinned. "Never read *The Times,* my dear. Get along better with *Sporting Magazine.* It keeps me up to date with all the really important issues in the world: horse racing, hunting, cockfighting and boxing!" He addressed Lord Rothwell. "Matter of fact, that's where Lady Leonora and I are off to now. A boxing match!"

As she faced the glare of Lord Rothwell's disapproval, Leonora unconsciously fingered his ring of gold filigree encircling her throat. "It . . . it sounds fun, Cameron!" she said weakly.

He raised a laconic eyebrow, and reached for the copy of *The Times.* "I trust you will enjoy yourself," he said curtly. "Pray do not allow me to detain you. I shall finish my coffee and wait for Melissa to join me. Good day, Sir Max."

As he escorted Leonora into the carriage, Sir Max remarked, "My, Lord Rothwell is in a glowering mood this morning. Do I suspect that he's had a tiff with his French widow?"

Leonora did not condescend to reply to this, but instead motioned the faithful Daisy into the carriage beside her.

Sir Max sighed as he regarded Daisy's sullen expression. "Good morning, Miss Longface!" he said grimacing at her.

"Good morning, Sir Storrac!" retorted Daisy.

Sir Max frowned. "Now what can that mean?" he demanded.

Leonora gave Daisy a sharp glance. She knew only too well that another of Daisy's verbal tricks was to pronounce words backwards. At her toilette that morning, Leonora had overheard Daisy complaining to Sarah at the prospect of her mistress being once more in the company of Sir Storrac.

"Carrots indeed!" Sarah had exclaimed. "I would remind you, Daisy, that you too have flaming red hair. So one could easily address you, too, as carrots!"

Leonora said hastily now to Sir Max, "Take no notice of Daisy. She is merely apprehensive of venturing into what she insists is the country."

"But we are only traveling to Hayes," laughed the Irishman. "That is a mere spit from London. You should count yourself fortunate, my girl, that your mistress does not choose to take herself off to a fashionable resort like Bath. The hills and dales round that part of the world represent *real* countryside!"

"I have heard of Bath," mused Daisy. "It sounds a wretched place. They say your teeth aren't safe in your head there, if you sleep with your mouth open!"

"That will do, Daisy," murmured Leonora, suppressing a smile. She turned to Sir Max. "You seem in high spirits this morning."

He raised a hand to his brow. "I assure you, it was only the thought of your delightful company that drove me to Grosvenor Street in such good time. The night was long. And very merry."

"More wagers won and lost?" enquired Leonora.

He replied, "Lord Tressler and I engaged in a long session of 'super nagulum.'" Observing Leonora's puzzled look, he explained, "It is a drinking game. After you have drunk your fill of wine, there comes the final test of a man's ability to hold his liquor. You down a mug of ale, then upend the tankard and let the last drop—pearl we call it—fall on to your thumbnail. If the pearl stays on your thumb, all well and good. But if it rolls off, it is a sign that you left too much ale in your mug. You are then compelled to drink another tankard, and another until the pearl remains upon your nail!"

Leonora thought this was the most absurd contest she had ever heard of. To change the subject, she remarked, "I have never before attended a fight, Sir Max. Indeed, I was not even aware that such an event was due to take place today. I have seen no advertisement of the matter."

Sir Max shook his red head. "No more you will. Because of the law, boxing matches are rarely advertised in advance. But word soon gets around to those in the know. And you would be surprised, Lady Leonora, how many people *are* in the know. Each bout draws the most amazing crowds."

As the road wound out of London, and through the fields toward Hayes, Leonora realized the truth of Sir Max's words. The route was soon crammed with coaches, gigs and carts, with horsemen riding between, all converging on an enormous field. The middle section had been roped off, and it was around this area that the crowd surged—laughing, chattering, jostling.

"Why, I have never in my life seen so many people!" exclaimed Leonora.

"Aye, there's thousands here today," commented Sir Max, taking her arm. "Now stay close to me. The place is teeming with thieves and rogues."

"Too true," muttered Daisy to herself, casting a baleful glance at Sir Max.

Having paid the entrance fee of three shillings each, Sir Max elbowed his way to an excellent position on the ropes. "You'll get a fine view from here, Lady Leonora."

Since the fight had not yet begun, Leonora's attention was focussed on the spectators. She was surprised, and reassured, to see so many of the *ton* present. There was Lady Pinsley in an absurd purple bonnet, and Lord Tressler, and the Duke of Westford. It appeared that coming to watch the bouts was really a quite fashionable activity. There had been no cause, then, for Cameron to look so disapproving, Leonora thought. She reflected she would enjoy telling him how many of the quality were present!

Sir Max was waiting impatiently for the bout to start. He flexed his muscles beneath the tweed coat. "I'll be happy to enlighten you on the finer points of the fight," he informed Leonora. "I'm a member of the Pugilistic Club, you know."

"Whatever is that?" queried Leonora.

"It was set up in Bond Street, by an old fighter called 'Gentleman' John Jackson," said Sir Max. "He coaches noblemen in the art of fisticuffs. I am surprised you have not heard of him. Even Lord Byron testifies to the excellence of his tuition."

"Lord Byron?" laughed Leonora. "But he puts his hair in papers at night to encourage the curl, and fasts to keep his romantic figure!"

"Nevertheless," insisted the Irishman, "if Mr. Jackson has taught him to box then you may rest assured that Lord Byron will acquit himself well."

Leonora said thoughtfully, "I wonder why it is that gentlemen are invariably aggressive toward one another?"

"Men will always quarrel," shrugged Sir Max. "It is in the nature of things. But one of the admirable facets of England is that arguments are settled honorably, with the fists."

"You mean instead of using more lethal weapons?" asked Leonora.

He nodded. "In Italy, they have the stiletto. In Holland the long knife. Whilst the French will resort to sticks and stones to seek revenge. But here in England grievances can be settled cleanly, in a fair, open fight." His face brightened. "Ah, here come the contestants! I do believe it is Jack Scroggins and Ned Turner. I can promise you some excellent sport with those two, Lady Leonora!"

Amid cheers from the crowd, the two men stepped over the ropes and entered the ring. Ned Turner was the first to strip off his shirt. He was a short, stumpy man, with bulging eyes set in a scarred, leathery face.

Sir Max gripped the rope. "Do you care for a wager, my lady? My money is on Jack Scroggins. Ned's a game fighter, but Jack is wily, and possesses more cunning."

"Thank you, no, I do not desire to wager," said Leonora firmly. She was aware of Daisy tugging violently at her arm. "What is it, Daisy?"

"My lady!" whispered the red-haired girl urgently. "That man in the ring. It's my Uncle Jack!"

Leonora suppressed a gasp of horror as Jack Scroggins turned to face her. That scowling, florid face! Those hard, ruthless eyes! Of course it was Uncle Jack!

Fearful of being recognized, Leonora shrank back behind Sir Max, and whispered to Daisy, "Keep well out of sight. We do not want him causing trouble if he realizes we are here!"

Daisy needed no second bidding, but dived behind a portly gentleman who was waving his arms, shouting for the fight to begin.

The two men in the ring shook hands, then separated to stand a yard or two away from one another. Ned Turner aimed the first blow, but Scroggins ducked, then planted a right and a left to his opponent's body. Turner countered with a vicious jab in Uncle Jack's left eye. Furious, Scroggins bore down on the bruiser, lashing at his mouth and drawing blood.

The crowd roared their approval. Leonora looked away. She felt sick at the spectacle, and dearly wished she had not come. For many, no doubt the sight of two men pulping one another was great sport. But Leonora could see no attraction in it whatsoever.

As the third round commenced between the two

men, Sir Max peered up at the sky. "Clouding up," he commented. "It'll be better if we get some rain. Cools down the contestants, and keeps them fresh. And it's amusing for us spectators to watch them slide about in the mud!"

At another excited cheer from the crowd, Leonora glanced toward the ring in time to see Jack Scroggins deliver a fearful blow.

"What a stomacher!" shouted Sir Max enthusiastically. "Follow it up, Jack! Keep the advantage!"

As if heeding the Irishman's instruction, Scroggins hauled his opponent to his feet and smashed him round the face. Leonora heard Daisy whimper.

The dazed Ned Turner had had enough. With his face and body bruised and bleeding, he ran for the ropes and pitched himself outside the ring. To the delighted shrieks of the crowd, Uncle Jack raised his hands above his head, grinning as he was formally declared the victor.

Sir Max whirled on Leonora. "Capital, was it now? My, a fight like that fair makes my blood race! I have half a mind to get in the ring and challenge Scroggins myself!"

Leonora paled. "You will kindly attempt no such thing whilst you are escorting me!" she instructed, with dignity.

Sir Max grinned. "Fear not, Lady Leonora. I tell you, if it were any other fighter in England, I'd be in that ring like a shot. But Jack Scroggins is the best. I admit I'm an impetuous man, but even I've got more sense than to take him on!" He looked once more up into the sky. "Besides, it's going to rain. Let us hurry back to the carriage."

Leonora was only too happy to agree. Once safely back on the road to London, she reflected on Sir Max's admiration of Uncle Jack's fighting prowess. The best in England, he said. A man whom even the hot-tempered Sir Max would not dare to challenge.

She fingered the filigree necklace at her throat. And

yet, on that night when she had gone alone to Covent Garden, Lord Rothwell had not hesitated to take on Uncle Jack. He had given him a sound thrashing, too!

As May gave way to a glorious June, Leonora saw very little of Lord Rothwell. He laughingly explained, on one of his rare visits to Grosvenor Street, that it was impossible to move a step beyond the front door. For the house was filled with boxes and packages containing Melissa's trousseau. But from Lord Rothwell's coolness of manner, Leonora suspected that the true reason he stayed away was that he was annoyed with her.

When she returned from the fight at Hayes, Leonora had been ready to admit to Lord Rothwell that she had not at all enjoyed the outing. And she would have liked to tell him about seeing Uncle Jack . . . and how impressed she was that Cameron had defeated a man who was a strong contender for the title of fight champion of England.

But when she broached the subject of Hayes, Lord Rothwell raised a laconic eyebrow, and made such lacerating comments about her choice of company, that Leonora immediately exclaimed defiantly:

"Oh, it was so amusing, Cameron! I was vastly entertained. I must confess, one of the things I find most attractive about Sir Max is the manner in which he finds such unusual diversions for me. One never has time to be bored in his company!"

Lord Rothwell's mouth tightened, and he abruptly left the house. For a moment, Leonora regretted her behavior toward Lord Rothwell.

Then she reasoned: *but it is all his own fault! He has such an abrasive manner at times. And then I cannot help but retaliate!*

Sadly, Daisy watched Lord Rothwell striding from the house. "Such a good, kind man, isn't he, my lady? And he gave you that beautiful gold necklace . . ."

"Which we must ensure is kept under lock and key," instructed Leonora. "I should be most distraught if my

154

lovely necklace was stolen. Although now I come to think of it, nothing has gone missing from the house for over two weeks."

Sir Max called every day, and late one sunny afternoon, Leonora agreed to accompany him on a ride in the park. The grass there was lush and green, with the trees just bursting into full leaf.

"What a glorious time of year this is!" exulted Leonora, her eyes sparkling as she guided her faithful chestnut mare into the park. "Did you notice, Sir Max, how all the gardens we passed on the way were massed with roses? The scent was so beguiling!"

"I regret that the beauty of the flowers escaped me," he replied with a practiced smile. "I had eyes only for you."

Indeed, all eyes were drawn to Leonora as the chestnut trotted under the oak trees. She was wearing a new riding habit in an unusual shade of cinnamon which enhanced the rare perfection of her amber eyes.

It was five o'clock, the most fashionable hour for ladies of quality to be seen in the park.

"Ah, there is the Countess of Jersey, waving regally at we lesser mortals," commented Sir Max. "She is the most delightful lady, but I confess that sometimes from the superior manner she affects, one would imagine she was the Princess of Wales herself."

"But did you not know," Leonora said laughing, "there is a rumor that when the Prince Regent married Princess Caroline, Lady Jersey was so jealous she put epsom salts in the Princess's soup on her wedding night!"

"That I can well believe," the Irishman said with a grin. "She is certainly a lady I would think twice before crossing. Though I understand she is now quite out of favor with the Prince. Lady Hertford holds all the aces at present. Yet I often wonder what *Lord* Hertford has to say about his wife's activities!"

Leonora tucked a stray lock of golden hair back beneath her plumed riding hat. "Oh, it is most amusing.

155

Day after day the Prince's yellow chariot draws up at Hertford House. The Marquis stands to receive him, and the two gentlemen exchange civil words. Then Lord Hertford tactfully bows himself backward out of the drawing room, leaving his wife ensconced on the couch with the royal guest!"

"Extraordinary!" marveled Sir Max. "That could never happen in Ireland. Passions run high there, you know. Royal guest or no, he would instantly be challenged to a duel. Mind, it seems to me," he gave Leonora a sidelong glance, "that if I were married I should ensure I kept my wife so happy that she would never desire to look at other men, even royal ones."

Leonora smiled to herself. *What a smooth talker you are, Sir Max! Thank heavens I have the sense not to believe you.*

Realizing that the conversation was too heavily inclined toward the dangerous area of marriage, Leonora diverted Sir Max's attention by pointing across the park with her crop. "Now tell me, Sir Max. Do you see that light blue carriage, conveying a lady dressed in pink? Are you acquainted with her at all?"

Sir Max narrowed his eyes as he considered the carriage. "I cannot say I recognize the lady. Yet she must be a person of quality, for her carriage bears a painted coronet on the door."

Leonora laughed. "I should have had a wager with you on that! You would not be the first to be deceived by that coat of arms, Sir Max. In truth, the lady is quite low born. And the coronet, on closer inspection, proves to be nothing more than an artfully painted basket of flowers!"

"What deception!" protested Sir Max indignantly.

Leonora's eyes danced as she reflected that the lady in the light blue carriage must surely have Irish blood!

Sir Max suddenly laid a hand on her arm. "Ah, there is my friend Lord Tressler. Is that not a magnificent stallion he is riding?"

Leonora nodded. "Indeed, he looks quite superb. Though he's too much on his toes to take kindly to standing still for long whilst Lord Tressler passes the time of day with Lady Pinsley. However, that single white leg marks him out as a good horse."

"I had no idea you were such a discerning judge of horseflesh, Lady Leonora," said an impressed Sir Max.

"Lord Rothwell has his own stud, you know, on his country estate. It is always an education to go there. I listen to the grooms, and learn a great deal. But I remember as a child, one of my first equestrian lessons was in the form of a rhyme:

> *Four white legs, keep him not a day,*
> *Three white legs, send him far away,*
> *Two white legs, give him to a friend,*
> *One white leg, keep him to the end."*

Sir Max was still gazing enviously at the stallion with the white leg. "I hire my horses from Mr. Tilbury in Mount Street. But I've got my eye on a superb thoroughbred at Tattersall's. It'll cost a thousand guineas. But I'm determined to have him. And soon!"

Leonora glanced away, so he should not observe her expression of fury and contempt. *Oh yes, Sir Max! No doubt you are planning all manner of extravagant purchases once you are wed to me, with my considerable fortune at your command!*

Her eyes flashed with anger as she recalled his despicable treatment of Clementina. *Well revel in your dreams, my Irish friend. They will soon turn to nightmares. Before long, you will be such a laughing stock that no lady of quality in London will so much as bow to you in the street, let alone walk up the aisle with you!*

Leonora was jolted out of her furious reverie by a frightened movement from her horse. Whinnying, the chestnut reared. Caught off guard, Leonora snatched at the reins. But to her alarm she found that the horse was quite out of control. With its eyes wild, and ears back, the mare sped into a gallop through the park, with Leonora clinging frantically to its neck.

Desperately, she tried to soothe the horse, and gain its confidence. But the chestnut careered on, heedless to the sound of her voice. The reins were useless. Leonora gripped tight to the chestnut mane, wondering feverishly what had come over her horse that it should behave like this. The mare had always before displayed such a placid, good-natured temperament. Yet now, out of the blue, it had turned into a wild, frightened animal, rushing Leonora along at breakneck speed.

Leonora was chilled with fear. Breakneck! Her hat had long since blown off, and her golden hair was flying free in the wind. She closed her eyes in despair. *If I do not stop her soon I shall be thrown! But how can I control her? She appears to have a terrifying will of her own, against which I am powerless!*

Suddenly, there came the furious sound of hooves, pounding along beside the chestnut. Opening her eyes, Leonora saw with amazement and relief that Lord Rothwell was drawing level on his gray. His face was grim, his mouth set in a firm, hard line.

"Hold on, Leonora!" he shouted.

"I'm trying!" she gasped, as the chestnut raced on. "But the horse seems crazed!"

Lord Rothwell spurred on his gray, then with a supreme effort leaned forward from his saddle and seized the dangling reins of the chestnut.

"Whoah, there!" he commanded. "Easy girl! Easy!"

The foaming chestnut slowed, attempted to rear, but was soon brought under control by Lord Rothwell's quietly authoritative handling.

"Oh Cameron!" cried Leonora. "I was so terrified! Thank heavens you were at hand! I am so grateful to you."

At that moment Sir Max came galloping up. His face

was livid. "No cause for you to have interfered, Rothwell! I'd have been at the lady's side in another minute, and rescued her myself."

"In another minute!" scorned Lord Rothwell. "Why, you were lumbering along as if you were riding a cart horse. And in another few seconds, Leonora could have been thrown, lying on the grass with her neck broken!"

Sir Max glared. "I'd have saved her, I tell you!"

"Well you were making very heavy weather of it!"

Leonora said hastily, smoothing down her tousled locks, "I simply do not understand why my chestnut should have behaved in such a manner. She has always been utterly reliable before."

The horse still looked fidgety and unsettled. Abruptly, Lord Rothwell dismounted, and reaching up, swept Leonora from the saddle.

"Why Cameron, what is wrong?" she asked breathlessly.

Without a word, he lifted her saddle and ran his fingers underneath. Then he said angrily, "This is what's wrong!" On his palm lay three steel pins.

"But no wonder my poor horse went mad with those sticking into her back!" cried Leonora. "Yet how did they get there, under the saddle?"

Lord Rothwell was staring accusingly at Sir Max. The Irishman shrugged. "You will observe that the park is infested with young urchins, who take a delight in this kind of mischievous prank. The main thing is that you are safe and well, Lady Leonora. Now I shall escort you home directly."

"On the contrary," snapped Lord Rothwell. "*I* shall see Leonora safely home!"

Leonora's head was beginning to throb. "Oh see!" she exclaimed with relief, "There is Melissa in the carriage. If you have no objection, kind sirs, I will beg a seat home with her. After the fright I have just had, I really just long to sit and be driven! Sir Max, thank you for your company. Cameron, I am so grateful for your prompt action in coming to my rescue!"

And with that she ran swiftly across the grass to Melissa—leaving the two men to continue arguing over who should take care of her chestnut.

Nine

A worried Melissa insisted that Leonora go straight home, and up to bed. "I'll order a tray of supper to be sent up to you. Perhaps some nourishing broth, and a nice light egg custard. Would that tempt you?" she asked anxiously.

Leonora laughed. "Melissa, I am not an invalid! I confess that I would like to rest, but my appetite is as healthy as ever. I want none of your insipid broth and egg custards! I should prefer cold roast chicken, and sliced tomatoes, and a baked potato. And to follow, some of Cook's delicious fruit trifle."

"Now I know you are really recovered from your ordeal," smiled Melissa. "I shall give instructions to Mrs. Harris directly."

As she sat up in bed that evening, nibbling at the excellent cold chicken, Leonora carefully reexamined the events leading up to the moment when her chestnut bolted. She did not for a moment believe Sir Max's assertion that a mischievous lad had inserted the steel pins under her saddle. Though it was quite true that at that hour, the park was infested with rogues, aware that with high society gathered there in force, there were rich pickings to be had.

But Sir Max was riding close to me, mused Leonora. Even if my attention had been distracted, it is unlikely that both of us would have failed to observe the boy as he stood close with the pins. No, there was no doubt about it, decided Leonora. Sir Max had placed those pins under the saddle himself, with the express purpose of unsettling her horse! And Leonora could well understand his motive in acting thus.

The Irishman had boasted that he would make Leonora his bride by the thirtieth of June. Yet May was now past, and he has still been unable to find a suitable moment to propose.

I have outmaneuvered him there, thought Leonora. By always insisting that Daisy is present at our meetings, I have never given him the opportunity to be alone with me, and press his suit!

She imagined that Sir Max had resolved to employ more dramatic tactics in pursuit of his goal. If Leonora's horse suddenly bolted and bore her off through the park at terrifying speed, would she not be eternally grateful to the gallant who rescued her? As she clung, sobbing, to his arm, would it not be the ideal time for Sir Max to coax from her an agreement to wed?

A fine plan! Leonora laughed. *But it went awry. You were too slow, Sir Max! It was Lord Rothwell who came thundering to my aid, whilst you limped home a poor second!*

However, the incident brought home to Leonora the fact that Sir Max would go to any lengths—however desperate or dangerous—to win her. Losing face over a rash boast, she realized, would be akin to losing an arm to Sir Max. Whereas any other man would give a philosophical shrug, and accept that one cannot be victorious all the time, Sir Max was a man obsessed with winning. He will allow nothing, and no one, to stand in his way.

Well fear not, Sir Max, mused Leonora. *I see what you are about. I know you are a desperate man. And I shall be watching you like a lynx from henceforth.*

But I shall need a level head and cool wits about me.

For I am convinced that the runaway horse drama is only the beginning. With less than a month to go to the end of June, Sir Max will be employing every devious ploy at his command to bring me to the altar!

In the meantime, there were more pleasant matters commanding Leonora's attention—the first being Daisy's birthday. Daisy had confided to Melissa's maid Sarah that her birthday was imminent, but she was surprised on the morning of the event to be greeted with an array of gaily wrapped packages.

From her fellow servants there were three pairs of precious silk stockings. Melissa gave her a pretty flowered shawl, and Leonora presented her with a delicate garnet necklace.

Daisy's eyes shone with delight. "It's the first proper jewelry I've ever owned, my lady. I promise I'll keep it safe. Oh, just look at the way the garnets shine in the light!"

But the gift which most amazed and overwhelmed her was a straw bonnet decorated with poppies—from none other than Lord Rothwell himself. It was delivered by Lord Rothwell's footman, with a personal note which Daisy proudly read aloud to Leonora:

"A small token of my gratitude for the loyalty and devotion you have shown to your mistress."

Daisy blushed as red as the poppies on the bonnet. "Fancy him doing a thing like that, my lady! Isn't that kind?"

"Lord Rothwell is an extremely thoughtful gentleman at all times," Leonora said smiling. "You understand his note perfectly, Daisy. But I had no notion you could read?"

"Uncle Jack's wife taught me my letters, my lady."

"It is a valuable asset," said Leonora. "You should read all you can. I shall lend you some books from my library." She laughed, realizing that Daisy was longing to run and try on her new bonnet. "You must wear it tomorrow. Sir Max is taking me on a picnic to Box Hill, and I should like you to accompany us."

Daisy fiddled with the ribbons on her bonnet. She was not looking forward to tomorrow. She had no urge to set foot outside London. She only felt at home in a city. Trees, grass, and wide open spaces unsettled her. Especially when she was in the company of that snake, Sir Max. Daisy glanced hopefully up at the sky, and prayed for rain.

But the day dawned bright and sunny. Daisy, grim-faced beneath her gay new bonnet, entered the carriage and sat in a corner as far removed as possible from Sir Max.

Leonora greatly enjoyed the journey. Although she loved London, it was a fact that on a summer's day like this, with the sky a cloudless blue and the sun warm on her face, she longed to escape from the city and enjoy the sweet fresh air of the countryside. Of all counties, Surrey had long been one of her favorites, with its wide variety of trees, and gentle landscape.

Though gentle was hardly the word for Box Hill, she mused, as the carriage zigzagged up the path that led to the summit.

"The hill must be all of five hundred feet high," she remarked to Sir Max. "What a marvelous view there will be from the top."

The view was breathtaking. Stepping from the carriage, Leonora gasped with delight as she surveyed the panorama of farms, fields, and woods stretching far below.

"See, over there is Dorking!" she exclaimed. "Why, from this height it resembles no more than a tiny toy town!"

Happy to be out in the fresh air, Leonora explored for a while some of the paths and tracks leading from the summit. With Sir Max at her side, and Daisy a watchful two paces behind, Leonora wandered contentedly among the bushes of elderberry and wild guelder rose. A meadow brown butterfly fluttered ahead of her, and she was delighted when she found a yellowhammer's nest, containing four spotted eggs. Leonora was careful not to disturb the nest, and readily agreed when Sir Max enquired if she would care for some refreshment.

Daisy fetched the hamper from the carriage and Leonora selected the picnic place. It was a little way down from the summit, sheltered from the wind and smelling deliciously of wild thyme.

A cloth was laid on the grass, and Daisy set out the cold meats, fruit, and pastries prepared by Cook. Sir Max opened a bottle of white wine.

"My, the fresh air has given me such an appetite!" confessed Leonora. "Tell me, Sir Max, how does the Surrey landscape compare with your native Ireland?"

He smiled. "Each has a charm of its own, Lady Leonora. Surrey is pretty, to be sure. But I admit there are times when I long for the misty hills of home. There is a particular view from the south wing of my mansion—"

"Your mansion?" queried Leonora shrewdly. "Forgive me, but from a previous conversation with you, I understood that your Irish home was a castle."

He sipped his wine. "Ah . . . yes . . . the castle, you see, is in Galway. But my family also owns a mansion in Kerry. When in Ireland, I divide my time between the two residences—my, this ham is delicious! Do try some, Lady Leonora. And allow me to help you to mustard. It brings out all the flavor of the meat."

One day, resolved Leonora, I shall discover the truth about Sir Max's mysterious Irish homes. I nearly caught him out over that matter of the castle, but he was quick-witted enough to cover his tracks.

She glanced round for Daisy. The girl had removed her hat and was collecting wild flowers. "Would you like something to eat and drink, Daisy?"

"No thank you, my lady. I want to gather a bouquet to take back for Mrs. Harris."

Leonora smiled. "Well do not wander too far."

"Have no fear," Daisy replied, looking sharply at Sir Max. "I'll not go out of sight!"

Sir Max stretched out his legs on the rug. "My, this is a pleasant way to spend the day. Quite restores the spirits. Don't mind telling you, I had a tedious dinner last night with old Bunbury. Are you acquainted with Sir Charles, Lady Leonora?"

She nodded. "Is he not a steward at Newmarket?"

"The very same. As I'm a racing man, it seemed as well to cultivate the fellow. But all he could talk about was horses! Now I'm as keen as the next chap on discussing horseflesh, but not for over four hours!"

Leonora laughed. "Poor Sir Charles. I am afraid horseflesh is the only topic with which he feels safe. He had an unfortunate marriage, you see."

"Tell me more," Sir Max said, grinning.

"His wife, Lady Sarah, hated their dull country Suffolk life, and ran off with Lord William Gordon. Sir Charles was livid, of course, and threatened to call Lord William out. But friends explained to him that it was fruitless fighting a duel with Lord William, as he was the tenth of Lady Sarah's lovers! In all fairness, poor Sir Charles would have been required to slay the other nine before taking on Lord William." Leonora smiled. "As some wag pointed out, Sir Charles was a better judge of horseflesh than of a spirited young lady!"

Sir Max laughed, and stood up, the better to admire the view across the Downs. Leonora closed her eyes, and drowsily lifted her face to the sun. Behind her she could hear Daisy humming to herself as she collected her wild flowers.

Suddenly, the humming escalated into a cry of anguish. "My bonnet! My pretty new bonnet has gone!"

Startled, Leonora enquired, "But where did you leave it, Daisy?"

"Over there, on the grass," cried Daisy in despair.

Sir Max snorted. "Foolish girl! I can see your bonnet. Look, it has rolled down the hillside. The wind must have got up and blown it away."

Daisy ran to the edge of the hillside and peered down. "Oh, it is caught on a broom bush. I'll slip down and fetch it."

Leonora sat up in alarm. She knew perfectly well that Daisy's hat could not possibly have been caught by the breeze. Had she not specially selected this picnic spot so they were safely out of the wind? She could not prove it, but Leonora was certain that Sir Max had taken the bonnet and deliberately thrown it over the hill! With Daisy frantically scrambling down after it, Sir Max was given the ideal opportunity to be alone with Leonora . . . and was not this pretty spot the perfect place for a proposal?

Leonora appreciated that it was useless calling to Daisy that she would buy her a new bonnet. Nothing, not even an earthquake, would prevent Daisy from rescuing Lord Rothwell's birthday gift. The bonnet, and the garnet necklace were Daisy's two most precious possessions.

Already, Sir Max was seating himself beside Leonora. In a few seconds, she knew he would be taking her hand, expressing his deepest affection . . .

Her mind was in a whirl. The time was not yet ripe for Sir Max to be allowed to proceed with his proposal. Leonora was looking forward to watching him suffer and fret as the end of June drew nigh, and society hostesses laughed as they enquired if he had yet bought the Lady Leonora's wedding ring!

What a fool I shall make you look, Sir Max! But meanwhile, what am I to do in this present situation, Leonora wondered feverishly. Last time he was about to propose, I pretended to faint. But I can hardly employ that ruse a second time!

Sir Max cleared his throat. His fingers reached out, and entwined with hers. His voice was low, and intimate, as he said, "Lady Leonora, my dear . . . this has been a day I shall treasure forever. Being with you is always such a delight. So much so, that when we are apart, my thoughts turn only to you. You mean so much to me, dearest—"

He broke off. Leonora had snatched away her hand, and jumped to her feet.

"Sir Max! Oh, I do believe I have been stung by a bee! Oh, the pain is quite unbearable!"

Out of the corner of her eye she observed his furious expression—quickly masked by one of concern. He advanced toward her, "My dear, allow me to assist you. Where . . ."

Leonora gave him no opportunity to come too close. As if agitated, and beside herself with pain, she seized her parasol and pretended to swat the offending bee.

Sir Max ducked and backed away as Leonora's parasol flailed wildly around his head.

"The wretched, beastly insect!" she cried. "It stung me on the neck. Sir Max, would you be so kind as to dampen your handkerchief in some wine so I may cool the sting?"

He had no choice but to do as she requested. As she held the handkerchief to her neck, Leonora ran to the edge of the hill. She was relieved to see that Daisy had retrieved her bonnet, and was now climbing doggedly up between the broom bushes.

"Daisy, come quickly! I have been stung, and urgently need your help!"

When the red-haired girl reached the top, Leonora whispered, "It is all a pretense! But I cannot reveal precisely why. Just trust me—and make a great fuss over me!"

Always eager to pull the wool over the Irishman's eyes, Daisy shrieked convincingly, "Oh my lady, what a horrid mark the bee has left! Here, allow me to draw the poison for you!"

They exchanged a smile as they observed a disconsolate Sir Max resignedly packing away the picnic hamper.

After a few minutes, Leonora returned to him. "I am

so very sorry to spoil our day, Sir Max. But if you do not mind, I should like to return home now. I can hardly move my head for the pain in my poor neck!"

Sir Max had no choice but to agree, and the party made its way back to the carriage. *Another round to me,* exulted Leonora. *But I was right. Sir Max is certainly growing desperate. It is plain that he intends to grasp every opportunity to press his suit. I must ensure I have all my wits about me as this fateful June progresses!*

But Leonora was wrong to imagine that the main adventure of the day was over—that she could now relax and enjoy an uneventful carriage ride home.

They were traveling across Epsom Common, which was covered in short, tough springy grass, and clumps of gorse bushes. Leonora clung to the leather strap as the carriage jolted and jarred over the ruts and potholes in the appalling road.

Suddenly, all the passengers were thrown from their seats as the carriage jerked to a halt. The driver could be heard arguing with someone outside.

Sir Max cursed softly, "Don't tell me the sap has run over a sheep, and the angry farmer is demanding compensation!" He flung open the carriage door, with the intention of investigating the matter.

"Oh no you don't, my fine Sir!" shouted a coarse voice.

Leonora gasped in horror. A pistol was leveled at Sir Max's head. It was held by a tall, masked man mounted on a large gray.

A highwayman! Of course, now she came to think of it, this area was notorious for holdups. In one week, all the stage coaches coming into Surrey had been robbed. Not one had escaped.

Leonora felt Daisy shrink back into the seat beside her. Oh, the daring of this highwayman, thought Leonora. To hold us up like this—in broad daylight!

The masked man was peering into the carriage. "As

169

I thought. The carriage carries a lady of quality. I see a fine necklace, and some pretty gold earrings. I'll relieve you of those, thank you, my lady!"

Before Leonora could make a move, Sir Max snapped, "Stay quite still, Lady Leonora! Give this foolish wretch nothing!"

The pistol came up once more, level with Sir Max's pale blue eyes.

"What the plague do you think you're at, my fine sir? Do you want you and your lady to end up dead on the Common? I assure you I am in earnest! Now hand over those jewels, or—"

"Hold your gibbering tongue, Tom Trubbler!" yelled Sir Max.

While the masked man was recovering from the shock of being recognized, Sir Max pushed past him, and walked across to a clump of gorse about twenty yards away from the carriage.

"Come over here!" commanded the Irishman. "There is much I wish to say to you!"

To Leonora's amazement, the highwayman meekly obeyed. She was disconcerted, however, to discover that the men were talking in low voices, and she could not hear a word.

"Daisy," she whispered, "can you lip read and tell me what they are saying?"

The red-haired girl shook her head sorrowfully. "They are keeping their chins well down, and their faces turned slightly away from us. I fear I cannot make out a thing, my lady."

"I wonder how Sir Max happened to know the masked man's name?" Leonora mused aloud. "And see, the highwayman is looking extremely crestfallen. All his bluster has completely evaporated. He appears almost humble now! Whatever can Sir Max have said to him?"

At that moment, Sir Max waved a dismissive hand, and the masked man turned and rode away fast across the Common. Sir Max strode back to the carriage, grim faced.

"Drive on!" he instructed the driver.

He seated himself in the carriage, and was silent for a while. Then he remarked conversationally, "Ah, it will not be long before we are within sight of the River Thames. I understand that a few winters ago, it was completely frozen over."

Leonora laughed. "Sir Max, you cannot be so heartless as to leave us in suspense like this! Why, one moment that masked man was threatening to leave us in a pool of blood on the Common. And the next, he had disappeared over the horizon in a cloud of dust! Whatever did you say to him?"

Sir Max shrugged. "It was an unfortunate episode. The man was, in fact, the valet of an acquaintance of mine, who had sadly fallen on hard times. He has been mixing with bad company. I recognized Trubbler almost immediately, and realized that he is not a born villain. I could quite easily have overpowered him and handed him over to the law. But it seemed more charitable to take him to one side, and give him a good talking to. I think the fellow has now seen the error of his ways."

"It was certainly not very intelligent to attempt to hold up a carriage in broad daylight," commented Leonora. "He might at least have had the wit to wait until dusk!"

"Well, no harm was done," said Sir Max. "And I fancy I have scared Trubbler off from highway robbery. It is obviously not as easy as he imagines!"

Leonora settled back in her seat with a sigh. "My, what an eventful day we have had! Melissa will never believe me."

Sir Max leaned forward, and said quickly, "If I were you, I should not mention this highwayman incident to Lady Melissa. It would only worry her."

"On the contrary!" laughed Leonora. "She will be

fascinated by every detail. How could she possibly be alarmed when I reveal how ably you coped with the situation?"

Later, in the privacy of her dressing room, Leonora remarked to Daisy, "I confess, I was surprised by Sir Max's modesty over his dispatch of the highwayman. Most gentlemen of my acquaintance would have been only too proud for intelligence of their gallantry to be spread abroad."

Daisy frowned. "If you'll allow me to say so, my lady, the whole affair smells fishy to me."

"Oh, what a suspicious mind you have!" scoffed Leonora. For her part, she was only too relieved that the earlier threat of the day, when Sir Max had attempted to propose to her, had been averted so successfully.

As it came about, Leonora had no opportunity to tell Melissa the following morning about her eventful day at Box Hill, for the count arrived early to take his fiancée to the goldsmiths, to choose her wedding ring.

Melissa's departure was speedily followed by the arrival of Lord Rothwell. He came armed with a list of houses which he thought might interest Leonora. He would be delighted to accompany her, he said, and was sure she would not object if they asked Madame Valbois to honor them with her presence, also.

Leonora had no choice but to agree. The day turned out as dismal as she had anticipated. They looked in all at five houses that morning, and Madame was quick to voice her opinion on each of them. Leonora found this so aggravating that she was unable to view any of the residences objectively. Instead, some stubborn streak in her dictated that she must disagree with everything Madame said.

At two o'clock the party arrived back at Madame's house in Hanover Square. They were all exhausted and out of temper.

"Really, Leonora," protested Lord Rothwell, "You

appear to be in a strange mood today. Usually you have such definite opinions on what you desire. But today you dithered and vacillated, and seemed infuriatingly woolly-minded over all those houses. Surely one of them must have appealed to you?"

"In my view," said Madame Valbois, ringing the bell for refreshments, "the little house in Hill Street was ideal. It was not too large, yet each of the rooms was perfectly proportioned."

Leonora, who had found the house quite agreeable, felt unaccountably prickly, and declared, "The windows were rather small. And the morning room was poorly situated, receiving no sun until the late afternoon."

Lord Rothwell sighed. "Clearly, this is going to be a longer task than I imagined!"

Madame accepted a glass of wine from the footman. "I confess, I am looking forward to a quiet afternoon. Today has been quite hectic, and yesterday, Lady Leonora, we were out in the fresh air. I expressed a desire to see your English game of cricket, and Lord Rothwell very kindly took me to Mr. Thomas Lord's cricket ground."

"How very enjoyable," said Leonora icily.

Lord Rothwell shook his dark head. "The turf was too ridged and furrowed for the game to be of a high standard. I was somewhat disappointed."

"Such a pity, then, that you both did not join Sir Max Fitzarren and myself. We had such a delightful picnic at Box Hill," said Leonora sweetly.

Lord Rothwell scowled. But Madame Valbois appeared full of interest. "It sounds the most charming place, Lady Leonora. I should so much like to go there. I love the country air! But unfortunately, my time in England is limited."

Leonora affected an expression of sorrow. "Surely you are not thinking of returning to France, Madame Valbois?"

"I regret that I must. I promised my brother that I would quit London at the end of July to prepare his chateau for his bride."

Leonora had to restrain herself from dancing around the room. Madame was leaving London! Oh joy! What wonderful news!

Madame went on, with a smile at Lord Rothwell, "But I shall be returning to England in September. I understand the English autumn is beautiful. And I am so looking forward to seeing the splendid beech avenues on Lord Rothwell's country estate."

Leonora hurried home and found Melissa seated at the writing table in the Blue Saloon. Throwing off her bonnet, Leonora exclaimed, "Melissa, I am extremely concerned about Cameron and Madame Valbois. Am I to understand that he has invited her to stay at his estate in Gloucestershire?"

Melissa laid down her quill and smiled. "Why, yes. In fact, it was I who suggested the plan. Madame is quite delighted."

"No doubt! But Melissa, how can you be so foolish as to encourage this relationship between your brother and the widow? She is clearly quite unsuitable, quite the wrong sort of woman for him."

Melissa laughed, "Oh Leonora, you are always so unreasonable about Madame! And after all, no one, not even I, can presuade Cameron to do something he does not wish to do. If he is constantly in Bettine's company, then one can only assume that it is by his own desire." She pushed aside her letters, and went on impatiently, "But let us not quarrel about Bettine and Cameron. I am longing to tell you about the wedding ring Edouard chose for me today. I do not have it with me, for the goldsmith is making it smaller, but it is quite exquisite. In Florentine style . . ."

Leonora gave Melissa her full attention, realizing that she was too much in love herself to be capable of thinking objectively about her brother and Madame. But the matter continued to vex Leonora.

After several days' serious reflection, she decided that, unpleasant though the task may be, it was her duty to quiz Cameron on the subject. She felt she must establish, once and for all, what his intentions were toward the Frenchwoman.

Accordingly, she called on Lord Rothwell one afternoon, and was ushered into the library. As she waited for him to enter, Leonora nervously justified her actions: I have known Cameron for many years. I am like a sister to him. I should never forgive myself if I did not speak out, and he married Madame, and doomed himself to a miserable existence.

Lord Rothwell smiled as she strode into the room. "Well, Leonora! How enchanting you look in blue! To what do I owe the honor of this call? Have you heard of another house on which you would like my opinion?"

Leonora drew a deep breath to lend her courage. "No, Cameron, it is not my personal affairs that I wished to discuss, but yours." She rushed on. "Please do not be angry with me for speaking thus, but I felt I must talk to you frankly about your . . . your friendship with Madame Valbois."

He lifted an eyebrow. His knuckles were white. "What about it?"

"Cameron, are your intentions serious toward her? Because if so, I feel I must warn you that she is not the kind of woman who will make you happy, I—"

Lord Rothwell had raised his hand. He said gravely, "Leonora, I appreciate that you are speaking out of friendship and concern. But I must ask you not to say another word on the matter."

"But—"

"I mean it, Leonora!"

His voice chilled her to silence. He went on, "After all, I would remind you that you are always quite adamant that I should not interfere in your choice of friends! I

175

have told you time and time again that I disapprove of Sir Max Fitzarren. Yet you continue to be seen in his company!"

"Cameron, I admit that Sir Max has certain . . . failings . . . of which I most certainly do not approve," said Leonora. "But I do believe in some respects you have misjudged him. Why, on our visit to Box Hill, we were accosted by a highwayman! Yet Sir Max defused the situation in the most admirable style."

Swiftly, Leonora outlined the episode on Epsom Common. Lord Rothwell paced up and down by the window. Then he said, "Tell me more about Sir Max. Where exactly are his estates in Ireland?"

"Well, he *says* there is a castle in Galway. And some kind of mansion in Kerry."

"I see," said Lord Rothwell thoughtfully. "And what of his people? Has he brothers, sisters . . . ?"

"I do not know," confessed Leonora. "He has certainly never mentioned any kin."

Leonora wondered why Cameron was expressing this sudden interest in Sir Max's background. But before she could say any more the footman announced that Madame Valbois had arrived, and had been shown into the drawing room.

Leonora rose immediately, and left the house with her head held high. It had been a wasted journey. Cameron had refused to listen to her. What's more, he now intended to spend the afternoon with the odious Madame. Yet Leonora was no nearer learning the truth about whether or not Lord Rothwell was in love with her.

Ten

A few days later, Melissa gaily announced at breakfast, "Leonora, I am aware that you do not hold Madame Valbois in the highest regard. But I am convinced that you will reverse your opinion when I tell you what she has planned for me."

Leonora sipped her coffee. "What is it, Melissa?"

"As you know," smiled Melissa, "It is my birthday on June 20. So Bettine has kindly proposed to hold a combined birthday and engagement ball for me at the house she has rented in Hanover Square."

"That is most handsome of her," agreed Leonora. "But the Hanover Square house is not overlarge. Has it the capacity for a ball?"

"Perhaps ball is too grand a word," admitted Melissa, buttering a piece of toast. "In fact, Bettine wishes the event to be quite select, with no more than a hundred guests invited. And as you so rightly say, the main saloon in the house will hold no more than that."

"I think it is a wonderful notion!" exclaimed Leonora. "Is it to be fancy dress? It is an age since I attended a costume ball!"

Melissa nodded. "Bettine proposes that the ladies should attire themselves in fancy dress, since she says all the females of her acquaintance love devising original costumes for themselves. The gentlemen, however, demur.

177

Both Cameron and Edouard loath dressing up as Cardinal Wolsey, or pirates, or whatever!"

"But it will look absurd if the ladies are in costume and the gentlemen are not!"

"Bettine has solved the problem by declaring that the gentlemen may wear their normal evening dress—but with the addition of masks. She feels this will lend a note of intrigue to the gathering!"

"Yes, that is an excellent notion," Leonora agreed. She thought for a moment, and then announced, "I shall attend the ball as a shepherdess. It is a becoming costume, yet not hot or cumbersome, so I shall be able to dance freely. What will you wear, Melissa? As the ball is in your honor, all eyes will be upon you!"

Melissa's cheeks were tinged pink. "I thought," she declared boldly, "that I would go to the ball as Madame Du Barry!"

Leonora's eyes widened. "But she was a notorious courtesan!"

"I am aware of that," said Melissa calmly. "But as I am soon to assume the mantle of a respectable married woman, I wish to indulge my fancies for just one evening, and present myself as a lady of dubious reputation. After all, it will be my last opportunity!"

Leonora laughed, and said warmly, "You will be the toast of all London, Melissa!"

Melissa pushed away her plate, and murmured hesitantly, "There is just one thing, Leonora dear. The fact is ... well, as you may be aware, Bettine regards Sir Max Fitzarren with extreme disfavor. I did point out to her that you would probably be pleased if he was invited to the ball, but I fear Bettine will not relent. Will you be dreadfully disappointed if he does not attend?"

"Why of course not!" cried Leonora, hiding a smile. Oh Melissa, she thought. If you only knew that, for once, I am totally in accord with Madame in her opinion of Sir Max!

"I am so relieved." Melissa took her hand. "I have

178

been so busy of late, arranging my wedding. I fear I have neglected you." She sighed. "Oh dear. This is such a delicate topic. I have no wish to sound like an interfering fusspot. But it troubles me that you cannot see how undesirable a companion Sir Max is for you. You are the loveliest girl in London. Yet you have steadfastly rebuffed all the eligible young beaux who have called on you these last few months. I am so worried when I see you leaving the house with Sir Max day after day . . ."

Touched by her friend's concern, Leonora said, "Now do not fret, Melissa. I give you my word that I have all my wits about me where Sir Max is concerned. And to put your mind at rest, I assure you that Sir Max will not be gracing London with his presence for very much longer!"

Melissa's face brightened. "Leonora, I am delighted to hear it! But why——"

Leonora raised a hand. "I can say no more at the present. Just trust me!"

"You are plotting something!" said Melissa suspiciously.

"Indeed I am!" laughed Leonora. "But when the time is right, I promise I shall reveal all to you!"

And refusing to say another word, Leonora slipped away to the Blue Saloon, and settled herself at the table with a new feather picture. As she sketched a design to incorporate some lustrous ostrich feathers which Daisy had dyed blue, Leonora sang softly to herself:

"Thirty days hath September, April, *June* and November . . ."

There were now less than three weeks of June remaining. Only nineteen days for Sir Max to propose, be accepted, and bring Leonora to the altar in order to fulfill the terms of his rash boast.

It will soon be time, mused Leonora, *for me to allow him to propose. What I must decide is when, exactly, I shall permit that interesting event to occur. Now let me see, Madame's ball is to be held on the twentieth. It would be pleasant for me to be able to enjoy the ball safe in the knowledge that Sir Max has been defeated. Then I shall be free to devote my attention to all the other young blades who have been dancing attendance on me these past few months! Yes, I shall kindly permit Sir Max to declare his undying love for me a day or two before the ball.*

But in the meantime, I think it would be amusing to keep my suitor nervously on tenterhooks. It is obvious from the incident over Daisy's bonnet at Box Hill that he will seize every opportunity to bring up the subject of marriage. Very well, I shall ensure that he has absolutely no occasion to be alone with me! Somehow, I shall make myself quite unavailable to him. But I must take care to devise a plan for my "disappearance" which will not arouse his suspicions.

After some minutes' thought, Leonora jumped up from the table, her eyes sparkling as she rang the bell and requested that the carriage be brought around.

Although Madame Valbois was surprised by Leonora's unexpected morning call, she possessed sufficient poise to conceal her disquiet. She laid aside the guest list she was preparing for the ball, and greeted her guest with the utmost civility, offering her the most comfortable chair in the morning room, and ringing for refreshment.

But Madame was unable to suppress a small gasp of astonishment when Leonora stated the purpose of her visit.

". . . So you see, Madame, with Melissa occupied with her wedding arrangements, and yourself still something of a stranger to London, I felt it my duty to offer my help for the organization of your ball."

"*Ma petite,* that is indeed most kind, most thoughtful of you," an aghast Madame replied slowly. "But I would not dream of imposing on you. You should be out with your beaux, enjoying yourself! I assure you, it will be no trouble for me to make the arrangements for the ball. I have done it many times before."

"In France, yes," replied Leonora sweetly, greatly relishing Madame's discomfiture. "There you are no doubt familiar with the best florists, musicians, and caterers for such an event. But here in London, you will find it difficult knowing which suppliers to choose. This is where I can assist you. If you follow my advice on these matters, I will save you a great deal of valuable time. And naturally, as the suppliers have respect for my name, it will be a safeguard against them attempting to charge you too high a price!"

Leonora affected to gaze out of the window—but from the corner of her eyes she was amused to watch Madame battling with herself. Madame Valbois, like Leonora, was a strong-willed woman with a mind of her own. She would have preferred to arrange her ball herself, imposing on it her own taste and ideas. And Madame would, therefore, gain all the credit for the success of the evening. The ball would undoubtedly establish her in London as a powerful society hostess. Yet if it became known that another lady was the guiding light behind the arrangements, then Madame would lose considerable prestige.

Madame Valbois was especially unhappy that the lady in question should be Lady Leonora Pagett: the woman she regarded, rightly or wrongly, as her rival for Lord Rothwell's affections. It was one thing for Madame to accompany Lord Rothwell and *choose* to be in Leonora's presence while viewing houses. But it was quite another matter for Leonora to arrive unannounced, and blithely declare that henceforth they would be much in one another's company, organizing the forthcoming ball!

And yet . . . Madame's cool, calculating brain began to override her resentment. It had to be admitted that Leonora was right in this question of her being cognizant with the best suppliers. If there was one thing Madame abhorred it was being cheated over money by impertinent tradespeople. Would it not, in fact, be more sensible to take advantage of Leonora's local knowledge, and patronage?

Then there was Lord Rothwell to be considered. Madame was eager to retain his approbation. But it would not look well for her if he heard that she had spurned Leonora's offer of help with the ball.

At last, Madame forced a smile to her frozen lips. "Well, my dear, if you are sure the burden will not overtax you, then I am delighted to accept your generous offer."

"I am so glad!" exclaimed Leonora. "Between us we shall organize a ball that will be the talk of all London for months to come!"

So it was that whenever Sir Max Fitzarren called at the house in Grosvenor Street, he was informed by a footman that the Lady Leonora was at Hanover Square. And on being admitted to Madame Valbois's house, he invariably found the two ladies busily consulting over guest lists, or interviewing caterers, or inspecting bales of silk which were to be hung from the walls of the Great Saloon.

There was much to do before the ball, and true to her word, Leonora set to work with a will. She could in no way come to feel affection for Madame, but Leonora discovered that working with the Frenchwoman was a great deal easier than merely socializing. Madame was blessed with good organizing ability, which Leonora complemented with her excellent taste and quick eye for detail.

As the days flew by, the conversation naturally turned to other balls and assemblies the ladies had attended.

"As you know," said Leonora one morning, "I grew up in Gloucestershire, and as a child I dreaded the annual ball held by my father. It was the custom in those days for all the walls to be washed down before such an event, and it left the house damp and cold for months afterwards!"

Madame glanced approvingly at Leonora's sketch-plan of the dining table centerpiece decoration. "I have heard that all English country houses are cold and drafty."

"It is a problem in winter," Leonora agreed. "My father was something of a scholar, and when the weather was icy he would order cognac to be mixed with the ink to prevent it from freezing."

Madame rolled her eyes at such sacrilege of fine cognac. "Well thank heavens it is June, and the weather in London is fine and warm." She consulted her guest list. "I do believe the ball is going to be a success, Lady Leonora. Everyone of quality will be present. Lady Holland's footman has just called with her acceptance. It is quite a feather in one's cap, is it not, to have Lady Holland gracing one's house?"

"I fear the Duke of Bedford would not agree with you," laughed Leonora. "Lady Holland once arrived at Woburn with an entourage of no less than sixteen people. And the Duke's servants were completely thrown into disarray by Lady Holland's insistence on bringing her own silver chamber pot!"

Madame looked puzzled. "But surely English servants are accustomed to such, er, conveniences?"

"Ah, but not silver ones," smiled Leonora. "You see, in English houses it is customary for the maids to clean all the china, whilst the under-bulters look after the silver. I hear there was a near revolution below stairs when the under-butlers were required to take responsibility for her ladyship's silver chamber pot!"

Madame shook her head in amazement. "Sometimes, I feel I will never understand you eccentric English! I do hope Lady Jersey has no such similar foibles. She too has accepted for the ball."

"The only trouble you will have with Lady Jersey will be to persuade her to stop dancing and go home," advised Leonora. "Her energy is legendary."

"Yet she is no longer young," replied the Frenchwoman tartly.

"No, but she is beautiful and gay. Lord Byron compared her to a gold and silver bird who sings joyously every hour of the day until it is time for rest. Lady Jersey herself has a less lyrical turn of phrase. She attributes her youthful appearance to the use of gruel instead of soap and water."

Madame Valbois shuddered. But she made a mental note to take the opportunity at the ball of inspecting at close quarters Lady Jersey's celebrated complexion.

Two days before the ball, Leonora stayed at home instead of going as usual to Hanover Square. She decided that Sir Max had been left long enough in suspense. Today, when he called, she would encourage him to declare himself!

She was confident that he would come to Grosvenor Street that day, for in the preceding weeks her absence had not daunted him. If Sir Max had not called himself, then his footman had arrived with flowers, and a note imploring her to be free that afternoon, or evening.

Accordingly, Leonora toyed with her feather picture in the Blue Saloon, and composed her eloquently acidic reply to the Irishman's proposal of marriage.

But the hours slipped away. Four o'clock chimed, and Sir Max did not come. Neither did his footman with flowers. Thoroughly perplexed, Leonora mentioned very casually to Melissa when she returned from her modiste that she was surprised to have seen nothing of Sir Max that day.

Melissa bit her lip. "Oh dear. I am so sorry, Leonora. There was a message left for you yesterday, but in all the rush to get my costume fitted I completely forgot about it. Sir Max asked me to tell you that he has been called out of town, but will wait on you without fail early in the afternoon of the twentieth."

The day of the ball, thought Leonora. How vexing! I was hoping to have the whole unsavory business over and done with well before then. However, it cannot be helped. Sir Max shall propose to me on the afternoon before the ball. I shall deliver my biting refusal, and go off to Hanover Square to dance the night away with a light and carefree heart!

Sir Max was as good as his word. At two o'clock on the afternoon of June twentieth, Melissa's footman ushered him into the drawing room where Leonora was waiting.

She greeted him with a smile. "Sir Max! How patient you have been with me over the past two weeks. I fear I have been so immersed in assisting Madame Valbois that I have had no time for social pleasures."

He replied with a bow, "I assure you, you have been ever in my thoughts, Lady Leonora. In fact, I have been busy on your behalf. If you are still interested in acquiring a house in this vicinity, I can show you one just off Park Lane which I am sure will meet with your approval."

Leonora arose. "I should be delighted to see it, Sir Max. How very kind of you."

She rang the bell and asked Daisy to bring her a bonnet and light shawl. "Will we be out for very long, my lady?" enquired the maid. "I have still to press your shepherdess costume for the ball tonight."

"Oh, I shall not require you to accompany me, thank you, Daisy," smiled Leonora. "You may iron the dress whilst I am out."

Leonora's eyes glimmered with amusement as she contemplated the contrasting expressions on the faces of the two people before her. Daisy—dismayed, and anxious about her mistress venturing abroad alone with the evil Sir Max. And the Irishman—smiling, confident, and faintly relieved.

I am convinced, thought Leonora as she entered his carriage, *that he had devised an elaborate plot to rid himself of Daisy on this outing. How lighthearted he must feel that his scheme will not now be necessary!*

"I should explain that the house we are going to view is at present still occupied," said Sir Max, as the carriage drew up outside a tall, elegant residence in the street leading from Park Lane. "But the owners are away this month, refurbishing their new villa, and they have kindly lent me the keys so I may show you around."

He opened the front door, and Leonora obediently

went through the motions of looking at the rooms. She praised the view from the drawing room, and wondered aloud if the music room would not be better sited on the south side of the house, away from the noise of passing traffic.

"No," she said thoughtfully, "on reflection that would not be a good notion. For the library is sited on the south side, and it is never a good plan to place a music room next to the library. Though what a gloomy library this is! My, how high the windows are set. I firmly believe, Sir Max, that libraries should be light, airy places . . ."

As she chattered on, Leonora was observing Sir Max closely. She strongly suspected that he was not listening to a word she uttered. Indeed, he appeared restless, and on edge, tapping his ringed fingers impatiently on the library mantelpiece.

Leonora decided to come to his aid. After all, she reasoned, I do not want this business of the proposal dragging on all afternoon. I must be back at Grosvenor Street in good time to prepare myself for the ball!

Turning from her examination of the dusty volumes on the shelves, she enquired, "Are you quite well, Sir Max? It appears to me that you are not quite your usual ebullient self."

As she expected, he eagerly took his cue. "I must confess, Lady Leonora, I feel quite overwhelmed at seeing you again. I have missed you most dreadfully whilst you have been so much with Madame Valbois at Hanover Square."

Leonora modestly cast down her eyes to the carpet.

Encouraged by her silence, Sir Max took her hand and said urgently, "My dearest Leonora, we have been much in one another's company in the last few months. And you must be aware that I have fallen hopelessly in love with you. I think about you night and day. The hours when I am not within your sight are a torment to me. You are so beautiful, so witty, so charming. Tell me, my dearest, sweetest Leonora, dare I presume to hope?"

186

This, thought Leonora angrily, *is how he must have wooed dear Clementina! How heartless! How cruel! For she, poor innocent, believed him. But I am made of stronger metal!*

Leonora fluttered her long eyelashes and murmured breathlessly, "Why, Sir Max! Am I to believe that you are proposing to me?"

He gripped her hand so hard she thought she would faint. "If you would consent to be my wife you would make me the happiest man in England . . . and Ireland . . . and the entire world! I should love you, and cherish you, and—"

"And then once we had returned from our wedding tour no doubt you would callously abandon me, as you once deserted Clementina Westlake!" Leonora's eyes were stormy, her voice as cold as steel.

Sir Max blanched. "What . . . I do not understand . . . what nonsense is this?" he blustered.

Leonora declared hotly, "You were unaware that Miss Westlake was a particular friend of mine. She revealed to me every detail of your dastardly behavior toward her. And then she died, Sir Max. She died of a broken heart!"

"I . . . I have never heard of the girl!" ranted Sir Max.

"You lie! I know the truth!" Leonora challenged scornfully. "And when I heard of your despicable boast that you would have me at the altar by the end of June, then I resolved to take revenge on Clementina's behalf. For months I have amused myself watching you pay court to me. And now you have asked me to become your bride. But not because you love me or indeed have any shred of affection for me. No, you feel no more for me than you did for Clementina. She you seduced, and then abandoned. But you had a more cunning plan for me! Oh, it would have made your reputation, wouldn't it? What a fine story to tell over the card tables at White's—how you redeemed your boast, and flattered Lady Leonora

187

Pagett into marrying you. And in the process, of course, you would have gained command of her not inconsiderable fortune!"

Sir Max roared, "You are deranged! I would advise you to seek the advice of a physician!"

"And I would advise you, Sir Max, to take the first boat back to Ireland! For by the end of the ball tonight, I shall ensure that everyone of quality in London knows the truth about you. They will all be aware that I have made a total fool of you. And my, how all London will rock with laughter at the intelligence!"

Sir Max's pale blue eyes were glittering dangerously. "I should have known! You were always a clever little minx!"

Leonora swept past him, and paused at the door. "What you should know, without any doubt," she said disdainfully, "is that there was never any question of my marrying you. Even if I had not been aware of your despicable treatment of Clementina. Even if you had loved me passionately, do you seriously imagine I could entrust my heart to a man who devotes most of his time to gambling, drinking, and carousing? Good day, and good-bye, Sir Max!"

"Not so fast!" In two strides he was at the door, barring her way. His face was contorted with anger as he turned the key in the lock.

"Open this door this instant!" Leonora demanded.

Sir Max snarled, "You are not leaving this room, my lady, until you have given me your solemn promise that we shall be wed!'

"I shall never give such a promise!" countered Leonora, speaking boldly, although panic was beginning to rise within her. She realized now that she had seriously misjudged Sir Max. She had certainly never expected him to become so violent.

Courageously, she lifted her head and commanded, "Let me pass at once!"

By way of reply, he took her by the shoulders and

flung her roughly across the room. "Don't try my patience too far!" he shouted. "I want that promise, and I want it soon! And if you won't give it freely, I'll damn well beat it out of you!"

"You would not dare lay a finger on me!" Leonora's heart was pounding with fear. Why, *why* had she been so foolish as to involve herself in such a nightmare situation as this?

She backed away as he waved a large fist in front of her face. "Wouldn't dare?" he bellowed. "I tell you I shall have my way in this matter! Yes, I admit, I did boast that I'd wed you and bed you! And I'll be damned if I'll have all London jeering at me because I was dished by a mere slip of a girl like you! I intend, therefore, that we shall arrive together at Madame Valbois's ball tonight. We shall then proceed to announce our engagement!"

"You . . . you have not been invited to the ball," stammered Leonora, still backing away across the library.

"But as your fiancé," grinned Sir Max, "naturally I shall be welcome. I shall expect dear Rothwell to greet me with open arms!"

Leonora was trembling from top to toe. But her fighting spirit had not deserted her. "I shall never agree to marry you! Never!"

His voice was heavy with menace. "Oh yes you will. Even if our pretty little shepherdess is obliged to go to the ball with her lovely white body covered in bruises!"

He snatched out a hand to seize her, but Leonora whirled away. As he pursued her around the library, Leonora frantically surveyed the room for a means of escape. The door was locked. One window was open, but it was set too high for her to jump through. The situation seemed hopeless!

With her eyes fixed on the window, she had not noticed the mahogany library stool in her path. She tripped over it and fell sprawling onto the carpet.

Sir Max laughed softly as he stood over her. "So.

189

You are now totally at my mercy! Why not surrender gracefully, and agree to become my bride?"

But he had reckoned without Leonora's cool head in an emergency. For a moment, her amber eyes rested thoughtfully on the mahogany stool. Then slowly, as if defeated, she rose to her feet.

"Perhaps," she murmured, "I have been a little hasty in my reactions."

He smiled triumphantly. "Now you are beginning to talk sense! I knew you'd be persuaded in the end. Shall we seal the bargain with a kiss?"

Observing that Sir Max had relaxed, and was slightly off-guard, Leonora launched her attack. First, she seized the firescreen and threw it with all her might at Sir Max's red head. As he reeled back in surprise, Leonora followed this up by hurling the brass fire tongs and poker at his shins.

He roared with pain. Leonora paid him no need, but speedily pushed the mahogany stool across the room, until it stood underneath the high open window. When she had stumbled over the stool, she had realized with relief that ingeniously concealed beneath it were a set of library steps, to enable the reader to reach the books on the top shelves.

While Sir Max was still bellowing and hopping round the room, Leonora unfolded the steps, ran up them and hoisted herself to blessed freedom through the open window. She caught her breath when she realized what a long way it was to the ground. But with Sir Max shrieking terrible threats from below, she had no choice but to utter a swift prayer, and jump.

She landed safely in the flower bed, narrowly missing the laurels. Leonora knew she must think quickly. Sir Max would be charging across the library, unlocking the door, then dashing for the garden entrance of the house. This would take him a few minutes, so for a very short while Leonora was aware that she held the advantage.

Wasting no more time, Leonora ran through the garden, and pushed open the wooden gate which led into the mews. The stableboys and grooms were quite naturally surprised to see her. She had lost her bonnet in the jump, and her hair fell in a tangled mass of golden curls around her lovely face.

She addressed one of the grooms. "Please," she gasped. "In which direction is Park Lane?"

He pointed. "Up to the end and turn right, my lady."

Thanking him, Leonora sped on. Only just in time, for as she turned into Park Lane she glanced behind into the mews and saw Sir Max in hot pursuit. Leonora lifted her skirts and ran as never before down fashionable Park Lane, oblivious of the amazed stares of the elegant ladies and gentlemen strolling up to the park.

The only thought in Leonora's head was that she must reach Lord Rothwell's house. There she knew she would be safe.

At last, the steps of Lord Rothwell's imposing residence were in sight. With a sob of relief she hurled herself at the front door, which to her surprise was wrenched open by Lord Rothwell himself.

"Leonora!" he cried. "I glanced out of the window and saw you hurtling down Park Lane! Whatever is wrong?"

Leonora flung herself into his arms. Just being in his presence gave her an overwhelming sense of security.

"Sir Max," she gasped. "He asked me to marry him. I refused, and he said he'd beat me until I agreed . . ."

"You are trembling," said Lord Rothwell, his handsome face full of concern. "Do not try to talk now. You are with me. You are safe."

Without another word, he picked her up in his arms and took her into the drawing room, where he gently laid her down on the sofa. He poured her a brandy, and watched over her while she drank it.

Gradually, the color returned to Leonora's ashen cheeks.

"Thank you, Cameron," Leonora faltered. Suddenly,

her eyes filled with tears. "Oh, I have been so foolish! You were right about Sir Max. I imagined him to be a mere rogue, and thought I would amuse myself by giving him his comeuppance. But I misjudged him. He is an extremely evil, menacing creature! You were right to warn me against him. How deeply I regret not listening to you!"

Lord Rothwell put his arm around her shoulders, and said soothingly, "Come, now Leonora. No harm can come to you. You are here in my house, under my protection. Why not tell me the whole story, from beginning to end?"

Warmed by the brandy, and reassured by Lord Rothwell's presence, Leonora told him everything. About Clementina. How she had never intended to marry Sir Max, but had resented Lord Rothwell's interference in the matter. Sir Max's boast about making Leonora marry him. And Leonora's decision to keep Sir Max dangling on a string, before humilating him.

"But my plans went hopelessly wrong!" exclaimed Leonora. "I had no notion that he would threaten me with violence!"

Lord Rothwell arose, and stood with his back to the fireplace. "Sir Max's character is just as I suspected. I knew of the insolent boast, of course. I told Melissa I intended to call the fellow out. But the notion upset her dreadfully. She said she was sure you had more sense than to be blarneyed into marriage with the Irishman. So, very reluctantly, I took no action. But I shall not make the same mistake again! I intend to set after Sir Max Fitzarren immediately!"

"No!" cried Leonora. "Please wait until after the ball, Cameron! Melissa would be so disappointed if you did not attend. Especially if the villainous Sir Max was the cause of your non-arrival!"

Lord Rothwell paced the floor. "I confess I am torn. My every instinct tells me I should waste no time in hunting down this blackguard who has dared to raise his fist against you! And yet I know that tonight, it is my duty to be at my sister's side at her engagement ball."

"You must not desert Melissa," said Leonora firmly. "But Cameron, I believe Sir Max will not be very far away from us tonight! I believe it is I who should absent myself from the ball. For Sir Max is bound to follow me there. Oh, I know he has not an invitation, but with all the gentlemen wearing masks it would not be difficult for him to gain entry. And he is aware that I shall be attending as a shepherdess."

Lord Rothwell shook his head. "Of course you must attend the ball. I am well aware how much you are looking forward to it. After your ordeal, it will be a tonic for you to dance and make merry all evening."

"But Sir Max will recognize me from my shepherdess costume," protested Leonora. "And even if I change my dress, and go as Anne Boleyn or suchlike, he will study the face and figure of every lady at the ball until he finds me. He is a determined man, Cameron! He will hunt me down, I am convinced of it!"

"All the more reason for you not to stay at home, then," declared Lord Rothwell. "I would rather you were at the ball where I can keep a watchful eye over you. And if Sir Max is unwise enough to put in an appearance, I can assure you it will give me great pleasure to tear him limb from limb!"

He rang the bell. "Now my orders for you are to go upstairs and rest. I shall send my footman to Grosvenor Street with instructions for Daisy to bring round your shepherdess costume."

"But—"

"No buts. Just do as I say." He turned to address the under-housekeeper as she answered his summons. "Kindly escort the Lady Leonora upstairs so she may sleep. Her maid will be arriving shortly. But on no account is Lady Leonora to be awoken until five-thirty."

Realizing that it was futile to protest, Leonora allowed herself to be taken upstairs. Although she was certain she would never sleep for the raging turmoil in her head, nevertheless, she fell into a deep slumber as soon as her head touched the pillow.

While Leonora slept, Lord Rothwell sent his carriage to Hanover Square. A little while later, a worried Madame Valbois arrived at Park Lane and entered into grave consultations with Lord Rothwell. When certain matters had been decided between them Lord Rothwell summoned Brockway, his faithful steward, and issued some precise instructions. Before long, footmen had been despatched from Park Lane to almost every fashionable address in London.

When the ladies within these elegant houses received Lord Rothwell's message, their first reaction was one of surprise and exasperation:

"Well really!" they cried indignantly. "This is too vexing of Lord Rothwell and Madame Valbois! How dare they oblige me to change all my plans like this, and right at the last minute, too!"

But after a moment's contemplation as they reclined on their sofas, the ladies began to smile. "Perhaps, after all, I have been hasty in criticizing Madame Valbois and Lord Rothwell," one lady reasoned. "Oh, of course, it will mean such a rush and bustle making all the arrangements in time. But what fun! And what a golden opportunity to prove that I am far more inventive and quick-witted than Lady Jersey, or Lady Holland! Very well, Lord Rothwell. I shall throw myself wholeheartedly into your extraordinary scheme for Madame Valbois's ball. My, what an entertaining evening it promises to be!"

While the ladies of society rang their bells, and whirled their maids into a flurry of activity, Sir Max Fitzarren was feverishly devising plans of his own.

"Impertinent bitch!" he ranted. "How dare she attempt to make an ass out of me! What effrontery! Well I will marry the minx—even if I have to seize her with my bare hands and spirit her away to Gretna Green!"

He scowled, and thoughtfully rubbed his chin. *Aye, Gretna Green,* he thought. *Now that might not be such a bad idea. After all, I've given her the opportunity of marrying me at a proper, formal wedding. Yet she had the audacity to fling my proposal back in my face! She spurned me, and scorned me, with the clear intention of making me look a prize fool in the eyes of London society! I'll not forgive her for that. My, when we're wed I'll bring her smartly to heel!*

Abduction. The more Sir Max considered the notion, the more it appealed to him. But the crucial problem remained: how was he to get close enough to Lady Leonora to kidnap her?

Without doubt she would by now have informed that infuriatingly watchful Lord Rothwell of the violent scene between herself and Sir Max in the library that afternoon. Inevitably, Lord Rothwell would not let Leonora out of his sight at the ball tonight. And tomorrow, sure as day followed night, Lord Rothwell would be out scouring London for the Irish villain who had dared to attack the Lady Leonora.

Sir Max attempted a grin at the thought of Lord Rothwell's wrath—but he could manage no more than a stiff grimace. Sir Max, in truth, was considerably in awe of Lord Rothwell. He was only too well aware that if the English nobleman did run him to earth, he would show him no mercy.

No, decided Sir Max, *it is imperative that by tomorrow morning Lady Leonora and I are safely on the road to Scotland, and our wedding! Which means I must abduct her from the ball tonight. But how?*

He pondered the problem for a long while, rejecting scheme after scheme. Then a slow smile spread across his face. He smashed his right fist into his left palm, and exclaimed, "Capital, capital! So simple! Yet so devastatingly effective!"

Accordingly, that evening Sir Max slipped into Hanover Square and positioned himself behind the stone pillar of the house next door to Madame Valbois's. Further along the square there walked a slim young woman. She was soberly dressed, and a casual onlooker would probably have judged her to be a respectable governess. Out of sight, around the corner, lurked a rogue named Tom Trubbler.

Sir Max regarded the lighted windows of Madame Valbois's house, and grinned. What a fiendishly clever plot he had devised! He was aware that Lady Leonora would be wearing a shepherdess costume to the ball tonight. It was also inevitable that she would arrive under heavy escort, accompanied by either Lord Rothwell himself, or the Lady Melissa's French fiancé.

Lord Rothwell will be expecting me to attempt to gain entry to the ball, mused Sir Max, his eyes glittering with malice. *But I shall take him unawares! As he assists Lady Leonora down from the carriage, he will not notice my white handkerchief fluttering to the ground as a signal to my accomplices. But he cannot fail to be aware of the fearful commotion suddenly issuing from the corner of the square. A decent, respectably dressed young governess will be heard screaming with terror. A dastardly rogue is attacking her!*

Impossible, then, for Lord Rothwell to ignore the plight of a lady in distress! Naturally, the gallant gentleman will dash to her aid. Lady Leonora, meanwhile, will continue her progress from the carriage to Madame Valbois's residence. But she will not reach the door of the house! For in those few short minutes whilst Lord Rothwell's attention is distracted, I shall throw a hood over the shepherdess's head, hurl her into my waiting gig and speed us away to catch the fast stagecoach.

The beauty of it is, that in all the confusion, it will take Lord Rothwell some time to discover that Lady Leonora has disappeared. After going to the governess's aid (her attacker will of course run off into the night at his approach) *he will assume that Lady Leonora entered the house and is occupied in the ladies' dressing room, depositing her cloak and prettying her hair.*

By my estimation, it will be a full half hour before the alarm is raised. And by that time, my bride to be and I will be on the stagecoach. Oh yes, it is an ingenious plan! How can it fail?

Sir Max hopped impatiently from foot to foot, glaring round the Square. "Damn it," he muttered, "the guests are the devil of a time arriving for this ball. What can have delayed them all?"

But after a few more minutes, he observed the first carriages bowling into Hanover Square, to draw up outside Madame's house. Sir Max leaned forward, tense with anticipation. Was this the Lady Leonora, beautifully robed in her shepherdess costume?

He relaxed. No, it was only Lord Tressler and Lord Pinsley. He was on the alert again as a second carriage arrived. But from this emerged Sir Frederick Darney, Lord Bilchester, and Sir Roger Lamprey.

After twenty minutes watching the carriages arrive, Sir Max was growing restive, and confused. He could not understand why no ladies were accompanying their menfolk. For every single carriage had so far carried only gentlemen. They crowded jovially into the house, putting on their velvet masks and clearly looking forward to an evening of gaiety and mirth.

But where are the ladies, wondered the Irishman, beginning to grow desperate. *Surely I have not mistaken the time, or the date, or the venue?* His hands and brow grew coldly clammy at the notion that perhaps he had made a terrible mistake. That the gathering in Hanover Square was a stag event, and the true fancy dress ball, at which Lady Leonora would be present, was taking place elsewhere!

In that case, thought Sir Max frantically, *I shall have missed my chance. For if I do not make off with Lady Leonora tonight, then there will be little opportunity tomorrow. For by first light Lord Rothwell will be hounding me, and I shall need all my wits about me to avoid ending up as pulp!*

Just as Sir Max was beginning to be engulfed in furious despair at his situation, three more carriages swept into Hanover Square. To his overwhelming relief, there issued from the carriages the welcome sound of female laughter. Sir Max breathed an enormous sigh of relief.

Eagerly he craned forward to watch the fancy-dressed ladies emerge from their carriages. But as the ladies descended, Sir Max stood and stared in horrified disbelief. There were twelve ladies in all. And each one of them was arrayed—quite delightfully—in the costume of a shepherdess!

Eleven

"Is this not the most charming notion?" trilled the Countess of Jersey, advancing across the ballroom and waving her shepherdess crook at Leonora. "I confess I was a little taken aback when I received the message this afternoon that the theme of the ball had changed. I had planned to appear as Diana the Huntress! It was a fearful rush finding a shepherdess costume. But what fun!"

"And how ingenious of Lord Rothwell to arrange for all the gentlemen to arrive first, and shower us ladies with rose petals as we made our entrance!" exclaimed Lady Holland. "I am enjoying it all immensely! And I do hope I win the diamond necklace!"

She whirled away across the brilliantly lit Grand Saloon. Leonora raised an enquiring eyebrow at Madame. "Diamond necklace?"

Madame, who as the hostess was not attired in costume, rapidly explained, "When Lord Rothwell informed me of his plan for all the ladies to appear as shepherdesses, I pointed out that there would be much dismay amongst my lady guests. They would have put much thought into devising original, witty costumes."

"Bettine felt, quite rightly, that some kind of compensation—or incentive, call it what you will—was required," said Lord Rothwell, looking extremely dashing in

199

a dark blue evening coat, embroidered waistcoat, and velvet mask.

The Frenchwoman nodded. "So Lord Rothwell kindly offered to donate a diamond necklace which will be awarded to the lady wearing the most fetching shepherdess costume."

"Cameron, how thoughtful and ingenious of you!" cried Leonora, who was an enchanting vision in a costume threaded with blue ribbons. "I confess, I could not believe my eyes when I entered the ballroom and saw so many shepherdesses! Only you could devise such a bold, imaginative scheme! Though you will have a difficult task deciding which is the most becoming costume. To my eye all the ladies look delightful." She smiled at Melissa, promenading on the far side of the ballroom with the count.

"If it were left to me, Cameron, I should award the diamond necklace to Melissa—as consolation. She was so looking forward to presenting herself as a courtesan!"

Lord Rothwell laughed. "I regret that Melissa is disqualified from the contest. We can hardly give the prize to Madame's future sister. It would smack too much of favoritism."

Leonora was glancing anxiously round, wondering if Sir Max had yet contrived to effect an entry. Lord Rothwell laid a reassuring hand on her arm.

"Do not fret. My men are stationed discreetly all through the house. And even if Sir Max does manage to outwit them, and gain admittance, he will have the Devil's own job sorting out which shepherdess is which!"

Leonora commented, with a light laugh, "But Cameron, if you are to be keeping a watchful eye on me all evening, how will you tell who I am when there are fifty other shepherdesses to choose from?"

"My dear Leonora," he replied, "were I blindfolded and placed in a ballroom with a thousand shepherdesses, I should still know instantly which was you."

Madame Valbois cleared her throat. "Er ... Cameron, all the guests have now arrived. I believe it is time for me to give the musicians the signal for the dancing to begin."

"Ah yes. What is the first dance to be, Bettine? A cotillion, or a minuet?"

"A minuet, I think," she said. "And later, we shall indulge ourselves with some waltzes." She fluttered her eyelashes coquettishly. "I seem to remember you waltzed divinely in Paris."

Leonora heard no more, for a cluster of young gentlemen were gathered round her, clamoring for the honor of the first dance. At a sign from Madame, the orchestra struck up a gentle minuet, and the ball was under way. Leonora, beautiful, amusing, and an excellent dancer, was never short of partners, and in the hours until midnight she was constantly on the dance floor.

After supper, however, she felt she had earned a rest. Taking a glass of white wine, she slipped upstairs to sit on the balcony which circled the edge of the Grand Saloon. It was an admirable vantage point from which to observe the revelers, all of whom were in festive high spirits. Yes, the ball was undoubtedly a success. Under the dazzling chandeliers, the white dresses of the shepherdesses looked delightful, especially when contrasted with the mysterious velvet masks and dark evening coats of the gentlemen.

Leonora smiled. Dear Cameron. Only he could have thought of such a daring, novel scheme—to transform every lady into a shepherdess! She watched him below her, dancing the waltz with Madame Valbois. The Frenchwoman, robed in pale green shot silk, murmured something, and Lord Rothwell threw back his head and laughed, his gray eyes alight with amusement.

It was a moment Leonora was to remember for the rest of her life. As she gazed on Lord Rothwell's handsome, smiling face, her heart seemed to miss a beat. She felt unaccountably breathless, and strangely light headed.

Confused, Leonora sought for the cause of this sudden affliction. Had Daisy laced the bodice of her dress too tightly? Or was the wine a little stronger than that to which she was accustomed?

Swaying, she clung to the rail of the balcony. She found she was unable to take her eyes from Lord Rothwell's rugged countenance, as he waltzed with Madame. He held the smiling Frenchwoman a little closer to guide her round a corner—and at that instant, Leonora felt as if she had been stabbed, betrayed, abandoned.

Ashen-faced and trembling, Leonora faced the truth.

Cameron and Madame Valbois! Oh, I cannot tolerate the sight of them together! And why? Because I love him! I love Cameron! But for all this time I have foolishly shut my ears to what my heart was trying to tell me. For years Cameron has watched over me, protected me, rescued me! And in return, I have treated him so carelessly, stupidly imagining that I felt for him as does a sister to a brother.

But I was wrong! Hopelessly, tragically wrong. For I know now that I love him as a woman loves a man— with fire and passion, and oh, such desire! But he is lost to me. He is in love with Madame. It is she he holds in his arms. She who will enjoy the ardor of his kisses! Oh, I cannot bear it!

Leonora turned away, closing her eyes in a vain attempt to quell the storm of jealous fury which consumed her. Every instinct urged her to rush down on to the dance floor, wrench the loathsome Frenchwoman from Cameron's arms, and declare her love for him.

But it would be senseless to expect him to return my passion, thought Leonora wretchedly. *He regards himself as my protector. Nothing more. In caring for me, he has been doing no more than his duty. To him, I am a mere headstrong girl. A nuisance. Whereas Madame Valbois is a mature, sophisticated woman. Of course she has won his heart! Whilst I have lost him. And all because of my own foolish blindness!*

Enveloped in misery, longing, and despair, Leonora

did not not notice the approach of the Comte de Selvigny.

"Ah, Lady Leonora," he smiled. "Are you fatigued? You certainly deserve to be, for I have observed you dancing with nearly every gentleman in the room!"

Leonora summoned a weak smile. "I do feel tired," she admitted. "I think I should like to go home."

More than anything she wanted to hide herself away from Lord Rothwell. She was terrified of what her face would reveal to him. He, who knew her so well, would immediately sense the dramatic change in her. And she could no longer suffer the sight of him dancing with Madame. Their laughter, their whispered intimate remarks served only to twist the knife in Leonora's anguished heart.

What irony, mused Leonora, *that I was amused because Madame regarded me as her rival for Lord Rothwell! Perhaps she has the uncanny ability to sense the truth in a situation before even those involved are aware of it. Did she suspect that I was certain to fall in love with Cameron before long? Did she hope to coax him to the altar before I understood the depth of my passion for him?*

Leonora raised a hand to her throbbing brow. Oh, it was all too much to contemplate. As if from a great distance, she heard the count declare, "Permit me to escort you home, Lady Leonora. In fact, Melissa is fatigued also, so it will be convenient for us all to return together in my carriage."

"Thank you," smiled Leonora wanly.

He went on, "Lord Rothwell has requested me to tell you that he would prefer you to stay at home and not venture a step outside the house until he has tracked down Sir Max Fitzarren."

Leonora laughed shakily, "I do not imagine that will take very long. All Cameron need do is tour White's, Buck's and Boodle's. Sir Max is certain to be found gambling and drinking at one of them!"

The count gave a dry chuckle. "Well it might be advisable for Lord Rothwell to take refuge in a gentleman's club for a few days. He has awarded Lady Holland the diamond necklace prize for the best shepherdess costume. And the Countess of Jersey is furious!"

But Leonora was wrong. Sir Max did not spend the night carousing at one of his clubs.

As he stood in Hanover Square watching the succession of laughing shepherdesses arriving at the ball, he had been consumed by a terrifying torrent of rage.

Between them, Lord Rothwell and Lady Leonora had outwitted him! *But not for long,* he resolved. *They shall have their comeuppance for this! I'll be damned if I'll be thwarted in my bid to wed that golden-haired minx.*

Speedily, he devised another plan. It was, admittedly, more dangerous than the first, because now he would have to wait until morning. But Sir Max was a gambler, and understood that when the stakes were high a man must play his cards boldly and fearlessly. To be faint-hearted was to invite defeat.

Accordingly, he paid his two acomplices and gave them fresh instructions. Then he hastened back to his lodgings to collect the items which would assist him in his scheme. He dare not remain there for the night, for Lord Rothwell would surely be breaking down the door first thing in the morning.

Stealthily, Sir Max made his way through the dark streets of Mayfair and admitted himself to a certain empty house. He smiled to himself. Tomorrow, a furious Lord Rothwell would be ransacking every London haunt of Sir Max's. He would assume that Lady Leonora, safe behind locked doors in Grosvenor Street, was securely out of the Irishman's reach.

Sir Max grinned. "I fear that is a rash assumption, Lord Rothwell! One you will have cause to regret!" Then he opened a flask of wine, and settled down to wait for the dawn.

204

Understandably, Leonora spent a restless night. It was hours before sleep claimed her, and then she tossed and turned, dreaming of Lord Rothwell. She was awake again soon after dawn, pacing up and down her chamber, berating herself for her folly in not realizing months ago that she was in love with him.

But I had no notion then what love was, thought Leonora frantically. *I have known Cameron for so long. We are so familiar to one another. We have quarreled so much! And yet, seeing him with Madame last night ... his hand in hers ... their eyes meeting in shared laughter ... oh what a fever of jealousy consumed me! Why, it was all I could do to stop myself from clawing her bright brown eyes out!*

Yes, then I knew for sure that this was love I felt for Cameron. I cannot stand to think of him associating with another woman! Any woman. But particularly Madame Valbois. Oh, why did she have to come to London? Why did Melissa have to fall in love with her brother? Why, oh why is my life so wretchedly complicated?

Leonora had an early, solitary breakfast as Melissa was sleeping late after the ball. All Leonora's instincts told her that the wisest course would be for her to go for a bracing walk in the park, to clear her head. But Lord Rothwell had instructed her not to leave the house.

At one time Leonora would have shrugged her slender shoulders, and thought nothing of disregarding Lord Rothwell's wishes. But now he had won her respect, and her love, she knew she must obey him. He had, she was forced to admit, been right from the very beginning about Sir Max. Time and time again Lord Rothwell had warned her not to associate with him. And Leonora had scoffed, imagining that, yes, Sir Max was a raffish rogue, but she alone could humble him. But there she had been disastrously wrong.

No, Leonora decided, *I must certainly not infuriate Cameron by venturing out of the house.* But a turn around the garden can do no harm. She slipped on a shawl, though soon discovered it was unnecessary as she felt the warm sun on her face. For a pleasant half hour, Leonora wandered through the lawns, admiring the flag-like yellow irises which had just come into bloom, savoring the heady scent of honeysuckle, and amused by the little robin which hopped along at a discreet distance behind her.

Soothed by the fragrant summer air, Leonora returned to the house and settled down in the Blue Saloon. I must not dwell on my hopeless passion for Cameron, she thought. If I concentrate quietly on my new feather picture, perhaps my torment will be eased for a while.

Leonora selected the blue ostrich feathers she intended to use in her design, and set them ready in a small china pot at her right hand. As she did so, the feathers fluttered slightly, indicating that there was a draft in the room. Leonora glanced round, wondering if she had left the window open. But no, it was firmly closed. Yet the manded harshly,

It was then that her attention was caught by the paneled wall. Leonora rubbed her eyes in disbelief. It could not be! It was impossible! Her fevered imagination was playing her tricks!

But when she looked again, she saw that she had not been mistaken. The white paneled wall was in motion! Slowly, the panels were inching to one side, revealing a dark, dank passageway.

Recovering from the shock, Leonora ran for the bell to summon assistance. But before she could reach out a hand, a familiar voice—a dreaded Irish voice—commanded harshly.

"Stay quite still, Lady Leonora! Or I shall be compelled to use force!"

Leonora froze as Sir Max Fitzarren stepped out from the gloomy opening into the elegant Blue Saloon. "I did warn you," he said mockingly, "that you would never escape me."

Leonora rushed for the bell. But he dashed across and forestalled her. "Oh no," he said softly, his eyes glittering evilly. "There is no one who can help you now!"

He saw Leonora glance toward the door, calculating when to make her run for it. Quickly, he seized the writing table from the corner, and pushed it in front of the door.

"There! Now you are, I fear, truly at my mercy!"

"What do you want?" demanded Leonora boldly. "I have told you plainly that I will not marry you. And when Lord Rothwell hears about this—"

Sir Max laughed. "By the time Rothwell receives the news, it will be too late. You will be rejoicing in the title of the Lady Leonora Fitzarren!"

Leonora paled. "You mean to abduct me? You would not dare!"

"On the contrary, my dear. It is not a question of daring, but of necessity. I've said, loud and clear to all London, that I'll wed you. And if I don't now drag you to the altar, I'll have the entire city bent double with mirth at my expense. Oh, no! I'll not allow you to make a fool out of me! Since you refuse to marry me of your own free will, I have no choice but to carry you off to Gretna Green."

Leonora gazed past him at the opening in the paneling. "I had no notion the wall was false. And neither, I am sure, did Melissa."

Sir Max grinned. "Some friends of mine discovered the passage by accident. It was blocked, and damp, with crumbling mortar and rotting wood. Considerable work was required to make it passable."

Leonora gasped. "That noise Melissa complained about all through the spring! It was not workmen refurbishing the house next door at all. It was your workmen chiseling out this passage. And when I came upon you by chance when I was viewing the neighboring house, you were no doubt checking on the progress of your men!"

"As usual, your intelligence astounds me," bowed Sir Max.

Leonora's amber eyes narrowed. "And did your low friends, by any chance, have anything to do with certain missing items of jewelry from Melissa's apartments?"

Sir Max laughed. "Ah, what a smart girl you are! I wondered when you would tumble to that one. I thought you might regard it as strange that it was always the Lady Melissa's jewelry that disappeared, never yours. Of course, there was no point in my men stealing your valuable trinkets, as when we are wed all you possess will belong to me!"

"What a reptilian creature you are!" scorned Leonora. "There are no words to describe how much I despise you!"

He replied calmly, "I did not come here to be admired, my dear. Or to pass the time of day with you. Now, if you would be so good as to sit down at your writing table, I shall dictate to you."

Leonora had no alternative but to do as he requested. He stood behind her, arms folded across his chest, and as she took up her pen he dictated:

"My dear Melissa, Do not be alarmed by my sudden departure from your house. It is simply that I awoke this morning and felt a longing to go home to Gloucestershire for a short while. I will write again when I am settled. With love, Leonora."

As Leonora wrote, her mind was working feverishly. When she reached the phrase *when I am settled,* she glanced up at Sir Max and gave him a conspiratorial smile.

"I shall never agree to marry you," she said softly, "but I must confess it is rather amusing being abducted! It will put poor Lord Rothwell into the most dreadful spin!"

As she anticipated, Sir Max looked gleeful at this intelligence. "I *am* sorry! To be sure, I owe him one for his ruse at the ball. By arranging for all you ladies to be dressed as shepherdesses, he confounded my plan to abduct you last night. However, I hid in the house next door,

208

and bided my time until this morning. Everything depended on your coming to sit in this pretty Blue Saloon. Then when I observed you walking in the garden, and then reentering this room by the garden door, I knew I'd soon have you safely in my net!"

Leonora said dismissively, "You are a fool if you think you will deceive Melissa for one instant with this note."

Sir Max glowered. "Why so?"

"Because," explained Leonora patiently, "no lady in my position would set out for Gloucestershire without leaving instructions for her maid to pack her personal possessions, and then follow on."

Sir Max scratched his chin. "Ah. Yes. I had not thought of that. You'd best add a short message to that glum-pot maid of yours. But no tricks, mind!"

Leonora looked up at him guilelessly, "You will read every word I write. How could I possibly deceive you?"

She added to the letter:

Daisy must pack all my muslins and a few silks. Please remind her to collect my new kid boots from Messrs G. Anterg. I shall not require her whilst I am in Gloucestershire. As you know, there is already a lady's maid in residence there. Perhaps you could arrange for one or t'other of your men to follow as soon as possible with my portmanteau. Leonora.

Leonora's heart was pounding as Sir Max snatched the note and scrutinized it carefully. The message was crammed with clues that something was seriously wrong. Leonora had ordered no new kid boots. And Melissa was well aware that Leonora retained no personal maid at her house in Gloucestershire. Leonora hoped Melissa would have the sense to show the note to Daisy, for then the red-haired girl would be sure to pounce on the telltale reverse lettering of G. Anterg. As for the phrase *one or t'other,* Leonora regarded that as a real flash of inspiration. Thank heavens she had remembered Daisy telling her that this was a rhyming expression meaning brother!

Nevertheless, Leonora held her breath as Sir Max read the note. He had, Leonora now suspected, strong connections with the underworld rogues who employed devious rhyming expressions and reverse lettering. By speaking thus, they were able to deceive any honest citizens who might be listening. But would Sir Max understand her clues? Leonora closed her eyes and prayed that being Irish, Sir Max would not yet be au fait with low London terms of speech.

At last, after an interminable wait, Sir Max nodded. "That seems plausible. Now come! We have dallied long enough!"

Leonora rose obediently to her feet. Turning a shoulder to Sir Max, she laid the letter to Melissa on the table, next to her feather picture. On top she rested a paperweight and one of the blue ostrich feathers from the china pot. The remainder of the feathers she tucked casually into the girdle of her muslin dress.

Sir Max seized hold of her arm and dragged her toward the passage.

Leonora protested, "Sir Max, if we are to travel up to Scotland I shall require at the very least a pelisse to keep the chill from me."

"That is all taken care of," he snapped, pushing her through into the cold, dank passage.

With what despair Leonora watched him slide back the paneling into its original position. The beautiful Blue Saloon, in which she had spent many a peaceful hour, disappeared from view. How long, she wondered, would it be before she was safely back there again?

Hastily, she reassured herself that there was really no cause for alarm. Melissa, with Daisy's help in deciphering the clues, would realise that she had been abducted to Gretna Green. Naturally, they would realize who the villain was. They would instantly send for Lord Rothwell, who would set out post haste to rescue her.

She smiled as a tinderbox flared and Sir Max lit a candle to guide them along the dark passage. *No doubt, my Irish friend, you are at this moment congratulating yourself on your bold, imaginative scheme. But I can assure you that when Lord Rothwell catches up with you, you will rue the day you ever set foot on English soil!*

After a few minutes they emerged from the gloom into a ground floor room in the neighboring house. The room was empty, apart from some unturned packing cases, and evidence that a hasty meal had been consumed there. Empty wine bottles lay discarded on the floor, along with some rotting apples and half a chicken pie.

Observing Leonora's curious glance, Sir Max grinned. "Aye, this house made a very useful base for me and my men. We'd rob the fashionable Mayfair residences, then scuttle back here and hole up for a few days. The authorities assumed we'd hit the road out of London—but there we were, right under their noses all the time!"

"You are nothing but a common scoundrel!" raged Leonora. "And I insist that you return all the Lady Melissa's jewelry to her."

He laughed. "My dear, you are hardly in a position to demand anything at the moment! However, to prove that I do have a decent streak to my nature, I promise that as soon as we are wed, the Lady Melissa's trinkets shall be returned. Providing, of course, that they have not already been sold."

A carriage had drawn up at the door. Leonora saw that it was plainly painted, with no distinguishing marks of any kind. "Ah! At last!" exclaimed Sir Max. "Now, my dear, here is a pelisse for you to wear, and a pretty bonnet too."

He picked up from the floor a drab pelisse, fashioned of shabby brown cloth. The bonnet was of black straw, unadorned, and to Leonora's discerning eye, monstrously ugly.

"Pretty!" she protested. "Why, it is quite the most hideous thing I ever saw. And this pelisse must have been styled for a fat, rustic dowd!"

211

"Do as I tell you, and put them on!" ordered Sir Max impatiently. "How can I take you all the way to Scotland in the coach with you looking your usual beautiful self? We would attract far too much attention. And I am sure you are astute enough to realize that attention is the last thing I crave on this journey. When we are married, you shall have all the finery you desire."

When we are wed. When we are married, mused Leonora, reluctantly slipping on the pelisse and bonnet. Oh what confidence you possess, Sir Max! I cannot wait to see your smile turn to terror when Lord Rothwell takes hold of you!

Sir Max wrenched open the front door, and hustled Leonora into the waiting carriage. She had time only for a brief longing glance at Melissa's house before the blinds were hastily pulled and the carriage drew away.

They had not far to journey. Before long, Sir Max released the blinds and Leonora saw that they were entering Gresham Street. She had already guessed that their first destination would be the Swan With Two Necks, the coaching inn in Lad Street.

The inn yard was seething with activity, as coaches were loaded and unloaded, orders shouted, dogs barked and horses neighed. Around three sides of the yard ran open galleries leading to the upstairs guest rooms. From these rooms emerged a flow of passengers with their parcels and luggage. Below, a cacophony echoed from the loose boxes, harness rooms, and hostlers' chambers.

Sir Max assisted Leonora down from the carriage, and keeping a firm grip on her arm, led her across to a brightly decorated yellow and green coach. Leonora's eyes widened in surprise as she observed the word *Oxford* painted on the side.

"I am quite well aware," commented Sir Max, "that Oxford is not on a direct route to Scotland. We are merely taking this coach as a precaution, in case your friend Lord Rothwell becomes suspicious. His first move will be to check at the London coaching inns to enquire about all couples taking the fast coach to Carlisle. And he will draw a blank. He will discover that no beautiful fair-haired maiden, and no red-haired Irishman, traveled together on any of those coaches. It will never, of course, occur to him to check the Oxford route!"

Leonora's heart sank. She had not dreamed that Sir Max was capable of devising such a devious plan. Naturally, she had assumed that he would rush her onto the first northbound coach, and that it would be an easy matter for Lord Rothwell to make enquiries, identify the route, and speed after them. But as Sir Max pointed out, Lord Rothwell would probably not think of checking on all the coaches not traveling directly north.

Her mind raced. Somehow, she must give Cameron an indication of the direction they had taken. And she must do it quickly, for the horses were already harnessed, and the coach would soon be ready to leave.

Fortunately, she was given a brief respite. An enormously fat man was engaged in a heated argument with the ruddy-faced coachman of the Oxford-bound vehicle. The fat man had, it appeared, instructed his footman to book him two seats, thus ensuring that his ample frame could travel in comfort. But the dim-witted footman had, to the fat man's fury, hired his master one seat inside the coach—and the other outside!

While this matter was being resolved with the coachman, Leonora noticed that the passengers' luggage for the journey was being loaded from beside a sign which read "Oxford." The wood of the sign was old, and split along the top. Quickly, under cover of her voluminous pelisse, Leonora withdrew one of the bright blue ostrich feathers from her girdle. Whilst Sir Max's attention was caught by the argument between the fat man and the coachman, Leonora slid her hand behind her back, and stuck the feather firmly in the Oxford sign.

This done, she glanced anxiously up at the clouds in

the sky. To her relief, she saw they were almost stationary, indicating that there was very little breeze. The last thing she desired was for a wind to gust up and blow the feather away.

She had no doubt that Lord Rothwell would recognize the feather as one of her own. Only recently he had remarked favorably on her current picture design. And had she not laid one of the blue ostrich feathers down on her letter to Melissa?

At last, the fat man's seating problem was resolved, and Leonora entered the coach with Sir Max. They were the only three passengers, and within minutes the coachman had climbed up into the front seat, and the coach was rolling out of the yard. Left behind was Leonora's blue ostrich feather, fluttering bravely in the gentle breeze.

As the coach rattled out of London, Leonora nursed a faint hope of being able to engage the fat man in conversation—and thus give him some hint of her plight. But to her chagrin, no sooner was he seated than he closed his eyes, and slept. He did not wake when the coach stopped at Uxbridge, but snored loudly all the way to High Wycombe. There he awoke with a start and shouted at the coachman to have his portmanteau removed from the top of the coach, for he had reached his destination.

When the fat man had disappeared from view, the coach rumbled on its way. Leonora, exhausted, fell into a fitful slumber. Her dreams were confused . . . the ballroom was on fire, and Leonora stood trapped at the top of the stairs. She called for Lord Rothwell, and saw him battling through the flames to save her . . . but suddenly the smoke enveloped him. And above her screams, Leonora heard only the mocking, merciless laughter of Madame Valbois.

"Hush! Hush!," muttered Sir Max, shaking Leonora's arm. "Wake up, now. We have arrived at Oxford."

But Leonora was allowed no time to exclaim over the beauty of this city. Waiting in the coaching inn yard was a small private carriage. As Sir Max hustled her toward it, Leonora stared at the driver's face. Surely she recognized this foxy-faced youth? It was only when he spoke that she remembered.

"You're late, Harry. I've been waitin' the best part of an hour!"

He was the youth, Leonora realized, who had approached Sir Max so urgently that evening at the Vauxhall Gardens. And Daisy, lip reading, had sworn that the boy addressed Sir Max as Harry. How foolish I was, thought Leonora ruefully, not to believe Daisy! Perhaps if I had initiated enquiries then, I should have discovered in time the true villainous nature of Sir Max. Or is it Sir Harry?

Urging her into the carriage, the Irishman spat at the youth, "Dolt! I told you the timing of my plan was uncertain, so I wasn't sure how early we'd catch a coach. We had best take the Drovers Road to Towcester. It'll be quicker."

As Oxford was left behind, and they headed along the narrow Drovers Road, Leonora enquired,

"Why did that youth address you as Harry, Sir Max?"

He scowled. "Never you mind. The trouble with you, dear, is that you are endowed with too much intelligence. In the future, I'll thank you to leave all the thinking to me. Is that clear, Leonora?"

"*Lady* Leonora, if you please!" she flared imperiously.

His angry retort was cut short as the carriage jolted to a halt. Sir Max peered from the window, and cursed. "Why, there's an infernal herd of cows blocking the road!"

Leonora smiled sweetly. "A not unexpected sight, surely, to a gentleman of your perspicacity? A Drovers Road is, after all, intended for the use of cattle, not carriages!"

Sir Max waved his fist at the cowherd. "Get those damned animals out of my way!"

215

To Leonora's delight the boy replied, with stolid country stubbornness, " 'Tis a Drovers Road, Sir. Cattle take preference here over wheeled vehicles. If 'twas speed you were after, you'd a done better to take the main highway!"

And Sir Max had no alternative but to sit in a towering rage while the cows, lowing softly, lumbered slowly past.

Leonora realized that every delay, however slight, was to her advantage, giving Lord Rothwell more time to catch up with them. While they waited, she put the time to good use, making her own plans.

Soon it would be dark. Sir Max must have resolved, therefore, to spend the night at an inn at Towcester. Leonora's spirits rose. Surely amidst all the hurly burly of inn life, she would be able to seize the chance to escape? Sir Max would be occupied giving orders to the foxy youth, arranging their meal and rooms. It would be impossible for him to watch over her for every minute. *All I require,* thought Leonora, her eyes shining, *is sixty short seconds—and I assure you, you will not see me for dust, Sir Max!*

With hope in her heart, Leonora leaned forward in her seat as the carriage proceeded along the Drovers Road, through the darkening night.

But when they drew to a halt it was not to the welcoming lights and bustle of a friendly inn. Instead, the carriage had halted outside a remote, ivy-covered farmhouse.

"Out, out!" ordered Sir Max, as Leonora stared round her in dismay. "Come along, girl! What are you waiting for? Or do you not desire any supper?"

He took her unceremoniously to the kitchen door, where they were received by a slim young woman with frightened eyes.

"This is Lady Leonora Pagett, Mrs. Trubbler," said Sir Max. "She is soon to become my wife. Treat her with

216

respect—but don't let her get up to any tricks. Have you prepared a room and food for her?"

"Aye, that I have, Harry," muttered the woman. From her scornful gaze as she regarded Sir Max, Leonora guessed that Mrs. Trubbler did not hold him in too high regard. And she, too, had addressed him as Harry!

They followed Mrs. Trubbler to a small, sparsely furnished room on the top floor. There, to Leonora's relief, Sir Max left them. He clattered back down the stairs, shouting instructions to Mrs. Trubbler about being sure to lock Lady Leonora's door.

Without a word, Mrs. Trubbler served Leonora with the cold supper waiting under a cloth on a rickety table in the room. Sensing that she might have found an ally in the woman, Leonora ventured with a smile,

"Your name seems familiar to me, Mrs. Trubbler. Yet I do not recall that we have met before?"

"You've not met me, my lady," muttered the woman, splashing coarse red wine into a glass for Leonora. "My husband more like. Harry's men rob the fancy Mayfair houses, while Tom and his cronies hold up the country coaches. It's all rich pickings, so they say," she finished sourly.

Of course, remembered Leonora. That day on Epsom Common with Sir Max! The pieces were all falling into place. They had been held up by none other than Tom Trubbler. And Sir Max, a villain himself, had instantly recognized one of his own kind. No wonder he had experienced no difficulty in sending Trubbler packing!

Leonora glanced at Mrs. Trubbler and said sympathetically, "It must be a hard life for you."

The woman nodded. "I hate it, my lady! I feel ashamed being involved in this sordid business, watching my menfolk rob and steal instead of earning an honest living." Shrewdly, she guessed what was in Leonora's mind. "But don't go thinking I'll help you to escape. If they found out, they'd kill me. Honest they would!"

Leonora believed her. Sir Max would show no mercy to anyone who stood in his path. "I understand," she said softly. "But tell me, why do you call Sir Max, Harry?"

Mrs Trubbler looked puzzled. "Why, because that's his name, of course!"

And with that she left the room, locking the door behind her.

Leonora paced round her cell, examining with distaste the lumpy bed, the unswept floor, the grimy window. She pushed the window open, but one look was enough to establish that it was too far to jump to the ground. And although the house was smothered in ivy, someone had climbed up and cut away all the creeper from below her window. There was to be no escape that way, either!

But Leonora was not one to give up hope. As the barn owls hooted, and the men below caroused over their ale, Leonora took a blue feather from her girdle and stuck it firmly in the ivy which had been left above her window.

"Please find me, Cameron," she whispered to the moonlit night. "Please see my signal, and rescue me!"

Twelve

Leonora was awakened at seven o'clock by Mrs. Trubbler, who brought her a frugal breakfast of bread, cheese, and coffee.

"I'm sorry I've nothing better to offer you, my lady," the woman apologized. "But I was given so little warning of your coming."

"Don't worry yourself. This is very kind of you," said Leonora, concealing a grimace as she tasted the bitter coffee. As Mrs. Trubbler drew back the curtains she forced herself into an optimistic frame of mind, and exclaimed, "Oh see, the mist is clearing. It is going to be a beautiful day!"

"Mrs Trubbler! Bring Lady Leonora downstairs directly!" shouted Sir Max from below. "It is time we were leaving."

Leonora pushed away her plate and stood up. Mrs. Trubbler said anxiously, "There, you have hardly eaten a morsel of your breakfast. Try and finish the cheese at least. It will give you strength. For heaven knows when that brute downstairs will allow you to stop for a decent meal."

Leonora saw the sense of her words. She was not in the least hungry, but knew she must keep up her stamina as well as retaining sharp wits if she were to avoid becoming Lady Fitzarren.

Sir Max was waiting impatiently in the hall, striding up and down, cracking his whip against his high leather boots.

"Come along. Hurry now!" he commanded, hustling Leonora toward the door.

"Where are we going?" she asked breathlessly, as he hurried her round to the stables.

"Northampton," he replied curtly, lifting her up and practically throwing her onto a horse. As he paused for a moment, adjusting the length of his stirrup, Leonora was sorely tempted to turn her horse and break for freedom.

But a moment's reflection convinced her that this was a foolish plan. Sir Max's mount was strong and spirited, and he would soon catch her. No, better to keep to her plan of pretending that this was all something of an adventure . . . and trusting that either the ideal opportunity would arise for her to escape, or that Lord Rothwell would come to rescue her.

As she trotted her horse through the farmyard gate, she glanced back, and was reassured to see the bright blue ostrich feather fluttering amongst the ivy.

Sir Max spoke little on the road to Northampton. She guessed that last night's reveling had left him with a sore head. Wisely, she too kept her silence and did not attempt to enter into any banter with him.

As they advanced into Northampton, Sir Max made straight for the Angel Inn, murmuring, "My God, we are only just in time!"

There in the yard was a mail coach, and Leonora realized that this was to be her transport for the rest of the journey to Gretna Green. Despite the shudder of horror that ran through her at the notion of her destination, Leonora could not quell a thrill of pride as she regarded the coach. How smart it looked, with its maroon and black body, and scarlet wheels. Emblazoned on the doors was the royal coat of arms, and inevitably, Leonora's thoughts whirled back to her evening at Park Lane with the Prince Regent. What an age ago that seemed now!

Leonora glanced round curiously, wondering who her fellow passengers might be. Perhaps there would be the opportunity for her to reveal her plight, or perhaps send a message to Lord Rothwell. She realized full well that Sir Max would be watching her for just such a move, and that one of the reasons he had chosen the mail coach was that it only carried a maximum of nine passengers, compared to sixteen on the stagecoach.

Today, however, it seemed as if Lady Luck was definitely smiling on Sir Max. Instead of nine passengers, there were only five. Besides Leonora and Sir Max, there were two pale-faced ladies, whom Leonora guessed to be governesses. They seemed extremely nervous, and on entering the coach huddled together in a corner and responded in a frightened whisper to Leonora's cheerful, "Good day to you, ladies!"

No, thought Leonora gloomily, *neither of them will serve my purpose. If I asked them to help me they would probably faint with terror.*

Leonora then cast a speculative eye on the fifth member of the party, a man of middle age with a florid complexion and portly appearance. But her heart sank as she observed him draw a flask from his pocket and take a long swallow. The man was plainly intending to tipple his way to Scotland. He would be totally unreliable. In fact, Leonora thought wryly, he will most like strike up a famous acquaintanceship with my liquor-loving Irish companion!

Now the luggage and parcels were loaded. Leonora settled herself in a corner seat. The guard, resplendent in his royal scarlet livery, climbed onto the boot on the back of the coach, and with his feet firmly on the locked mail box, blew his long, shiny brass horn. Onlookers scattered to the side of the yard as the magnificent mail coach swept out, and headed north.

The portly gentleman introduced himself as Dr. Burten. He was in semi-retirement now, he explained, and traveled a great deal around the country, visiting his five daughters and their families.

Sir Max responded by declaring his name to be Mr. Galway. Leonora was presented as his sister, much to her annoyance. That anyone should link her blood with the odious Sir Max Fitzarren! The two nervous governesses did not volunteer their names at all, but shrank into the corner and conversed in low tones amongst themselves.

Dr. Burten seemed anxious to impress everyone with his vast traveling experience. Before long, he had embarked on a tale about his incredible adventures on the Exeter Mail.

"We'd just left Salisbury," he declared, reaching for his flask, "when I noticed a large calf trotting along beside the horses. After a while, it was obvious that the horses were disturbed by this, so the guard very sensibly stopped. Well at this point, the calf seized hold of one of the horses, and seemed intent on devouring the wretched animal! Pandemonium broke out. The guard was about to fire his blunderbuss, when we realized that the calf wasn't a calf at all. It was a lioness!"

One of the governesses screamed.

Dr. Burten nodded. "It's as true as I sit here before you. A lioness escaped from a local menagerie. Well, in the end a net was thrown over the lioness, and the beast returned safely to the animal house."

"What about the horse?" enquired Leonora. "Was it harmed?"

"Shocked more than anything," said Dr. Burten. "But it soon recovered. These mail horses are quite a special breed, you know, Miss Galway. They don't scare easily."

The smaller of the two governesses plucked up courage to speak: "Too true, Dr. Burten. When Jemima and I were traveling across Dartmoor last summer, we felt the coach jolt rather sharply. Then the horses broke into a gallop. We were terrified, but hung on grimly, assuming that the coachman was trying to make up time. It was only when we stopped at a toll gate that we discovered we were completely alone on the coach! The driver and guard had been toppled from their seats miles back, by a heap of stones in the road. But the horses had kept to their route, and made no attempt to break free or cross the wilds of the moor!"

Leonora was amused to notice that Dr. Burten looked annoyed at the governess usurping his position as the experienced traveler. He took out a large leather bag, and delving into its interior, commented,

"Good food is such a comfort! Look what I've got here. Scotch shortbread, Grantham gingerbread, a Banbury cake, Bath buns and a Cheddar cheese. And when I went to visit my daughter in York I came home with the most succulent York ham. Always take my own food on a journey like this, you know. The inns are so atrocious."

The little governess said eagerly, "Oh I do so agree, Doctor. The meat is invariably tough, the linen dirty, and the knives filthy. The chambermaids are impertinent, and even the innkeepers themselves seem to be such an insolent breed." She leaned forward and touched Leonora's arm. "Be sure to lock your door at the inn tonight, Miss Galway!"

Before Leonora could reply, Sir Max commented, "Fortunately, Miss Galway will not be troubled by the horrors of an inn. My sister and I shall be traveling overnight."

Dr. Burten nodded. "Sensible of you, Galway. By far the best arrangement. I'm doing the same."

Leonora glanced out of the window to mask her disappointment. An inn would have provided some respite —some delay—perhaps given Lord Rothwell an opportunity to catch up with them. But Sir Max had clearly decided that speed was of the essence. They were to travel all night and all tomorrow, arriving after dark at Gretna Green.

Sir Max whispered in her ear. "And we shall be

married at first light, my dearest Leonora. Now there is something for you to look forward to!"

At five o'clock they stopped for dinner in Ashbourne. Sir Max kept Leonora close by him throughout the meal, warning her not to say a single unnecessary word to the innkeeper or serving wenches. There was scarcely time to eat the food before the guard was chivvying them back into the coach, waving his impressive timepiece, complaining that they could delay no longer. When the passengers were seated once more, he completed his routine inspection of the wheels and axles of the coach, then blew his horn. The mail coach was under way once more.

Dr. Burten, who had remained in the coach to consume his repast, smiled in sympathy as the two governesses protested that they had not had sufficient time to complete their repast.

"Always the same on the mail coaches," he remarked, wiping gingerbread crumbs from his mouth. "The guard would lose his job if he allowed the mail to arrive late."

Leonora nodded. "Is there not a saying, *as right as the mails?*" Indeed, she remembered Madame Valbois commenting that the English mail coaches were celebrated throughout Europe for their accurate timekeeping.

The little governess leaned forward, her face alight. "I recall when the Royal Mail brought us the news of the victory at Waterloo. The coach was decked with flags and laurel leaves, and the guard blew his horn in triumph all the way across Dartmoor!"

Sir Max slapped his thigh. "Come along now, ladies! I'll teach you a song about Waterloo. It concerns a mail guard, newly married, who is off to fight Boney." Throwing back his head he sang lustily,

"I've had many a hug at the sign of the Bear,
In the Sun courted morning and noon,

224

And when night put an end to my happiness there
I'd a sweet little girl in the Moon."

The governesses blushed, but Sir Max continued,

"Once guard to the mail, I'm now guard to the fair,
But while my commission's laid down,
Yet while the King's arms I'm permitted to bear,
Like a lion I'll fight for the crown!"

"Bravo!" applauded Dr. Burten. "It is heartwarming to have a man as cheerful as yourself along on this journey, Sir. Mind you, it has to be admitted that many of these mail guards are sheer rogues. They're in league with all the poachers. And the London newspapers pay them handsomely for tidbits of information about their rich passengers."

The governess called Jemima said anxiously, "Oh dear. I do hope our guard is a reliable man. There are so many villains aboard. I have heard that if one is traveling with a large amount of money, one should cut the banknotes in two, and post one half to one's destination."

Dr. Burten nodded sagely, "It is mainly jewels these blackguards are interested in. Why, it is not unknown for them to creep up by night, and cut a hole in the back of the stagecoach, the better to snatch the ladies' necklaces!"

The governesses clutched one another in fear. Seeing that Sir Max was looking highly amused at this account of his, and his friends' activities, Leonora said tartly, "At least one has the consolation of knowing that very few highwaymen die peacefully in their beds. Most of them suffer a public hanging in the end!"

Leonora had the satisfaction of observing the smile freeze on Sir Max's face. Before he could devise a suitable retort, she closed her eyes and feigned sleep.

Sleep, however, was to prove elusive as the mail coach rushed on through the night. Whereas from the outside, the lamplit speeding coach resembled a romantic chariot from fairyland, for the passengers inside, it was cold, cramped, and uncomfortable.

Somewhere toward midnight Leonora was shaken awake from her light doze by a rush of cold air as the doors opened and the governesses departed into an inn. There were shouts, and banging as the coachman knocked up the bleary eyed inn-keeper. Luggage was hauled down, wooden shoes clogged round the yard, and horses drank thirstily from waiting tubs. Leonora was dimly aware of another passenger entering the coach, then the doors slammed, and they were hurtling through the darkness once more.

As dawn broke, Leonora awoke to discover that the new passenger was a tall, thin gentleman who sat huddled in a corner, showing no interest in his fellow passengers.

Sir Max, however, was in high spirits, and suggested they play a game to pass the time.

"How about it, Burten," he said eagerly. "We'll toss for who takes which side of the coach, and we each score points for the objects we see. You score seven points for a donkey, five for a cat, ten for a cat in a window, five for a gray horse, one for a black sheep, a pig, or a magpie. We'll lay a wager . . ."

Leonora sighed, and took no part. Her ears were pricked for the sound of galloping hooves that would herald the arrival of Lord Rothwell. But the hours passed, and no horsemen either overtook, or drew level with the fast Royal Mail.

As the day progressed, and they approached Carlisle, Dr. Burten, having lost his wager to Sir Max, remarked, "Nearly at the Scottish border, then. My, I recall one time on this route, we had a young man and his girl on the run to Gretna Green."

Leonora could not resist an involuntary gasp, and felt Sir Max's hand gripping her wrist tightly.

226

Dr. Burten continued blithely, "Great excitement there was in the coach. We were all urging the young man to action, goading him to seize the reins and lash the horses on to Gretna Green!" He glanced at Leonora. "I say, Miss Galway! You look very pale. Have I said something to upset you?"

With Sir Max's fingers bruising her wrist, Leonora said faintly, "Pray do not alarm yourself, Doctor. I was merely thinking of the time when the Marquis of Abercorn discovered that his wife intended to elope. He was a most fearful stickler for good form, you know. He immediately dashed off a note to his wife, urging her to use the family carriage, lest it be said that his wife had left home in the shame of a hired coach!"

Dr. Burten laughed. "Ah yes. Was it not the same finicky marquis who required his housemaids to wear white kid gloves when they made his bed!"

It was dusk as they arrived at the Bush Inn at Carlisle, and Leonora was almost dropping with fatigue. But there was to be no rest for her yet. Grim faced, Sir Max whisked her straight from the carriage to a pair of waiting horses. Within the hour they were on the road again, heading for the Scottish border.

As night fell, so did the temperature, which was a blessing for Leonora as the cool air helped to keep her awake. She was dimly aware of money changing hands between Sir Max and the border guards, and then they set off once more, with only nine more miles to cover to Gretna Green.

When they arrived at the small Scottish village, Sir Max took her straight to a dimly lit inn. Any hopes Leonora had harbored of a friendly welcome, and allies for her escape, were dashed as she regarded the dour innkeeper and his wife.

The woman took immediate charge of her. "I'll take her to a room and lock her in for the night," she informed Sir Max. "You'll be wanting to talk to the village

227

blacksmith. He does na' charge much to marry you. Give him a guinea, and a bottle of whisky, and he'll be content!"

With that, she grasped Leonora by the arm and marched her upstairs to a small attic room. A tray of cold meats, fruit, and cheese lay on the plain deal table beside the bed.

"You'll stay here till morning," commanded the woman, shoving Leonora into the room and locking the door behind her. There were bolts on the inside of the door. Leonora pulled them across, for added protection.

She was nibbling at the cold meat, when she heard the doorhandle rattle, and Sir Max shouting, "Have you bolted this door, you insolent wench?"

"Yes, I have!" retorted Leonora. "You shall not enter!"

He laughed cruelly. "I merely came to inform you that we shall be wed tomorrow morning. It is all arranged. Tomorrow night, you shall share my bed, my pretty young bride! And I assure you, no bolted doors will deter me. I'll break the door down if I have to!"

"At least no one will be in any doubt of my feelings for you!" called Leonora. "They will tell from the color of my dress."

Sir Max sounded puzzled. "Are you fevered? What the deuce do you mean?"

By way of an answer, Leonora sang defiantly:

"Married in white, you have chosen all right,
Married in black, you will wish yourself back.
Married in red, you will wish yourself dead.
Married in green, ashamed to be seen.
Married in blue, you will always be true.
Married in pearl you will live in a whirl.
Married in yellow, ashamed of your fellow.
Married in brown you will live out of town.
Married in pink, your fortunes will sink.

"My dress is of primrose yellow, Sir Max. When they view us tomorrow, all the residents of Gretna Green will know how much I loathe and despise you!"

He hammered on the door, and roared, "I'll whip you for your damned impertinence! By God, once you're married to me, I'll teach you to curb your high-handed ways!"

Leonora sank onto the narrow bed, and blew out the candle. Oh, how menacing Sir Max had sounded! What an evil, cruel man he was. Leonora knew that these hours before dawn were her last opportunity to plan her escape. She must think and plot as never before!

But Leonora had forgotten her state of physical exhaustion. As soon as her head touched the pillow, her eyelids drooped, and she fell instantly into a deep slumber. When she awoke, the sun was shining and the birds sang joyously outside her window.

It was her wedding morn.

Leonora scrambled to her feet. It was morning. She was in Gretna Green. Yet still Cameron had not come! Never before had be failed her. Leonora had not realized how much she had come to depend on him, to rely on his strong, reassuring presence in her life. Right from that first moment when she had discovered Sir Max in the Blue Saloon with her, and learned of his evil intentions, Leonora had not in her heart of hearts, taken the threat of abduction seriously. She had been so sure that, providing she could send a message to Cameron, he would come to her aid. Had he not saved her so many times in the past?

It was this thought which had kept her cheerful and optimistic during the long, fatiguing journey to Gretna Green. This which had kept her spirits high when Sir Max had talked to her of their forthcoming marriage.

But in an hour—even less—Sir Max would be dragging her before the village blacksmith: the unknown man who was to perform the ceremony, and doom her for life, in return for a guinea and a bottle of whisky. Why, oh why had Cameron not come?

As Leonora slipped on her travel-stained dress, there came a loud banging at the door. A chill of terror struck her. It was Sir Max come to make her his bride!

Boldly, she lifted her voice and called defiantly, "You may knock and hammer for as long as you like, Sir Max. You will never take me willingly as your wife! If you wish to wed me, you will have to break the door down. And even then I shall fight and claw and scratch you every inch of the way to the blacksmith!"

His answer was a roar of laughter. And yet . . . Leonora stood rooted to the spot, every nerve tingling. That was not Sir Max's laugh! It was . . . it was . . .

"Leonora, will you kindly open this door!" instructed the familiar tones of Lord Rothwell. "Your breakfast is getting cold downstairs!"

Oh, with what joy did Leonora draw back the bolts! Cameron, dear, wonderful Cameron, was here! He had not failed her after all!

With trembling fingers she flung wide the door, and without a second thought, flung herself into his arms.

"Cameron! Oh, I am so very glad to see you. Oh, Cameron!"

His gray eyes held hers for a moment. Then he bent his head, and kissed her. It was not the greeting of a brother to a sister. Neither was it the kindly embrace of a family friend. No, this was the kiss of a man to a woman. A kiss of such abandoned rapture that it left Leonora trembling and breathless, when at last he released her.

She could not meet his eyes. Oh, she reproached herself, why did you respond to him in such a wanton fashion? For now Cameron can be in no doubt of the depth of your feelings for him. You have placed him in an impossible, embarrassing situation . . . for it cannot be long before his engagement is announced to Madame Valbois.

But he kissed me. Oh how he kissed me!

You are deceiving yourself, replied the cold voice of reason. He was merely expressing his relief at finding you alive and well. You would be foolish to read too much into one unexpected embrace!

With an effort, Leonora composed herself, and followed Lord Rothwell downstairs. "Cameron, what about Sir Max?" she enquired anxiously. "Oh, you would not believe what I have discovered about him! He is involved with a gang of rogues . . . Melissa's jewelry . . . the paneling in the Blue Saloon . . ." the tale came spilling out in a rush.

"I know the full story," smiled Lord Rothwell, guiding her into the breakfast parlor, where to her surprise Leonora found Daisy waiting.

"Daisy refused to be left behind," laughed Lord Rothwell, as Leonora sat down.

While Daisy served her mistress with freshly made toast, ham, and coffee, Lord Rothwell said grimly, "This may come as something of a shock, Leonora. But I have to advise you that Sir Max Fitzarren is an impostor. He is plain Mr. Harry Fitzarren, a notorious villain from Galway."

"Oh!" Leonora's amber eyes were huge with indignation. "But he told me he owned land . . . a mansion . . . even a castle!"

She burst into laughter as she observed Lord Rothwell's mocking expression. "Oh, very well Cameron. I mind that you warned me about him. But I never intended to marry him, you know. And in truth, I did enjoy watching you become irate every time you saw me in his company!"

Leonora bit into a piece of toast, and enquired, "But where is Sir—Mr. Fitzarren now? Oh Cameron, when you came knocking at the door, I feared it was he come to drag me off to be wed!"

Daisy could contain herself no longer. "My lady!" she blurted, her eyes alight with admiration as she regarded Lord Rothwell. "You should have seen the pair of them fighting! Lord Rothwell came marching in here, grabbed Mr. Fitzarren by the scruff of the neck, and threw him out into the garden. Mr. Fitzarren staggered to his feet, fists up and a stream of oaths on his lips. But Lord Rothwell went at him, and gave him such a milling as I've never seen in all my days. By the end of it Sir Storrac was covered in blood, and his face was so bruised—"

"That will do, Daisy," said Lord Rothwell quietly. "As I said, the important thing is that we'll not be troubled any more with this Irish impostor."

Leonora said breathlessly, "How did you know about the gang of rogues, and their thefts?"

"That was thanks to you," explained Lord Rothwell. "And your ingenious letter. Daisy realized instantly, through that strange reverse lettering, that you had been taken to Gretna Green. I, of course, rushed down to the Swan With Two Necks—and drew a mystifying blank."

"Because Mr. Fitzarren had cleverly routed us through Oxford," sighed Leonora.

"Fortunately, I observed your blue ostrich feather sticking from the Oxford sign," smiled Lord Rothwell. "After that, it was really a simple matter of following the feathers you left at each stopping place. A very cunning ruse, Leonora. Though I must confess I was surprised when they led me to the ivy covered farmhouse in Towcester."

"That was how you discovered about the gang?"

Lord Rothwell nodded. "I made a few enquiries at the farm. Naturally, they denied having seen you. But I felt that something was wrong. And Daisy here was convinced of it."

"I had that cold, prickly feeling down my spine, my lady," said Daisy. "It's always a sure sign there's something fishy going on."

"I alerted the local Watch," said Lord Rothwell, "and when they raided the farmhouse they found valuable silver, glassware, and jewelry from a score of fashionable houses in Mayfair."

Leonora sighed contentedly. "I cannot believe this is

all happening! What a beautiful day it has turned out to be."

Lord Rothwell stood up. "Come, let us take a turn around the garden. The fine Scottish air is like champagne, so they say."

They walked in silence for a while across the springy grass. Leonora lifted her head, reveling in the soft breeze ruffling her golden hair. "And to think," she said softly, "that I awoke this morning with dread in my heart, because I believed it to be my wedding day."

Lord Rothwell took her hand. His voice was low. "If you wish it, Leonora, this can still be your wedding morn."

For a heart-stopping moment, she stared up at him. "I—I don't understand," she faltered.

"I am asking you to marry me," he said quietly, gazing into her eyes. "I love you, Leonora. And from the manner in which you returned my kiss earlier on, I firmly believe that you love me too!"

Leonora clung to him. "Oh, of course I love you! With all my heart and soul! But what about Madame Valbois? I thought . . ."

He drew her close to him. "I have never, at any time, been in love with Madame Valbois."

"But in Paris," protested Leonora. "You yourself admitted that you fell in love with a French widow!"

"I had a brief romance with a lady," said Lord Rothwell. "It lasted for six months, and then the flame died between us. I assure you, I feel nothing for her now but a distant, nostalgic affection. Later, she married a wealthy, and extremely influential duke. She begged me not to mention to anyone that we had been romantically involved. Evidently the duke was a friend of her late husband's, and he fondly believed that she had been faithful to his memory! Naturally, I kept my word to the lady, and remained silent about our affair. As for Madame Valbois, she was a friend of the lady concerned. I knew Bettine in Paris, and when she came to London she naturally called on me."

Leonora had lost interest in Madame. It was enough that Cameron had never loved her. How foolish I was, thought Leonora, to have been so jealous!

She said hesitantly, "This lady in Paris. You loved her—"

"It was a lighthearted affair," he reassured her. "I promise you, I have felt for no one what I feel for you. Oh Leonora, have you no idea that I have been in love with you since you were a schoolgirl?"

"Cameron! Have you really? But I had no notion . . . in fact, as I recall, for the past few years you have been most unloving toward me! You have treated me in the most arrogant, high-handed fashion. Do you call that love?"

He smiled at her outrage. "Leonora, think back. I could quite easily have courted you when you were seventeen, and just *out*. I am older than you, more sophisticated, more worldly wise. It would have been a simple matter for me to sweep you off your feet and make you my bride."

"Then why did you not?"

"It would not have been fair to you. I would have been taking advantage of your youth and innocence. I wanted you to have the opportunity first to enjoy yourself as a young girl should . . . whirling through the London Season, attending balls, theaters, assemblies, with dashing young men dancing attendance on you."

"Yes," smiled Leonora. "I certainly had my fill of London's social pleasures. And then, one evening, I looked at you, and it was as if I was seeing you for the first time. In a single, blazing instant, I knew it was you I loved. I realized, too, that for all these years I have been measuring my beaux against you—and finding them all wanting."

He crushed her into his arms, and then his mouth was on hers, possessing her with a passion which could not be denied. Willingly, Leonora yielded to the torrent

234

of desire that raged within her. From this moment on she knew she belonged to this man—body and soul. Gladly, rapturously, she abandoned herself to the exquisite intimacy of her lover's embrace.

At last he whispered. "Shall we be married today?"

"Oh yes!" breathed Leonora ecstatically. "But that horrid blacksmith! I should not want him to marry us."

"No, no," smiled Lord Rothwell. "There is a church in the village. We shall be wed there, in the sight of God."

"How romantic it all is!" Then Leonora's face clouded. "Oh, but look at this appalling dress. It is yellow, and travel stained. I cannot be wed wearing such a rag!"

"Daisy thought of that," said Lord Rothwell. "She insisted on bringing one of your favorite blue dresses with her."

Leonora's eyes widened. "You mean you told her you intended to marry me at Gretna Green?"

"One never needs to tell Daisy anything," he laughed. "She just knew!" He urged her toward the inn. "Now away with you and dress, whilst I make the arrangements at the church."

Leonora ran upstairs, where Daisy was laying out the delicate blue dress.

"Oh, my lady! I'm so happy for you!" beamed Daisy. "I can tell from the radiant look on your face that everything's come right between you and his lordship. Oh, and before I forget, the Lady Melissa asked me to give you this, most privately."

She handed Leonora a letter.

Intrigued, Leonora broke the seal, and read:

"My dearest Leonora, How I wish I could be with you today! I wanted to come, truly I did, but Cameron said I would only complain about the rutted roads, and slow him down, and then he might not reach you in time. He did tell me, however, that he intends to whisk you off to be married with no more delay, before you land yourself in any more perilous situations from which he has to rescue you!

"I have known for years, you see, that Cameron was in love with you. (Sisters always do understand these things about their brothers!) But he was so familiar to you, I feared that you looked upon him merely as a brother. Hence my ruse with Madame Valbois. Strictly between ourselves (as she is shortly to become my sister by marriage) I share your low opinion of her. But I pretended to like her, and encouraged you to imagine that Cameron was fond of her, in the hope of making you jealous enough to realize that you loved him!

"Forgive me for deceiving you. But I always knew that you and Cameron would make the ideal couple.

"I wish you every happiness, my dear. My thoughts are with you on this, your wedding day.—Melissa."

Leonora's eyes misted as she refolded the letter. *Dear Melissa. I could not have wished for a kinder, more sweet-natured sister by marriage.*

While Daisy tied the blue silk girdle round Leonora's tiny waist, the golden-haired bride suddenly laughed.

"My, what a game of pretense we have all been involved in, Daisy! Nothing has been what it seemed. You are in the habit of pronouncing words backwards, or in rhyme, to disguise their meanings."

Daisy grinned, and Leonora continued, "I pretended to be enamoured with Sir Max—who was not Sir Max at all, but a plain mister! Then for years, Cameron has concealed from me the depth of his love. And Melissa has been codding us all that she held Madame Valbois in high esteem! So we have all, it seems, been masquerading in one way or another."

"But only in the best interests of love, my lady," smiled Daisy. She sighed. "Oh, how enchanting you look in that blue silk! I'm sure no other bride has ever looked as lovely!"

It was a sentiment echoed by Lord Rothwell who stood waiting by the inn gate. The tall, handsome lord took Leonora's hand and raised it to his lips. "I am the most fortunate man in the world," he told her. Then he pointed across the flower-strewn meadow. "See, there is the church where we shall be married. I will have a carriage brought round for you."

"No," smiled Leonora. "After the nightmare ride here with Harry Fitzarren, I confess I cannot abide yet awhile the sight of another coach or carriage. Especially on my wedding morn. If you have no objection, I should much prefer to walk to the church."

"It shall be as you wish," he smiled.

Leonora paused, and exclaimed, "Oh, but I have no flowers! No bridal posy!"

But Daisy had been busy. "Here, my lady. I have fashioned a bouquet for you, from the flowers by the hedgerow. See, there are wild roses, sweet smelling honeysuckle, and pretty blue borage to match your dress!"

"Daisy, how thoughtful! Why, it is the most beautiful bouquet I have ever set eyes on!"

Lord Rothwell said, "Are you quite sure, Leonora, that you are content to be wed at this remote little Scottish church? If you desire, we can always be cut and carried instead at a fashionable ceremony in Mayfair."

Leonora laughed. "I can tell you have been much in Daisy's company over the past day or so, Cameron! But even I am aware that cut and carried is Daisy's rhyme for married!" Her eyes were luminous as she gazed up at him and said softly, "No, Cameron. I want no hectic Mayfair marriage. No jam of carriages, no craning of titled heads in the church to see what the rest of the ton are wearing. That little church at Gretna has such a tranquil, ageless air. It is there that I wish to make my vows to you."

He kissed her. Then with the red-haired maid dancing attendance, Lord Rothwell led Leonora through the daisy-starred meadow to her Gretna Green wedding.

ABOUT THE AUTHOR

Caroline Courtney was born in India, the youngest daughter of a British Army Colonel stationed there in the troubled years after the First World War. Her first husband, a Royal Air Force pilot, was tragically killed in the closing stages of the Second World War. She later remarried and now lives with her second husband, a retired barrister, in a beautiful 17th century house in Cornwall. They have three children, two sons and a daughter, all of whom are now married, and four grandchildren.

On the rare occasions that Caroline Courtney takes time off from her writing, she enjoys gardening and listening to music, particularly opera. She is also an avid reader of romantic poetry and has an ever-growing collection of poems she has composed herself.

Caroline Courtney is destined to be one of this country's leading romantic novelists. She has written an enormous number of novels over the years—purely for pleasure—and has never before been interested in seeing them reach publication. However, at her family's insistence she has now relented, and Warner Books are proud to be issuing a selection in this uniform edition.

YOUR WARNER LIBRARY OF REGENCY ROMANCE